Christmas at Willoughby Close

Christmas at
Willoughby Close

A Return to Willoughby Close Romance

KATE HEWITT

TULE
PUBLISHING

Chapter One

BELINDA JAMISON GAZED at the gleaming parquet of the floor, newly varnished, and couldn't keep a swell of pride from practically lifting her off her toes.

Poised to take a few balletic steps into the room, she stopped herself just in time. The varnish needed at least a week before anyone so much as put a toe on it, and she certainly had no intention of scuffing its pristine surface, not before her first class, anyway. After that there would be plenty of scuff marks, and that would be fine. That would be wonderful.

With a grin spreading over her face, she switched off the lights and turned from the room. As she clattered down the stairs, her landlady Monica poked her head around the till of Wychwood Waggy Tails, the shop she ran and that Lindy rented a room above.

"All finished?" she asked cheerfully as she cradled a mug of tea.

"Yes, for now. It needs a week of simply sitting pretty and then I'll jazz it up a bit." She already had a wall of mirrors planned for one side. "It's going to be perfect."

"You're very optimistic. I like that."

"I have to be," Lindy said simply. Perhaps it was the way she was born, or simply the way she'd chosen to live, but she wasn't going to let a few unexpected bends or bumps in the road get her down—and there had been a few since she'd moved to Wychwood-on-Lea in June, over two months ago now.

Moving to a small village in the Cotswolds hadn't been in Lindy's life plan, and yet when she'd made the decision last April it had felt suddenly and wonderfully right. She'd been working in Manchester as an accountant for over a decade, and the years had started to feel as if they were slipping away from her.

Thirty-six come December, and she hadn't had much to show for it besides a nondescript flat and a stellar CV. Yes, she had a handful of lovely work colleagues and she was friendly with her neighbours, but thanks to the way her life had gone—and she wouldn't let herself regret a bit of it— that tribe of kindred spirits and cosy relations most people took for granted had completely passed her by. She was pretty much all alone, and she realised she didn't want to log the lonely nine to five for the rest of her life.

Then her friend Ellie had suggested she move down south, just as she had done herself three years before.

"It's so lovely here, and people are really friendly. I mean *really* friendly. They will absolutely insist you be friends with them."

"Now you're starting to scare me," Lindy had joked, even though secretly she thought it all sounded rather wonderful—the bevy of kindly friends, the impossibly quaint village, the stable yard of converted cottages where Ellie had assured her there was space. Willoughby Close, it was called, and it had already sounded like home.

And so, somewhat recklessly, Lindy had agreed. Thanks to parents who had worked hard all their lives and loved their only child devotedly, not to mention her own respectable savings, she didn't have to worry too much about money. She could rent number two, Willoughby Close, and pursue her pet project for at least a year or two without having to count pennies—or at least not count them too carefully.

"Cup of tea?" Monica asked and Lindy nodded. It was only half past five, and she had nowhere to go but home that evening.

"Thanks, Monica, that would be lovely."

As Monica went to the tiny kitchen in the back of the shop to make her a brew, Lindy perched on a stool and considered all the last two months had—and hadn't— brought.

When Ellie had suggested the move, Lindy had made sure to get everything in place before she signed on the dotted line, because as impulsive as she could be, she still liked to be prepared. Ten years of accountancy work counted for something.

She'd rented the cottage in Willoughby Close, and made a verbal agreement with Wychwood-on-Lea's parish council to rent out their newly refurbished village hall for her classes. And it had all looked as if it was going to go swimmingly when she'd arrived in June with a moving van in tow and a head full of dreams, just in time to offer a few free lessons at the summer gala up at the manor.

But then it had all suddenly fallen apart, and over the wretched floors, of all things. Someone on the parish council decided they didn't want people tapping their toes or really, digging in their heels, on the village hall's gleaming new parquet floor, and the council had, sorrowfully but firmly, revoked their offer of hosting Lindy's classes.

Lindy had done her best not to get down, even though it soon became apparent that there was no other suitable space in all of Wychwood, or any other nearby village, to host the dream she'd been cherishing—Take a Twirl School of Ballroom Dancing.

She'd had to cancel her already booked schedule of summer classes, including her tiny tots holiday week that she'd been especially looking forward to. She'd scrambled to look for a space, and in mid-August Monica Dewbury had offered her the room over her pet shop and dog bakery, which was small but adequate and the only space she could find.

An elegant woman in her fifties with a silver bob and a ready smile, Monica had followed her dream by opening a dog bakery of all things, and now she wanted the same for Lindy. She'd assured her she didn't use the upstairs, and this would be putting it to good use. Lindy promised her free dance classes, to which Monica laughed and said she had two left feet.

"So you must be ready soon," Monica said now as she handed Lindy her cup of tea. "When is your first class?"

"Not for a few weeks. I still have to get all the publicity out—" which she'd had to revise, thanks to the change of venue "—and I'm still hoping to put up the wall of mirrors. Ava's husband Jace said he might be able to do it."

Lindy had been wonderfully overwhelmed by the outpouring of friendship she'd encountered almost from the moment she'd driven into Willoughby Close. Her neighbours in the close, Olivia and Emily, had both welcomed her with casseroles, bottles of wine, and an invitation to go to the pub with a whole bevy of former residents.

"It'll have to be The Three Pennies," Emily had said with a wry little grimace, "unless you're willing to sit outside."

"Emily's boyfriend Owen runs a pop-up pub," Olivia had chimed in. "Man with a Van. It's brilliant."

There had been so many people to meet and names to learn—Olivia's fiancé Simon was a music teacher at the primary school, and then there was Ava and Jace and their little boy William, plus Alice and Henry up at the manor, and Harriet and her family in the village. And of course there was Ellie, living in Oxford with her husband Oliver.

Lindy had met Ellie when they'd got to chatting on the bus into Manchester, both commuting daily for work. She'd been hoping to see more of her now that she'd moved to Wychwood, but she hadn't quite twigged until she'd arrived that Ellie lived over half an hour away, worked in Oxford, and was generally very busy with her daughter Abby doing GCSEs and a husband who had a demanding job at the university, and was a viscount to boot.

But that was okay. Lindy was used to having to fit in to other people's busy lives, and it had never bothered her before. She wouldn't let it now—because although she'd made a lot of friends in the two months she'd been living at Willoughby Close, they were all friends with boyfriends or husbands, children or pets or both, and when it came to a Friday night or a Saturday afternoon, they tended to be rather busy. Which was fine, because Lindy was busy too. Mostly. She certainly would be busy when she finally got her school up and running—or really, up and dancing.

"I think it's brilliant you're doing this," Monica said. "Following your dream, no matter what. I love it."

Lindy smiled her thanks. She knew more than one eyebrow had sceptically risen when she'd arrived in the village, planning to start a school for ballroom dancing. She wasn't exactly the expected model for the teacher of such a school—standing at just over six feet without shoes, and with a figure that was more statuesque than supermodel, Lindy was surprisingly light on her feet, but also a perfectly satisfied size fourteen. Still, she knew people had been expecting someone a bit, well, tinier.

"Have you had many people enrolling yet?" Monica asked.

"A few. I need to do more publicity." Lindy was trying not to worry about the lack of enrolment. After she'd done her sample lessons at the charity gala back in June she'd had a whole host of sign-ups that she'd had to postpone when the village hall made their unfortunate U-turn.

Now that she had a new location, only a handful of those previously booked had bothered to re-enrol, despite her determination to contact each and every person. Lindy wasn't worried about money, but she knew the importance of having a critical mass to get the momentum of enthusiasm she'd need for the school to be a success. She hated the thought of having it limp along for a few months before she had to close up shop.

But she was getting ahead of—or really, behind—herself in thinking that way. Her first class, an evening class for beginners, was still a fortnight away.

"Well, I for one hope it will be a success," Monica said firmly. "And I tell everyone who comes into the shop about it, as well."

"You've been wonderful, Monica, thank you."

Lindy finished her tea before taking both her and Monica's mugs and washing them in the kitchen in the back of the shop.

"I should get going," she told the older woman brightly. "I've still got quite a lot of paperwork to sort through."

"That's not a very exciting plan for a Friday evening," Monica said with a wry grimace, and Lindy shrugged.

"Needs must, I'm afraid." She still had a great deal of work to get through before she officially opened—insurance forms, health and safety checks, and putting the finishing touches on her website. "See you next week," she told Monica, and then she headed out into the still-bright light of an August evening.

Everything looked golden, not quite twilight, the sun slowly sinking towards the horizon, spreading out like melted butter. Lindy headed down the high street, enjoying the pretty sight of the terraced shops of golden Cotswold stone, the village green a verdant square at the bottom of the street.

Wychwood-on-Lea was impossibly quaint compared to the Manchester suburb where she'd lived for the last ten years. It reminded her a little bit of her childhood, when she'd lived in a topsy-turvy cottage that had been four hundred years old, on the edge of the rugged Peak District, the only place she'd ever really called home.

She let herself feel a single, nostalgic pang for that lovely house and all the happy memories it contained before she made herself move on. In actuality, despite being rural, this village was very different from the one she grew up in. There were no peaks, for a start, and the prettiness of the village was decidedly of the gleaming Land Rover and pristine Farrow and Ball variety, every house like something out of *Country Living*, the wealth of the area on quietly ostentatious display.

Not that she minded…it took all sorts, and Lindy tried not to begrudge anyone anything. And, she hoped, the well-heeled residents of Wychwood-on-Lea would be willing to turn up those heels at a dancing school.

As she left the village behind for the Willoughby Manor estate where she rented number two in the Close, she wondered how she could drum up some more business. Right now she only had three people for her evening class, and three little girls and a boy for her junior one on a Saturday morning. She'd been hoping to run four or five classes a week, but that seemed like a distant dream at the moment.

Still, she was determined to be optimistic. It was just like her dad used to say, why be pessimistic when you can always hope? Lindy was most definitely in the glass-is-half-full camp. As far as she was concerned, the glass was overflowing no matter what was or wasn't in it. It was all a matter of perspective.

Humming a little under her breath, she turned into Willoughby Close as the shadows started to lengthen. She could see Olivia and Simon in the lighted windows of number four, eating dinner and no doubt talking about their wedding plans. Emily's cottage was dark, and Lindy suspected her neighbour was at her boyfriend Owen's house on the other side of the village, where she spent a lot of her evenings. Number three hadn't been rented yet, but Lindy was looking forward to another neighbour, when they came. Perhaps it would be someone single, like her.

Her mobile phone started to ring just as she unlocked the door to number two and stepped into her own cottage—laid out exactly like the other three, with an open kitchen and a living area with a wood burner and French windows leading out to a tiny terrace and garden.

"Hello," Lindy sang out as she nudged the front door closed with her hip, her mobile cradled between her ear and her shoulder.

"Am I speaking to the proprietor of the Take a Twirl School of Ballroom Dancing?" a rather stern voice asked.

"Indeed you are," Lindy answered after a second's surprised pause at the slightly aggressive tone of her caller. "May I help you?"

"I am ringing to enquire about availability in Monday's evening class for adult beginners," the man answered in that same stern, slightly supercilious tone that both intrigued and irritated Lindy in equal measure. Who *was* this guy?

"Yes, there is availability," she answered. "Are you interested in learning how to dance?" Although, judging by his voice, the man seemed like the least likely candidate for a ballroom dancing aficionado that she could imagine.

"I am not," the man replied rather severely, startling

Lindy with his vehemence. "That is to say, I am not at *all* interested in learning how to dance."

Oh-kay. She took a second to gather her scattered thoughts. "You're not interested?" she repeated. "Then why…are you calling?"

"As I said, I am ringing to enquire about *availability*," he told her, now beginning to sound a bit annoyed. "Did I not make that clear?"

Lindy stayed silent for a moment, unsure how to respond to the question he'd asked as if he thought the answer were glaringly obvious. This had to be the most bizarre conversation she'd ever had. "You did make that clear," she said finally, speaking carefully, as if to an animal that might startle or attack, "but then you told me you weren't interested in learning how to dance. So I must confess, I am a bit confused." She gave a little laugh, to take any possible sting from her words. This man, whoever he was, seemed like the sort of person to be easily offended.

A second's arctic pause followed, and Lindy feared, despite her best efforts, she'd offended the man, after all. "I am *not* interested in learning how to dance," he emphasised, "but I am *still* enquiring about availability. Do you or do you not have any space in your Monday evening class for adult beginners in ballroom dancing?"

Lindy was starting to feel as if she were in a comedy sketch. Was there a camera somewhere, filming her reactions for some weird YouTube stunt? Or was this man just being strange? Amusement warred with exasperation. "As I said, there is availability. Do you or do you not want to register?"

She'd meant to sound friendly, gently mimicking him, but the question came out with a bit more hostility than she had intended. With all the challenges she'd faced in getting her school up and running, and the fact that it was nearly seven on a Friday evening when she could really do with some ice cream, wine, and Netflix, she did not need some random pedant arguing with her over the phone.

"I do wish to register," the man answered in a tone stiff with both dignity and affront. "But that is not what you originally asked."

"What—"

"You asked if I was interested in learning to dance, and I am not. I thought I made both points equally clear."

"Funnily enough, you didn't," Lindy answered and then she started to laugh. She didn't mean to; she knew already it would offend the man excessively, and yet somehow she couldn't stop. The giggles escaped her like bubbles, and she knew she was on the verge of losing it completely, and starting in with the kind of breathless, belly-aching laughs that went on for at least five minutes. This was so not good.

"I fail to see what is so amusing," the man answered, after several seconds of her helpless laughter. Now he definitely sounded offended.

"I'm sorry," Lindy gasped as she tried to stifle the laughter that was now coming out in little hiccups. Tears streamed down her face. "I'm so sorry. But surely you can see how funny this conversation is? I feel like I'm in the middle of a Laurel and Hardy sketch." Her tone, she hoped, invited him to see the joke, but of course he didn't see it at all. He most likely never did.

"I do not know to whom you are referring," the man replied. He did not sound quite as offended, but he was definitely still annoyed, or perhaps just perplexed. His sense of humour, if he'd ever had one, must have been surgically removed some time ago.

Lindy's laughter morphed into a sigh. "Never mind," she said. "You have said you're interested in registering, and I am interested in having you register. Why don't you give me your details, and I'll put your name down for the class?"

"Very well," the man answered. "My name is Roger Wentworth and I will be attending the class with Ellen Wentworth. I trust there is space in the Monday evening class for adult beginners for two individuals?"

"There is," Lindy confirmed. Her urge to laugh had, quite suddenly, completely deserted her; she now felt quite flat, although she couldn't have said why. "The first class is on September seventh," she added dutifully. "Is that all right?"

"I have already marked down the dates of all the classes in my calendar," Roger Wentworth replied with some asperity. "I hardly would have taken the time to ring you and enquire about availability, if I did not believe I could attend the classes as they were scheduled in your promotional material."

Of course not, Lindy thought with an inward sigh. Already she could tell he was the sort of man to schedule everything, including his own trips to the toilet, no doubt. Having him in her dancing class was going to be interesting, to say the least. Excruciating was probably more like it.

"If you come on the first Monday a few minutes early, you can fill out the registration form," she told him. "The class starts at seven, and we should be finished by nine." No doubt he knew that already, and was about to tell her so, but fortunately Roger Wentworth seemed to have had enough of verbal nitpicking for he simply said, "Thank you," and then, quite abruptly, he hung up.

Lindy was left holding her mobile, shaking her head at the surreal nature of the call, and wondering if Roger Wentworth—as well as Ellen—would actually show up two weeks from Monday. She couldn't decide if she wanted them to or not.

Chapter Two

"COME ON, DARLING, this is going to be *so* much fun."
That, Roger reflected, was an inaccurate statement, if not an actual out-and-out untruth. This was not going to be fun at *all*. It was going to be humiliating and horrendous, and he was under absolutely no illusion whatsoever that any part of it would amuse him in the least. Quite the opposite.

Ellen beckoned to him appealingly, one hand held out, a half-smile on her face, as they both stood on the pavement before the ridiculously named Waggy Tails Bakery. The Take a Twirl School of Ballroom Dancing—also a ridiculous name—took place above it, according to the promotional material Roger had in his possession. It seemed to him an unlikely pairing—although *dog* and *bakery* was also an unlikely pairing, so perhaps he did not understand what sort of things belonged together.

"Please, Rog," Ellen said. "I don't want to be late. You're the one who signed us up, after all."

And she knew precisely why he'd done that, Roger

thought, not that he would ever verbalise it. They spoke about the C-word as little as possible, which suited him fine, even if Ellen insisted upon bringing the subject up on unfortunate occasions, as if she were his therapist rather than his mother.

Yes, she was his mother. He, a thirty-eight-year-old unmarried man, was actually taking ballroom dancing lessons with his *mother*. He was either pathetic or strange or even a bit scary, in an unpleasant Norman Bates-like fashion. Whichever it was, and perhaps it was all three, he knew that coming to this class did not put him in a good light. At all.

The exceedingly awkward telephone conversation he'd had with the school's proprietor hadn't, either. Even two weeks later Roger mentally cringed at how ridiculously pompous he'd sounded on the phone, like a complete prat basically, which was always how he sounded when he was out of his comfort zone, which was about ninety-eight per cent of the time, at least in dealing with other people.

"Rog?" His mother was still waiting for him to enter the building, which he was reluctant to do. Yet the fact that he'd signed up for the classes, given his card details by email, *and* embarrassed himself in the process, compelled him onwards. He'd got this far. Why not go a little farther, and make his humiliation complete?

Roger Wentworth was not a dancer. This was a gross understatement. He had not been sporty in school; quite the opposite. Some teachers had called him clumsy. And when he'd thankfully outgrown the clumsy stage—there had been a period of four or five years when he'd been nothing but sharp-angled elbows and knobbly knees—he had still remained stiff and awkward, a man who seemed uncomfortable in his own body, although he wasn't, not particularly. He just didn't how to *be*.

Unless he had a spreadsheet or a crossword in front of him, Roger did not know how to act. He tried, heaven knew, and often his attempts were at least somewhat successful. He had learned the art of at least appearing to know how to make chitchat, and he managed to get by at work with the usual social niceties, although to say he was *friendly* with his colleagues would be something of an overstatement, although perhaps not a gross one.

"*Rog.*" His mother was starting to look exasperated, and Rog could hardly blame her. He'd been standing on the pavement for at least ten minutes, which was just another sign of his inherent awkwardness. He followed his mother into the bakery, which did not have any of the usual pleasant olfactory associations with the word, but rather smelled like a pet shop or a vet's, and then up a narrow, rickety set of stairs to the room above. Roger bumped his head on the ceiling. Twice. He was still rubbing it as he emerged into a narrow corridor, the premises of Take a Twirl School of Ballroom Dancing ahead of him.

As he stepped into the room, a wall of mirrors greeted him and he immediately balked. He did not want to look at himself for the next two hours, but it was difficult not to when there he was, looming up, all gangly six feet four of him. Next to him his mother looked tiny and wizened; the chemo had reduced her body weight by nearly a third.

"You must be the Wentworths, Ellen and Roger."

He turned at the sound of a voice he recognised, husky and rich—the voice of the woman on the phone, the proprietor of the school. She came towards them with a wide smile, and Roger blinked at the sight of her.

She was at least six feet tall, if not a little more, and nearly his height in the pink platform shoes she was wearing. She'd matched the shoes with an even more outrageous outfit—a poodle skirt in hot pink satin, cinched tight at the waist, with a white silk blouse tucked into it and unbuttoned enough to reveal a generous portion of her even more generous cleavage. Roger, somewhat inexplicably, felt himself blush.

Her hair tumbled halfway to her waist, a rich golden brown, and there was something so impossibly sensual and earthy about her that she seemed to take up all the air in the room. Certainly he seemed to be having trouble remembering how to breathe.

"Rog?" Ellen asked a bit anxiously. "Are you all right?"

He cleared his throat. "I'm fine," he said tightly. He nodded at the woman standing in front of him, still taking up too much air.

"Pleased to meet you. I'm Belinda Jamison, but everyone

calls me Lindy."

"I'm Roger Wentworth," he responded somewhat mechanically. "As you must know, since you just said it." Her eyes, a bright blue green, seemed to be laughing at him. No doubt she was remembering how idiotic he'd sounded on the phone, blustering on about how he wasn't interested in learning to dance. Whenever he was nervous, he became pedantic. Even aware of this weakness, he seemed utterly unable to amend it.

"Well, now that we're all here, why don't we get started?" Lindy said as she moved to stand in front of the mirror, her bright skirt swishing about her long, athletic-looking legs. "If you need to fill out any forms, you can do so at the tea break, or at the end of the class. I think it's important to get moving as soon as we can."

Roger glanced around the room, appalled to realise how small the class was. Besides him and his mother, there were just three other people present—a couple who were clearly together, and an old woman who was so hunched over, Roger wondered how she could walk, never mind dance. Perhaps he wouldn't be the worst one in the class.

No, he would. No matter what, he would.

"Right." Lindy clapped her hands lightly, looking around at her five pupils with a wide, beaming smile. "Now I know you are all coming to this class with different experiences and expectations, and there are some of you who can't wait to tango—" amazingly, she directed this comment to the hunched-over woman "—and some of you who would prefer to stick to the basic box step." Her gaze skimmed over Roger, and he felt himself flush. Again. Good heavens, but this was actually going to be hell.

"But I think it's always important to start with the basics, to build a good foundation of skills and get your confidence going. So we're going to start with the waltz, which might seem a bit old-fashioned, but it never steers you wrong. Don't worry, Maureen," she said to the older woman, "we'll be doing the salsa in no time."

The salsa? Wasn't that a food? Judging by the way Lindy waggled her eyebrows, Roger thought it was not a dance he would be interested in learning. The last thing he wanted to do was attempt to shimmy and shake, especially with his mother. This really was going to be torture. Unmitigated, absolute torture.

IF LINDY HAD had to pick Roger Wentworth out of a line-up, she thought she'd be able to do it easily. He was *exactly* what she'd expected—stern-looking, buttoned up, and undoubtedly boring. Priggish, too, judging by the scandalised look he'd given when she'd mentioned the salsa. Oh, dear. He wasn't going to have much fun in her class, not unless she was able to pry open that fussy shell he'd crammed himself into. She was certainly going to try.

She glanced at him again as she demonstrated the basic

box step of the waltz; he was frowning slightly as he watched her, looking as if he was following a complicated chemistry experiment. He was, she acknowledged as her gaze slid away from him, good-looking in an entirely *normal* sort of way—tall, muscular, brown hair, brown eyes. Forgettable, but still handsome. Sort of. She looked at him again, and his whisky-brown gaze caught hers, and for some reason she felt jolted, like missing the last step in a staircase, and she actually stumbled in her box step, something she never did.

"Oops, sorry!" She let out a breathless sort of laugh. "But you get the idea. I'll put some music on, and everyone can have a go. Maureen, shall I partner you? With my height, I'm used to being the man."

She went to her phone, which was connected to a speaker, and put on the classic waltz number, Strauss's 'The Blue Danube.' The famous first strains, and then the wonderful swelling of music, caused her a sweet pang of memory of dancing around the kitchen with her dad, standing on his feet while he showed her the steps.

"All right, everyone, let's take it slowly. One, two, three, one, two, three!" With a smile for Maureen, who was bent over nearly double and yet still determined to dance, Lindy took the older woman's claw-like hand in her own, and rested the other on her waist. When Maureen approached Lindy at the summer gala up at Willoughby Manor and said she'd once been the tango champion of Newcastle, Lindy had been slightly incredulous, but also delightfully charmed.

"It's been awhile since I've tried to tango," Maureen declared, "but you should have seen me back in the day. The men couldn't keep their eyes off me, along with other things."

"I'm sure they couldn't," Lindy had agreed. "So you're looking for a...refresher course?"

"I know I can't move much, because of this blasted arthritis," Maureen explained, "but I want to give it a go."

Now, Lindy moved her partner around in a careful box step, afraid of dancing too fast and injuring Maureen, who was shuffling more than waltzing.

"Is this all right?" she asked, and Maureen threw her an irritated look.

"Don't mollycoddle me, dearie. I may be twisted up like an old pretzel, but I know how to move."

"I'm sure you do," Lindy answered, and picked up the pace slightly. She glanced at the other two couples—Simon and Olivia, who seemed to have two left feet each and were stumbling around rather adorably, clearly happy simply to be in each other's arms, and then Roger and Ellen, whom Lindy assumed was his mother or maybe an aunt; she was smiling easily, seemingly impervious to his expression of utter torment. Roger was moving so stiffly around the floor that his posture suggested there was a poker involved, placed in an uncomfortable position.

He caught her eye—again—and Lindy tried for an encouraging smile. Roger's expression of torment did not alter in the least. Lindy don't know whether to laugh or groan. He was clearly going to be hard work, but at least he was here— which begged the question why. Why on earth had he signed up for this class? Was it for Ellen's sake? Either he was the most dutiful relative ever or something weird was going on, perhaps blackmail.

The waltz ended, and Lindy extricated herself from Maureen's rather bony clutches to switch off the music, before turning to everyone with a light, friendly clap. "Wonderful effort, everyone! Now, to mix things up a bit, why don't we change partners?"

Dutifully everyone came apart, looking around each other with the sort of shy uncertainty of a twelve-year-old being chosen for a team sport in PE. Lindy decided to take control. "Simon, why don't you go with Maureen, and Olivia, you can go with…" She was about to say Roger when she saw his utterly stricken look, and decided quickly to change. "Ellen. I'll take Roger." She gave him what she hoped was a smiling, encouraging look but his expression of something close to terror had turned to a more predictable scowl. *What was with this man?* Lindy wondered. He was the proverbial riddle wrapped in an enigma. She couldn't understand him at all, or why he was here.

Simon and Olivia, Maureen and Ellen all gamely took their places, and Lindy put another waltz on her phone. As the strains came through the speakers, she turned to her partner.

"So now I'm the woman, and you're the man," she said, and Roger gave her an incredulous look.

"I did not realise such a thing was in any doubt."

Lindy swallowed her instinctive gurgle of laughter. "I only meant, because I was dancing as the man with Maureen."

"But you're not with Maureen," he pointed out, and Lindy only just kept from rolling her eyes.

"Right. So, as you're the man, you're meant to lead." She took his hand—warm, dry, strong, she couldn't help but notice—in hers and placed her other hand on his shoulder. Also warm, dry, strong. And his aftershave, if that's what it was, was quite a nice smell. Understated and old-fashioned, perhaps bay rum. "You put your hand on my waist," she reminded him, and with a look on his face that made him seem as if he were reaching into a pit of wriggling snakes with his bare hand, Roger planted his palm on the dip of her waist.

"Very good," Lindy encouraged. If she felt a little frisson of something at the feel of his hand on her waist, it had to be merely relief that he was coping okay so far. Everyone else had started shuffling around, but she and Roger still had their feet glued to the floor. At least they were in position.

"And now you lead," Lindy continued in a tone similar to one she suspected was used when soothing a wild horse. "Right foot forward, left foot side, right to left, and back—"

Somehow, with a bit of stumbling and jerky steps, they got through the basics. "And now again," Lindy said as once more they went through the box step. "See, this is easy."

"I would have to disagree on that point," Roger replied dryly, so dryly that Lindy thought he was simply making a statement rather than being wry. Or was he? She looked up, scanning his face for clues and finding none.

Then Roger glanced down at her, his warm, whisky-brown gaze meeting her own for a second that felt weirdly jolting, making Lindy's hand spasm a little on his shoulder. What was *wrong* with her?

She wasn't sure who looked away first; she had a feeling they'd both jerked their gazes away as fast as they could, the same way you might yank your hand back from an open flame. And in truth it had, very oddly, felt a little bit like that. Lindy could make absolutely no sense of her reaction. It wasn't as if…no, she couldn't even think that. It was ridiculous. Utterly ridiculous.

"You're doing very well," she told him and Roger moved his gaze back to hers with obvious reluctance.

"I am not. Please don't humour me."

"You're not enjoying yourself?" she dared to tease, and his serious expression did not flicker in the least.

"I am not."

"Why did you register, then?" Lindy couldn't help but ask. "Was it just for your mum's sake? She is your mum, isn't she?"

A tiny pause, like a flinch, although Roger's expression didn't change. Lindy was starting to think it very rarely changed. "Yes, she is, and yes, that is more or less the reason," he said, the words offered reluctantly, making Lindy wonder.

The waltz was coming to an end, and so with a quick, apologetic smile, Lindy stepped back from Roger and then hurried over to turn the music off.

"Right, everyone, that was a brilliant start," she sang out cheerfully. "How are you all feeling?"

"Brilliant," Ellen parroted back enthusiastically while Maureen rubbed her lower back.

"Like I'm a bit creaky," she said in her no-nonsense, al-most brusque way. "But then I am, and more than a bit."

"Why don't we have a tea break?" Lindy suggested. They'd only been going for half an hour, but she felt the need for a cuppa, and she thought her pupils did, as well. "And then we'll start again."

She glanced at Roger—she wasn't sure why—but he wasn't looking at her. He had gone over to his mother, and was stooping slightly to speak to her, a look of concern on his face, making Lindy wonder. Again.

As if sensing her speculative gaze on him, he looked up, right at her—and frowned. No jolt this time, unless it was of embarrassment. Lindy quickly turned away, wondering yet again just what intrigued her about Roger Wentworth, when he had to be one of the dullest, most staid people she'd ever met.

Chapter Three

THE DOOR TO Tea on the Lea, Olivia James's bakery and teashop, jangled merrily as Lindy followed her friends Ava, Harriet, Alice and Emily inside. It was a rainy Saturday afternoon, nearly a week since she'd started her dancing classes, and she'd been more or less strong-armed into joining everyone for a Saturday afternoon cream tea. Lindy was game enough, although she wished Ellie had been able to make it. She'd only seen her friend once since she'd moved down south, and while she understood that Ellie was busy, it still felt a bit disappointing.

"So, Lindy," Harriet said as she pushed two small wrought-iron tables together and then began arranging chairs, clearly a woman in charge, "you've got to dish all the gossip on who is dancing with whom."

"I don't think there's any gossip to dish," Lindy replied with a smile. Monday's class had gone well enough—after practising the waltz for another half hour, she'd moved on to a basic cross step. Maureen had had to stop midway because her arthritis was playing up, and Simon and Olivia had been fairly hopeless if cheerfully willing. As for Roger and El-len…every time Lindy thought of them she fought an urge to laugh, or at least smile.

Ellen had been so relentlessly chipper, and Roger had looked…tortured. Perhaps constipated. Actually, both. She hadn't really had a chance to talk to him again beyond giving him instructions, and yet she had been weirdly curious about a man who seemed to be the definition of 'what it says on the tin.' Surely there were no hidden depths to a man like Roger Wentworth. Most people would call him a bore, if not a downright pillock. He was pedantic, sanctimonious, stuffy, *and* grumpy.

When Lindy had been making the tea, he'd wiped the inside of the mugs with his handkerchief. Admittedly the cups had looked a bit tea-stained and grotty, but still. Something about his prim fussiness got right up her nose, and yet he made her curious.

"You seem like the sort of man who is in possession of a cotton handkerchief," she'd teased him as she'd brought out the tea, and he'd given her a blankly uncomprehending look before replying, "I would prefer to be a man with a cotton handkerchief than one without."

Again Lindy had wondered if this was his deadpan hu-mour, but she had a feeling he was just being serious. Very serious.

"There must be some gossip," Harriet insisted as they all sat down and Olivia came from behind the counter to take their orders.

"Well, there are two lovebirds in my class," Lindy said in the voice of someone telling a secret. She grinned at Olivia who smiled and blushed. "They're completely smitten."

Harriet rolled her eyes. "You must mean Simon and Olivia, and we all know *that*. How could we not?" She gave Olivia an affectionate look. "The wedding is only three months away now."

"Three and a half," Olivia corrected with a smile. "Don't panic me, Harriet! I've still got so much to do, but it's not until after Christmas. Now what is everyone having?"

"Cream teas all around, I think," Harriet said with an enquiring glance for everyone at the table. "Clotted cream and jam, please, and two scones each."

"Two!" Ava exclaimed in mock horror. "Harriet, are you trying to fatten us all up?"

"One simply isn't enough," Harriet declared in the tone of someone stating a universal truth. Lindy decided not to contest the point. She could put away two scones easily, even if her waistline wouldn't thank her for it.

As Olivia bustled away to prepare their cream teas and everyone settled more comfortably into their seats, Lindy glanced covertly at the group of women she was only just coming to call friends. There was Harriet, clearly a leader both of this little tribe as well as in the village; Lindy had already heard of the organisations she was running and the PR business she'd started.

Ava was another leader, in her own, understated way—oozing confidence and sex appeal in equal measure, voluptuous in the fourth month of her pregnancy.

Then there was Alice, who seemed younger than the others, with a fragile, blonde beauty and an ethereal air. She seemed to be growing into her role as lady of the manor, possessing a shy confidence that only occasionally wilted. Lastly there was Emily, the other resident of Willoughby Close; she'd moved in just a few months before Lindy. Like Alice, Emily was younger, quieter, possessing a sense of containment that bordered on wariness, although from all the snippets Lindy had heard, she seemed to have relaxed since coming to Wychwood-on-Lea and starting to date Owen Jones, the former owner of the village's 'rougher' pub, which was now a pop-up pub in a van.

They all, Lindy suspected, had grown into themselves since moving to Wychwood-on-Lea, something Olivia had confirmed when Lindy had mentioned it.

"Willoughby Close seems to have that effect on people," she'd said with a laugh. "At least it did on me."

Which had, of course, made Lindy wonder if her new home would have a similar, magical effect on her. Would she grow in confidence? Gain a sense of serenity? Or maybe find true love?

She was smiling rather wryly to herself at the thought of any of those, but especially the last one, when Harriet once again broke in with a request for gossip. "So who *is* taking the ballroom dancing class?" she asked. "Besides Olivia and Simon?"

"Only a few other people." Lindy took in all the avid expressions and wondered at divulging any personal details. "A variety of beginners," she said in a tone that suggested she was done with the conversation, but Harriet didn't seem to take the hint.

"Anyone interesting?" she asked with an over-the-top waggle of her eyebrows. "Anyone single?" For some stupid reason Lindy thought of Roger Wentworth and started to blush. "There is someone!" Harriet crowed gleefully and everyone leaned forward in expectant interest. Even worse, Lindy started to laugh. It tended to be her default in a lot of situations in life, which was sometimes good and sometimes—not.

"Who is it?" Ava asked with a throaty gurgle of laughter. "Because your face is on *fire*."

"No, honestly, there's no one," Lindy managed when she'd got her gasps of laughter under control. "Absolutely no one. There's one single man in the class and he's—" She stopped abruptly, not wanting to gossip, and even more importantly, not wanting to say anything blatantly unkind about Roger Wentworth.

"He's what?" Harriet asked and Lindy shook her head firmly.

"He's not suitable."

"That makes him all the more interesting," Ava protested

with a wicked glint in her eye and Lindy decided she needed to nip this one in the bud.

"No, really, he isn't anyone I'd ever think that way about at *all*. Which is good, really, because he's a pupil of mine and it would be inappropriate. So." She let out a huff of breath, hoping she'd convinced everyone. They were looking somewhat sceptical.

"Olivia?" Harriet called finally, towards the counter where Olivia was assembling the pots of cream and jam. "What do you think? Who is this oh-so-unsuitable man in your dancing class?"

"There's no one unsuitable, per se," Olivia returned with a sympathetic look for Lindy, "although we're all beginners."

Laughingly Harriet threw up her hands. "I'm looking forward to meeting this guy. He sounds intriguing."

Thankfully, and helpfully, Alice moved the conversation on, with an effort akin to pushing a very large boulder up a very steep hill. "You're doing a children's class too, aren't you, Lindy?"

Lindy threw her a grateful look. "Yes, it starts next week."

"Any other classes?" Harriet asked, and regretfully Lindy shook her head.

"No, sadly not. I was hoping for an intermediate class but there haven't been any takers yet."

"How did you get interested in ballroom dancing?" Ava interjected. "It's such a cool hobby."

"My dad, actually," Lindy said. "He was a great dancer, and he taught me pretty much everything I know." She smiled in memory. "When I got a bit older, I started taking lessons on my own, and I joined a ballroom dancing club up in Manchester."

"Your dad must be so proud then," Emily told her with a warm smile, and Lindy hesitated for a fraction of a second before surrendering to the inevitable.

"I know he would be," she said in the firm, upbeat tone she'd learned to adopt for moments like these. "Unfortunately he died a long time ago. My mum, too." Might as well get it over with in one fell swoop. Lindy was half-amazed this conversation hadn't happened earlier; she'd been living here for two months, after all, but somehow the subject of her orphan status hadn't come up. It didn't always, when you hit your midthirties. Often she discovered she wasn't the only one, which was a sight different from when she'd been nineteen and completely alone.

"Oh, I'm so sorry," Emily blurted, looking horrified by her seeming faux pas, and Lindy smiled at her in reassurance.

"Like I said, it was a long time ago." She registered the usual spectrum of expressions, from stricken to sympathetic with a hefty dose of awkward thrown in. She was used to it. She was also used to the unabashed relief that washed everyone's expressions clean when she told them it was a long time ago, implying she was completely over it. She certainly tried to be.

"I'm sure he would be proud," Ava said quietly, giving Lindy a look that suggested she had some inkling of what she really felt. Lindy smiled back, and then looked away, because whenever she skirted too close to the grief she'd firmly put away more than fifteen years ago, she felt her throat go tight and her eyes start to sting, and she definitely didn't want to go there. Life was for living, for enjoying, for wringing the zest out of. It wasn't for looking back.

Olivia started bringing over their cream teas, which looked delicious, and thankfully the chatter moved on to talk of bumps and babies and weddings—all of which was completely outside Lindy's experience.

They were just setting to slathering scones in several heart attacks' worth of clotted cream when the bells on the door jangled again, and to her surprise and then dawning horror, considering what she'd just said about him, Lindy saw Roger Wentworth coming into the teashop. And even more alarmingly, he saw her.

ROGER'S GAZE ZEROED in on Lindy sitting in the back of the shop with a gaggle of women and his heart seemed to bump in his chest before doing a sickly plummet towards his toes. This was definitely not good.

Could he just pretend he hadn't seen her? Difficult, when they'd most certainly made eye contact. Somewhat surprisingly, considering how often he suspected he appeared to be, Roger didn't like to seem rude. And ignoring Lindy now, when she was still gazing at him, wide-eyed and open-mouthed, would be rude indeed.

But the alternative was surely not to be contemplated. To walk across the room and say hello—with not one or two but *four* women all watching him with goggle-eyed speculation—was surely impossible. Literally impossible. His feet felt as if they were stuck to the floor.

The more rational part of his brain reminded him that he was thirty-eight years old, not thirteen; he was in charge of an entire department at work; he was perfectly capable of basic social niceties, or even more advanced ones, at least on occasion. In other words, he could do this.

And yet…all four women had looked up to gaze at him with such blatant curiosity, and Lindy…Lindy looked amazing, Roger acknowledged as his heart, in addition to bumping and then plummeting, seemed to do a weird little flip in his chest. Technically impossible, but still.

That's what it felt like when he looked at her—her golden-brown hair tumbling halfway down her back, bright blue-green eyes fringed with luxuriant lashes. She had, he noticed, a little mole at the corner of her mouth. She was dressed in a far less ridiculous outfit than when she'd been leading the dance class—a plain white T-shirt and a loose, dark green cardigan that was half-sliding off her shoulder, with a pair of skinny jeans that made the most of her generous curves.

Roger noticed all this in a heart-stopping instant—yes,

his heart now felt frozen on top of all the other sensations he'd experienced—and with a smile that he knew must look more like a rictus, he began to walk stiffly over to the table, keeping his gaze on Lindy who, unfortunately, was now looking as if she'd rather he'd stayed where he was, that initial smile sliding off her face just like the cardigan was off her shoulder, her eyes clouding in a way he didn't understand but felt fairly certain had to be ominous.

Had he read the social cues incorrectly? Would it *not* have been rude to ignore her? Perhaps this act of approaching her—a teacher, not an acquaintance or friend—was actually the rude thing to do. Inappropriate, violating her personal time and space. Roger realised he had no idea, and he hated the swamping at-sea feeling that created in him—a sensation he was, unfortunately, well used to when it came to moments like these.

"Roger." Lindy's voice and accompanying smile both sounded a bit forced. "How nice to see you."

"I'm just picking something up for my mother." Inwardly Roger cringed at the words that emitted from him almost robotically. Could he sound more awkward, more *weird*?

"For Ellen?" Lindy said, her smile looking slightly less fixed, and Roger nodded.

"Yes. Scones. She likes the cheese ones in particular." As if that was in any way relevant to this abysmal conversation. He really needed to stop. He had this most unfortunate habit—a kind of tic—to simply state facts and consider it conversation. He pressed his lips together to keep from saying anything more. He could already feel the women all looking at him with a curiosity that was both amused and a bit horrified, something else he was well used to. He couldn't see any of the other women, because he was refusing to make eye contact, which he realised belatedly was most likely another weird thing, since he seemed to be staring at Lindy so fixedly, but he could feel their transfixed curiosity.

He forced himself to move his gaze a little bit to the left, where there was a rather garish plate fixed to the wall from the Queen's Jubilee. He studied it with an intensity he didn't remotely feel.

"You must be from Lindy's dance class," a woman said, her voice so obviously laced with rich amusement that Roger tensed even more. The woman sounded as if she knew all about him. Had Lindy been talking about him? Laughing about him? He knew he shouldn't even be surprised, and yet some part of him felt not surprised, but…no. He didn't feel anything. Why should he?

He turned to gaze at the woman who'd spoken—about his age, with a knowing manner, her eyes alight, her head cocked to one side.

"Yes, I am from the dance class," he said stiffly, and fortunately he managed to leave it at that. He did not want to say anything that would either embarrass or implicate him further.

"Roger is attending with his mother Ellen," Lindy explained. "Doing her a favour, I think." She smiled at him, inviting him to share the joke, and Roger knew—in his head, at least—that this would be a perfect opportunity to lighten the moment, to ruefully say something about how he'd been dragged to the dance class, how he had not two but actually three left feet, how Lindy just might make a tango-er of him yet. Something. Anything. He could see the script running through his head, and yet somehow it was beyond him to articulate any of it.

What he said was, in the rather petulant voice of a little boy, "I don't like dancing."

Everyone stared.

"We'll see how you are at the end of the term!" Lindy returned brightly, and after another excruciating pause, Roger decided they'd all had enough.

"Yes. Well. I shall see you on Monday." He nodded stiffly, not meeting anyone's eye, and then retreated to the counter. The silence in the shop felt suffocating, as if a lead blanket was draped over the room. Roger focused on his breathing, staring straight ahead, as Olivia came to the counter with a smile.

"Roger! Four cheese scones as usual?"

"Yes, please."

"How is Ellen?"

"Fine."

"It was lovely to see you at the dance class," she said quietly, a look of sympathy in her eyes, and Roger just nodded.

Olivia fetched the scones and Roger stayed where he was, conscious of the women all huddled together in the back of the shop, silent and seemingly expectant, no doubt waiting for him to leave so they could gossip about him.

"Well," one of them said after a moment in what he suspected was meant to be a whisper he wasn't supposed to hear, "I get what you mean about him being *unsuitable*." This was followed by a hasty 'shh' and then some smothered laughter.

Olivia handed him the scones and Roger paid without speaking. He left the shop without a word or a glance for the women. He knew, of course, that they'd been talking about him—it seemed Lindy had said he was *unsuitable*. For what? Dancing? *Dating?*

Roger couldn't bear to think about it. He burned with humiliation just at the thought of them gossiping about him, as well as his own lamentable behaviour. *I don't like dancing.* What was *wrong* with him?

It was a question he'd asked himself many times over the years. Why did he have to be so awkward in social groups? Why couldn't he joke and laugh and chat as easily as everyone else seemed to do? Why did he have to sound so pompous when he wanted to be light and wry?

When he'd been a child, maybe eight or nine, he recalled having a set of medical assessments that had turned up nothing, no diagnosis for what, at that point, had just been an average, run-of-the-mill awkwardness. Back then autism hadn't really been known or talked about, and it had certainly never crossed his or his parents' minds.

Then, after university, when everyone was talking about 'being on the spectrum,' he'd considered seriously whether he was. He'd even booked an appointment with his GP, which had been awkward in the extreme, as he'd explained his symptoms and asked his doctor if he thought he was worthy of a diagnosis.

"Honestly, Roger," his GP had said in a rather jovial tone, "everyone is on the spectrum somewhere. It's just a matter of where. I don't think you have anything to be too concerned about, really."

Which hadn't been an answer at all. He shouldn't be *too* concerned? Did that mean he should be somewhat concerned?

His mother had always done her best to allay his unvoiced concerns.

"Roger, you're just like your father. Still waters run deep. Don't worry so much, darling. You're an amazing person."

Such reassurance might have worked when he was twelve; not so much when he was pushing forty. He wasn't just quiet; he was awkward. He knew he was. Sometimes he managed to make a joke of it, which made everyone look humiliatingly relieved. It was somewhat acceptable to be awkward as long as you realised you were, apparently. Unfortunately he didn't always realise, and worse, he couldn't stop it even when he did. At the end of it all, Roger had done his best to make peace with who he was—and who he wasn't. He knew well enough he couldn't change, not that much anyway.

Various people—mainly hopeful women—had tried over the years. Girlfriends who longed to possess some sort of key to unlock him, only to become frustrated, disappointed, or bitter when he proved to be too intractable. Not that there had been that many girlfriends. Two, to be precise, which considering his age was a bit on the pathetic side, but Roger wasn't looking for a relationship right now.

He'd put all that behind him after the last disaster a few years ago, when his last girlfriend, Laurel, had thrown a glass of wine in his face and told him tearfully that he was a cold-hearted bastard. He hadn't even realised he'd done anything wrong.

He still wasn't sure what had offended Laurel so much— his forgetting their three-month anniversary? His insistence that it was not a particularly significant date? Or his refusal to buy the most expensive bottle of champagne in the restaurant to celebrate what he felt was a non-occasion? Perhaps all three, and more.

"Darling?" Ellen's voice floated from the sitting room as Roger came into his mother's cottage. He spent most of his Saturdays with Ellen; although she protested he needed to 'get out,' there weren't many places Roger actually went. Besides, he hated the thought of his mum suffering alone— tired, ill, afraid.

This afternoon, despite the warmth of the September sun, she was lying on the settee in the sitting room, wrapped up in a crocheted afghan, looking wan and pale even as she smiled at him.

Roger poked his head in the doorway as he held up the paper bag. "Scones."

"You're an angel, Roger."

"Would you like one now? With a cup of tea?"

His mother made a rueful face. "I'm not very hungry just now. Maybe later."

Which meant the scones would most likely go uneaten. His mother, Roger knew, was wasting away, slowly but surely, no matter how many nourishing soups and stews he made, or cups of tea he brewed, or scones he bought. He also knew it was pointless to argue with her over the matter.

"Did you see anyone in town?" Ellen asked hopefully as Roger took the scones into the kitchen. "Anyone interesting?"

His mother always seemed to be hoping he'd run into the love of his life while buying milk or putting petrol in his car. Roger placed the scones in the breadbox as the memory of those four laughing women—and Lindy—flashed through his mind.

"No," he called back rather flatly. "No one at all."

Chapter Four

"IS THIS THE dance class?"

A harried-looking woman with sunglasses pushed on top of her highlighted blonde hair poked her head into the dance studio as Lindy offered her best and brightest smile—a somewhat difficult feat, as she'd been inexplicably feeling a little low this last week.

Well, not so inexplicably, unfortunately. She knew exactly why she was feeling low. She just didn't like the reason.

"Yes, it is." Lindy focused her attention on the girl of about six or so who was peeping from behind her mother's legs, offering her a shy smile like a gift. She had blonde ringlets and blue eyes and was wearing a gauzy pink tutu. "You must be Emma...or Zoe...or Carys?" There were three girls and one boy in her juniors' class so far, although she was hoping more might join in time.

"Zoe." The woman was looking around the room a bit dubiously, frowning at the garishly bright *Strictly Ballroom* poster Lindy had put up on one wall. "This *is* a ballet class, isn't it?"

Ballet? "No, it's a ballroom dancing class," Lindy corrected with another attempt at a bright and breezy smile. "Waltz…tango…foxtrot…that sort of thing."

"What?" The woman looked alarmed and even appalled as she gazed at Lindy with something like suspicion. "Ballroom dancing for *children?* But I thought it was ballet!"

"No, sorry." Where, Lindy wondered, had the woman got that idea? All her advertising, every single brochure and poster, not to mention her website, spelled out ballroom dancing in great, glaring letters. She'd even decorated it with some clip art of a waltzing couple.

"I was sure it was ballet." Now the woman sounded accusing, as if Lindy had conspired to trick her. Great. This was not an auspicious start to her first children's class.

She held on to her smile with some effort. "Ballroom dancing is fun," she said in the jolly tone of a PE teacher. "And it helps with coordination and gets kids up and moving."

The woman didn't look convinced, but before she could respond, someone else had come in, and Lindy soon discovered she'd thought it was a ballet class, as well. Within a few minutes it became all too apparent that all four parents had thought they were signing up for a ballet, rather than ballroom dancing, class, and were all in various degrees of displeasure to realise that wasn't the case.

"I only signed up because Twirling Tots is full," the first woman, Zoe's mum, told the others as she gave Lindy a withering glance. *This was her fault how…?*

Lindy tried to be understanding—a quick, harried glance at a brochure, the assumption that six-year-olds wanted to wear tutus and do pirouettes rather than tango or foxtrot, was understandable.

Fortunately, three of the parents were happy for their children to attend a ballroom dancing class instead, deciding that an hour's free time while their child bounced around was good enough for them; Zoe's mother, however, chose to leave in a huff.

"It's just as well," Emma's mother, Ishbel, said with a conspiratorial smile. "She's a bit of a nightmare, to be honest."

"Zoe or her mother?" Lindy half-joked, and Ishbel looked at her seriously.

"Both."

Ishbel and the other two parents soon left, happy to be footloose and fancy free on a Saturday morning, and Lindy turned to her three remaining pupils with determined delight. She'd been so excited for this class, and the fact that Carys was looking decidedly baleful was not going to dent her enthusiasm one bit.

It had been dented enough already, what with that awful, *awful* exchange in Tea on the Lea a week ago. Lindy wasn't even sure why it had bothered her so much—Roger had been characteristically awkward and fairly unlikeable, but Harriet's hushed whisper about him being unsuitable, followed with such a telling laugh, had made Lindy's face burn with mortification.

She'd been able to tell immediately that Roger had heard, although she wasn't even sure how she knew such a thing. He certainly hadn't looked at them; he hadn't even moved, and yet she'd *known*. He'd walked quickly out of the shop with his four cheese scones and she'd felt wretched, more wretched than she'd expected to feel. Harriet had been a bit abashed but fairly unrepentant, claiming he couldn't have heard, and even if he had, he wouldn't have known what the remark meant. Lindy wasn't so sure.

She'd tried a fumbling apology to him on Monday's class, although what she was apologising for she couldn't even say—that she'd considered him an unsuitable person to date? That she'd said so? That her friends had laughed about it? None of it was anything she actually wanted to admit, never mind apologise for, and in the end she'd barely begun her faltering apology before Roger had cut her off.

"About the other day…" she'd started, and he'd given her a freezing look and said coldly, "I apologise for my conduct. I realised belatedly that you were off duty, so to speak. I shouldn't have said hello, and for that I am sorry."

Lindy had stared at him, appalled by his assessment, and she tried to protest. "No, no, it wasn't that—" she began, but Roger had already turned away, and there had been no further opportunity to talk, not that Lindy would have even know what to say. She told herself it was silly to feel so badly about it—it had been nothing more than a moment, and no doubt Roger would find her just as unsuitable as she found him. Really, the whole thing was ridiculous, and yet a week later the memory of that moment felt like a thorn in her flesh, a slight but constant, nagging discomfort.

"Are we going to dance?" Emma—or maybe it was Carys—demanded, hands on hips, and Lindy decided it was time to stop thinking about Roger.

"We certainly are," she declared brightly, and went to turn on the music.

An hour later, three happy children—Emma, Carys, and Ollie—tumbled out of her class, fizzing with excitement about having learned the basic box step, although most of the hour had been spent careening around the room or making faces in the mirror. Still, they'd all had fun. At least, Lindy hoped they had.

"This is such a fun idea," Ishbel enthused as she collected Emma. "You should think about offering classes in school—I think every Year Six pupil should know how to waltz before heading to secondary!"

"There's an idea," Lindy answered with a laugh, and Ollie's father, Will, looked at her seriously.

"Actually, I think it's a brilliant idea. I'm a governor at the school—I'll run it by the head teacher if you're interested?"

"Oh, um…" Lindy was startled but pleased. "All right," she said, because why not? "Thanks."

All three parents—Ishbel, Will, and Liz—seemed very pleased with the class, and promised to return next week. Lindy's mood was decidedly more upbeat as she headed back to Willoughby Close, although as she came into the courtyard—empty as usual on a Saturday afternoon—she felt her spirits start to, if not flag, then at least wilt just a little.

She'd been in Wychwood-on-Lea for two and a half months, and it didn't feel like home yet, no matter how welcoming everyone had been. No place, Lindy had acknowledged, had ever felt like home, save for a tumbledown cottage nestled in the Peak District that was crammed with curios and antiques and had been brimming with love.

She sighed as she unlocked the door to her cottage, determined not to feel down. Upbeat was her thing, optimism her motto. She didn't *do* sad or depressed, because it wasn't in her nature. And it never helped, anyway.

But sometimes, Lindy acknowledged as she stepped into her sitting room, such feelings couldn't be contained. Perhaps it was all the time she had on her hands. Back in Manchester, she'd worked from eight to six Monday to Friday, and the weekends had been spent catching up on housework, errands and shopping. Her weekly dance class and occasional drinks with work friends had been social life enough. She'd been happy.

So why had she moved? To follow a dream that felt as if it were flagging, before it had achieved any real lift-off? She'd taught all of three classes. She couldn't give up yet, or even think about giving up. She wasn't going to. She was just having a little moan in the quiet of her own mind, and she'd be fine in a few minutes. She always was.

Yet her lowering spirits didn't lift as she looked around her little sitting room—pretty enough with its squashy sofa and patchwork throw, the big comfy chair she loved to curl up in facing the French windows. Admittedly, compared to the happy chaos she'd grown up with, it all looked a little bare, but that had been something of a deliberate choice. She couldn't replicate her childhood home, and she wasn't going to try.

There was plenty she could do now, Lindy reminded herself. She could update her website, or go food shopping, or simply take a walk through the wood or along the Lea River. Normally, she'd be content to do any of those things, yet for some reason right now she was feeling a bit restless. A bit alone.

Lindy let out another sigh as she gazed through the French windows to the postage stamp of garden outside. Olivia was working this afternoon, and Alice and Henry were away for the weekend. Emily was out with Owen, and Lindy didn't feel she knew Harriet or Ava well enough to see what they were up to. She'd left a voicemail with Ellie last night, and so far she hadn't had a response. Who else was there to call, to see?

She had a handful of friends from work in Manchester, and she was sure some of them would be happy to hear from her now, but Lindy knew the conversation would require some heavy lifting on her part and right now she wanted to be with someone who knew her. The kind of person you could be silent with and have it not matter.

Unfortunately, since her parents died, there had been no one like that in her life, which was a depressing thought and one she usually chose not to dwell on.

Lindy's gaze rested on the orange-and-black-striped cat sitting elegantly on her fence post—Cass, Emily's cat. Emily adored him, and the feeling was clearly mutual.

There was an idea, Lindy thought suddenly. What if she got a cat, or even a dog? She'd always liked pets, although they'd never been able to have one when she was growing up, because of how much they'd travelled. But why not now? She had time on her hands and was home during the day, unlike when she'd been living and working in Manchester, when a pet hadn't been a possibility.

But now…she could have a companion; dog or cat, it didn't really matter. She liked both equally well. The idea filled her with pleasure, and more importantly, with hope. She didn't have to be alone. She didn't have to sit here stewing in her cottage, struggling not to feel lonely when all she wanted was to be happy and get on with her life. Why not get a cat or dog, even today?

"Hey there, boy."

Roger stroked the greyhound's sleek head as he gave him a sympathetic smile. Toby had only just joined the rehoming centre, and he was still a bit skittish. Roger knew the feeling.

He straightened and closed the door to Toby's kennel before moving on to the next one. He volunteered twice a month at the Blue Cross Rehoming Centre just outside Burford, and he loved the quiet hours he spent there, helping to socialise animals and occasionally dealing with people. He preferred the animals. He knew what to do with them, how to make them happy, and it was an added bonus that they didn't talk.

He'd considered taking a break from volunteering after his mother's diagnosis, but she'd been insistent he continue.

"You love it so much, Roger, and you've already sacrificed so much for me. I don't want you to sacrifice anything more."

Roger wasn't sure he'd sacrificed all that much—a soulless flat in Oxford? He much preferred his cottage off the high street, just around the corner from his mother's. Admittedly the commute was a bit more substantial, but he could live with that, and it got him on his bike, which took care of exercise…along with the ballroom dancing he'd been doing once a week.

Roger winced as he remembered Monday's rather excruciating lesson. Lindy had tried to apologise for whatever had happened in the teashop, and Roger hadn't been able to stand it. It had been such a small thing anyway, at least small to most people.

In any case, he'd brushed off her apology and done his best to avoid her for the rest of the class, which was somewhat difficult when she was the instructor and he was a rather poor pupil. Still, he'd managed it, and he'd wondered if Lindy had been relieved. She certainly hadn't tried to seek him out again, which was fine. *Fine.*

His mother had noticed, however, and asked him if anything had happened, to which Roger had replied, rather sharply, that of course nothing had. And nothing ever would.

"You are enjoying the classes, aren't you, Roger?" Ellen had asked anxiously, and Roger had forced a smile. Normally his nature compelled him to an often awkward honesty, but with his mother he could lie, because he loved her.

"Actually, I am," he said, and she gave a sorrowful little laugh and stood on her tiptoes to kiss his cheek.

"Oh, Roger, I know you're not, not really, but thank you for saying so. And thank you for going to the classes with me. You're the kindest and most loving son a mother could ever ask for."

Which was the kind of talk that alarmed Roger, along with the C-word. So he'd muttered something about it being nothing, and his mother had just smiled, and the conversation had thankfully moved on, without Roger having to mention either cancer or Lindy, which was a plus.

Having said hello to the dozen or so animals currently in

residence at the centre, Roger retreated to the front desk to greet any enquiring customers who might come through the door and also to look through the charity's books, something he did for free since he was an accountant.

He'd been sitting there for about twenty minutes, scanning the monthly figures, when the door opened and he heard an audible gasp. He looked up, and felt that weird heart thing—a flip, a flutter, a jolt or jerk, maybe all four—as he saw Lindy Jamison coming through the door.

Chapter Five

THE LOOK OF horror on Roger Wentworth's face was comical. Almost. Lindy suspected she had a similar expression on her face, although she quickly masked it with a smile. At least, she hoped she did. She realised she was actually rather pleased to see him, despite what had and hadn't passed between them before.

"Roger! What are you doing here?" she asked as she came into the reception area of the rehoming centre, a small space with a couple of chairs and a counter that Roger stood behind.

"I volunteer here," he answered in a well-duh sort of tone. "Two Saturdays a month, afternoons only."

"I didn't know," Lindy said, and Roger gave her a blank look.

"That is to be expected, considering I never imparted the information."

"Right." She smiled, struggling not to laugh, because his deadpan manner was surprisingly charming if still slightly odd. "I suppose there's a lot I don't know about you, except that you don't like dancing. I haven't changed your mind on that one yet?"

Roger managed a tight smile. "No, you have not."

"It's very kind of you, to come with your mother."

He inclined his head, saying nothing, and Lindy wondered if that was something of a no-go area. He was a very difficult man to read.

"You do like animals, I suppose?"

"Yes."

"Have you got a pet of your own?"

"No, that would be quite impossible, with the amount I work."

"What do you do?" Lindy was starting to feel like an interrogator, but she really was curious.

"I'm an accountant."

"Oh, wow, are you? That's what I did up in Manchester, before I started Take a Twirl." He gave her a look of blank incomprehension, as if he could not imagine such a thing, and Lindy let out a gurgle of laughter. "What, do I not seem like an accountant?"

"I did not consider your previous employment one way or the other," Roger answered.

"Still," Lindy teased, "you seem surprised."

"I confess, if I'd had to take a guess as to what profession you'd been involved in formerly, I would most likely not have considered accountancy."

"Hmm." Lindy tapped her chin thoughtfully. "You don't

seem like a man prone to taking guesses." She realised, with an electric jolt of shock, that she sounded as if she were flirting, but she couldn't be, surely. Roger Wentworth was, after all, so *unsuitable.*

Colour had risen in Roger's cheeks, and Lindy suspected he didn't know how to respond to her flirtatious manner. She didn't even know why she'd adopted it; it really wasn't like her. She'd had precisely one romantic relationship in her life, and it had fizzled out after just a few months. Flirting was not her forte, and that was probably obvious, even to Roger.

"Guesses should be based on probability," Roger replied after a moment. "And so I'd consider them rather as informed estimations, which are perfectly reasonable to give."

"Spoken like a true accountant."

He gave a little nod, and Lindy wondered what she was hoping to achieve through this conversation. A smile, she supposed, would be nice.

"I presume you're here for a particular reason?" he asked, and it was clear their conversation, such as it had been, was over.

"Yes, I am, actually. I was hoping to adopt a pet. A cat or a dog, in particular."

"You wish to rehome one of our animals currently in residence?" he verified, and Lindy nodded.

"That is correct." She realised she might sound as if she was mocking him with her serious tone, but she wasn't. It was just difficult not to talk like Roger when she was with him. It was similar to how she felt after watching a Jane Austen adaptation on the BBC—she suddenly had an urge to say things like 'prithee, sir' and to curtsey.

"The process must begin with you filling out an online application, which is then reviewed by the staff," Roger explained, sounding slightly censorious of her ignorance of this matter. Lindy supposed she should have looked it up online before haring out here, but she'd been so excited to enact her plan.

"I see," she said after a second's pause. "Could I do that now?"

"I suppose that would be possible, but as I have already said, the application will need to be reviewed by a member of staff. I'm only a volunteer."

"Oh. Right. Of course." Lindy fought against the stupid, sweeping sense of disappointment this news caused. Of course you couldn't just pop in and get a puppy. Nothing worked that way anymore.

"If you like," Roger said stiffly, "I could show you the animals we currently have in residence."

"Oh, could you?" Lindy couldn't keep from sounding as if he'd just offered her the moon, making Roger look a bit taken aback. "That would be fab."

"Very well." He came out from behind the desk; unlike every time she'd seen him before, he was not wearing a suit. He wore a navy-blue polo shirt with the Blue Cross logo, and a pair of tan khakis. Boring clothes, and yet even so Lindy couldn't keep from noticing how fit he was—a broad chest, muscled arms, powerful legs. It helped that he was well over six feet, probably pushing six three or six four. But why on earth was she thinking this way? This was Roger. Unsuitable, somewhat annoying Roger.

"Come this way," Roger instructed, and obediently Lindy followed him to a heavy metal door that led to the kennels.

"How long have you been working here?" she asked as he unlocked the door.

"Six years, I believe."

"You live in Wychwood-on-Lea?"

"Yes."

He wasn't particularly chatty, Lindy acknowledged, but he didn't sound as if he minded her questions all that much, and so she kept at it.

"You grew up in Wychwood?" she asked as she followed him through the door to a concrete hallway with kennels on either side. The ensuing yapping, barking, and meowing kept Roger from replying for a moment and Lindy looked around in both dismay and wonder—the animals were all lovely, but many looked battered and bruised, victims of circumstance or even cruelty.

"Oh, what a sweetie." She stopped in front of the first kennel that housed a Yorkshire terrier with huge eyes and white, fluffy fur. "May I pet her? Or is it a him?"

A heavy pause ensued as Roger gazed into the kennel, his expression impossible to read. "It's a her, and very well," he said at last, and he unlocked the kennel, crouching down as he began to speak to the tiny Yorkshire terrier in a soothing voice, his gentle tone quite unlike any other that Lindy had heard from him.

"Hello, sweetheart. Aren't you excited today." His large hands fondled the dog's silky ears and something in Lindy melted like chocolate under the summer sun. She was strangely mesmerised by the sight of Roger's hands—strong, capable hands, with neat, clipped nails. He glanced up at her, his expression as stiff and serious as ever. "This is Poppy. She was abandoned by the side of the road three months ago, with a broken leg. She's doing much better, as you can see."

"Oh…" A lump formed in Lindy's throat. "How could anyone do such a thing?"

"It happens all too frequently." He straightened to let her come closer, and carefully Lindy stroked the terrier, who yapped excitedly and licked her hand.

"It's so cruel, to just abandon an animal like that."

"People are often cruel," Roger replied, and Lindy glanced up at him, wondering what exactly he meant by that. She hadn't realised as she'd been petting the dog how close she was to him, and as she looked up her hair brushed his cheek, their faces—and more crucially, their lips—only inches apart. Roger took a hasty step backwards, banging into the kennel door, and Lindy stumbled back, falling flat onto her bottom. Poppy, seeing her way to freedom, scampered out of the kennel and raced down the hallway. Every other animal in the place started up with another chorus.

"Damn it," Roger muttered under his breath, looking more flustered than Lindy had ever seen him, his hair mussed, his face flushed. He shot her a quick, apologetic look. "Sorry…"

"It's fine," Lindy assured him although her bottom might beg to differ. The concrete floor was *hard*.

Roger hurried after Poppy, and Lindy watched as he managed to catch the little dog, speaking gently to her all the while, and then brought her back to her kennel.

"Technically, I'm not actually allowed to open the kennels to visitors," he said in his stiff way as he locked Poppy's kennel. "So perhaps you should just view the rest."

"I'm sorry, I should have realised." Had Roger actually bent the rules for her? The thought was both surprising and strangely thrilling.

"There is no reason why you should have known the rules of this establishment." He glanced down at her; she was still sitting rather inelegantly on the floor. "Are you hurt?"

"My pride, I think, although my tail bone might be a bit bruised." She smiled wryly and Roger extended a hand.

"Let me help you up."

She took his hand, enjoying the way his fingers closed around hers. He pulled her up easily, considering that she was six feet tall and weighed eleven stone—so easily in fact that she took a step forward to balance herself and they nearly bumped noses. Again.

It was impossible for Lindy to ignore the frisson of awareness that rippled through her at his nearness. Okay, so she was attracted to him. Despite his stiff way of speaking, his awkwardness and his occasional pompousness, she found him undeniably attractive. She'd felt it the first time she'd met him, and then when they'd danced, and she felt it now. It didn't have to be a big deal. Physical attraction— chemistry—was just a part of life, a physical response to pheromones or whatever. And yet it had been a long time since Lindy had felt it for anyone, never mind this strongly.

"Would you like to see the other animals?" Roger asked after a pause, his gaze somewhere to the left of her head, colour still touching his cheeks, and Lindy nodded. Was he feeling it too? she wondered. This frisson of…something?

Roger moved past her to the next kennel, and Lindy followed him, determined to focus on the animals rather than the sight of Roger's broad shoulders, or the fact that her insides were feeling all fluttery from what had just happened, which was really basically nothing.

"This is Toby, a rescue greyhound," Roger began as he gestured to a sleek, brown dog in the next kennel who was nudging his nose through the wire with a meltingly sweet look. "He was racing until last year, and he is a bit skittish as a result."

"Oh…" Lindy looked into the greyhound's liquid eyes

and felt her heart suffuse with love. "What a sweetie."

"And this is Mary…" Roger continued, his voice a bit monotone as he went through all the animals, not looking at Lindy once. She wished she knew what he was thinking. Feeling. And then she wondered why she cared. She might be attracted to him, but it wasn't as if she wanted to *date* him or something. The idea was absurd.

One by one he took her through all the animals—a Rottweiler mix, a battered-looking Staffie, another greyhound, a cat with a missing ear and a bare patch on his side. There was a horse in a stall outside and several rabbits in a hutch, and an adorable little brown and white hamster. They were all wonderful in their own individual ways, and each one made Lindy's heart both break and melt.

"I wish I could rescue them all," she told Roger as they headed back to the front of the centre.

"That would be quite impractical." Lindy smiled at that and Roger continued, "They'll be able to stay here until they are rehomed. Fortunately this is a no-kill shelter." He glanced at her, his expression unreadable as always, as blank a slate as Lindy had ever seen. "Was there an animal you preferred, if you were to make an application?"

"I think I'm partial to Toby," she admitted. "The dark greyhound. I know he's a bit skittish but there was just something about him…"

To her surprised delight, Roger's expression softened and his mouth quirked in a tiny smile, the first he'd ever given her. "He's my favourite, too," he said, and something in Lindy fizzed. When Roger smiled…she felt as if she'd swallowed a firework. An over-the-top reaction, undoubtedly, but one she couldn't help but feel—and enjoy.

"When do you finish your shift here?" she blurted and Roger's eyes widened a fraction, clearly taken aback by her sudden question.

"I finish at four." He glanced at the clock. "In two hours and thirteen minutes."

Of course he was so precise. It was rather a long time to wait, but emboldened and a bit reckless, Lindy still asked rather stiltedly, "Would you…would you like to get a cup of coffee in Burford, after you're done? I was going to wander around the town anyway…"

Roger stared at her for a moment, looking completely uncomprehending. "I don't drink coffee," he said at last, and Lindy didn't know whether to laugh or groan. Was he trying to let her down nicely, or simply stating a fact?

"A cup of tea, then?" she persevered. "Or something cold? Whatever." Now she probably sounded desperate, and the truth was she didn't even care. She just wanted him to say yes, even if all that resulted was an undeniably awkward conversation over cups of tea.

Roger stared at her for another endless moment, as if he really couldn't fathom what she was getting at. Lindy waited, trying not to blush or feel stupider than she already did.

"Something cold would be refreshing," he finally said.

"Thank you." He made it sound as if she was going to buy him a Coke and then send him on his way. Perhaps that was what he was expecting.

"Great." She smiled, realising as she did so how pleased she was he'd accepted. Was she that lonely, or did she actually like him? Lindy didn't even know. "Where shall I meet you? You probably know Burford better than I do."

"I doubt that, but I am familiar with a café on the high street—Huffkins."

"I know it." She'd only driven through Burford a couple of times, but she recalled the sign above the bow window in the middle of the high street. "Shall we meet there a little after four?"

Another pause as Roger seemed to absorb her suggestion. "All right," he said finally. "Yes."

"Great."

"And will you be making an application to rehome one of our animals?" Roger asked, sounding like such a salesman that Lindy had to smile.

"Yes, I believe I will be. I'll do it online, as you suggested."

Lindy was mentally shaking her head at herself as she drove the few miles back to Burford, coming down the wonderfully quaint high street lined with terraced cottages and shops, some dating back to medieval times, with crooked timbers and drooping eaves. The small town was considered the gateway to the Cotswolds, or at least one of them, and on a sunny Saturday afternoon in September it was filled with happily window-shopping tourists.

With still two hours to kill, Lindy took her time wandering past shops selling expensive antiques and willow baskets full of ornaments and other trinkets. She spent a few moments looking in the window of a clothing shop that sold hundred-pound Wellington boots and even more expensive walking sticks. Burford clearly catered to a well-heeled clientele.

An hour passed slowly enough in this manner, with Lindy checking her watch far too often. Roger had her mobile number, thanks to the dancing class—would he call her if he'd decided to back out? *Would* he back out? Somehow she couldn't actually picture him showing up. She wasn't even sure she wanted him to show up.

Conversation was sure to be stilted and awkward, coming in difficult fits and starts, and for what purpose? A moment's chemical reaction when they'd got too close in the kennel?

Yet just remembering that moment made everything in Lindy fizz…again. And actually, she realised, despite his often stiff and awkward manner, Roger was someone she liked. At least she thought she could like him, maybe, if given a chance. She didn't know if she would get one.

She walked down the high street all the way to the stone, single-track bridge that was congested with tourist traffic, and then back up again. The sun was warm on her back and her T-shirt was sticking to her shoulder blades. She checked her watch again. Twenty more minutes. What did Roger think of her, willing to wander through really a rather tiny town for two *hours* just so they could have a drink? She felt ridiculous.

She spent the last fifteen minutes wandering through the churchyard, inspecting tumbled-down headstones and trying not to feel melancholy. Both her parents were buried in a similar little churchyard up in Derbyshire. She hardly ever went there.

At four o'clock exactly she started making her way to Huffkins, taking her time because she knew Roger would need to lock up at the rehoming centre, drive into Burford, and find a parking space. He might not be at the café till half past, but she didn't want to miss him.

Why, she wondered, was she so nervous? Her heart was fluttering as if this was a date, and maybe it was. A cold drink with a man she found attractive? What else was she meant to call it? And yet the thought of dating a man like Roger Wentworth seemed—well, ludicrous. He was so…well, what was he? A man who liked animals? Who was kind to his mother? And who was awkward and pedantic and pompous and sometimes rude. Really, Lindy had no idea what to make of him. She couldn't imagine dating him, although admittedly she couldn't imagine dating anyone, since it had been so long. She supposed she just wanted to spend time with him, to see what happened. Most likely, considering the pair of them, nothing would.

Huffkins was only half full as she came into the café, scanning the tables just in case, but Roger wasn't there. She took a seat by the window so she could watch the street, trying not to seem too anxious and eager, and, she suspected, failing at both.

Ten endless minutes passed; it was quarter past the hour. How long should she wait? She'd told the waitress she wouldn't order until Roger came, but the woman had been giving her questioning and slightly accusing looks, no doubt for wasting so much time. Lindy checked her watch again.

She looked up—and her heart lifted like a balloon in the breeze. Roger was striding down the street, a set, almost grim look on his face, as if he were marching to his doom, or perhaps just something unpleasant. But he'd come! Lindy realised she was grinning as she waved to catch his attention, and as Roger caught sight of her, he looked, she realised, grimmer than ever.

Chapter Six

ROGER HAD SPENT the last two hours and thirteen minutes in an agony of uncertainty and indecision and, frankly, plain old fear. He hadn't understood Lindy's behaviour at Blue Cross at all—from how pleased she'd been to see him, to the way she'd seemed to be flirting with him, to the entirely unexpected invitation to go out for a drink.

He'd had women flirt with him before, usually, Roger suspected, to amuse themselves rather than out of any genuine interest in him, or perhaps out of curiosity, to see how he responded. His girlfriends—all two of them—had tried to change him, and when they hadn't been successful they'd given up on him, which was just as well.

He'd thought at first that Lindy was doing something similar—flirting with him out of curiosity or amusement, and he'd done his best to pretend it wasn't happening, to play a straight bat as he always did, because he couldn't engage in those sorts of mind games at all, and flirting of any sort was utterly beyond him so he never even tried.

But then her hair had brushed his cheek and she'd been

close enough to kiss and Roger had felt as if his mind and body had both short-circuited, so for a few torturous seconds he hadn't been able to think. At least, he hadn't been able to think about anything but kissing her, which of course he was absolutely not been going to do. Even thinking about it had caused mortification to scorch through him, to imagine her reaction if he'd done such a wildly inappropriate and undoubtedly unexpected thing.

And then the invitation to go out for a drink, made with such a seemingly genuine enthusiasm…*that* had left him speechless and uncertain and yet strangely, sweetly wanting, and so he'd said yes, because even if he wasn't sure how this was all going to go, even if he felt more than a little apprehensive, he knew some small part of him at least wanted a chance to *see*.

Lindy had half-risen from her seat as he came into the café, her generous mouth curved into a wide smile. Her hair was piled on top of her head in the messiest bun Roger had ever seen, so strands and tendrils tumbled over her shoulders and brushed her cheeks. She was wearing a long, flowing skirt in a wild floral pattern that hurt Roger's eyes and a white top that revealed an inch of taut, golden belly as she waved.

"You came," she said as she sat down again and Roger forced what he hoped was the approximation of a smile.

"Did you think I wouldn't?"

"I wasn't sure, to be honest."

He sat down, his body rigid, his hands resting on his thighs, feeling the heavy, uneven beat of his heart as he tried to arrange his expression into some semblance of relaxed friendliness. "I'm a man of my word."

"That I believe." Her blue-green gaze swept over him teasingly, making Roger want to look away. There were so very many ways this meeting could go so very wrong. In fact, the eventual wrongness of the ensuing conversation was almost a certainty. If guesses were informed estimations as he had told her earlier, then his guess was that he was going to thoroughly humiliate himself in some way before he'd finished his Coke—or perhaps even before he'd ordered it.

"So your refreshing drink," Lindy said, her eyes seeming to dance and sparkle. "What would you like?"

"A Coca-Cola, please." He sounded as if he were about ten.

"Do you like Coke?" She sounded strangely pleased by this notion. "Because I love it. Everyone tells me my teeth are going to fall out or dissolve or something, but I can't stop drinking it. I usually have one a day, for breakfast."

She grinned, almost conspiratorially, and Roger longed to smile back as if they shared some delicious secret, but instead he heard himself say rather pompously, "You really should try to limit yourself. As an occasional refreshment, it may not do much harm, but if drunk on a daily basis…" Thankfully he lapsed into silence then. What was he, a PSA for good nutrition? A *dentist*? Someone please shut him up.

Lindy looked for a second as if she wanted to laugh, but then her expression turned serious and she nodded soberly. "I know. It's a terrible habit. Does it help that I have fruit and yogurt for breakfast, as well?"

"Fruit also contains a great deal of sugar."

She propped her chin on her hand. "What *should* I have for breakfast, then?"

Why were they talking about this? Roger stared at her in unhappy bewilderment. "I have no opinions on what you should have for breakfast," he said finally, and Lindy let out a laugh—a delighted sort of gurgle that made something in Roger tingle.

"But you do. You don't think I should have Coke."

"I was merely observing that having soda on a daily basis is not nutritionally advisable."

"Right."

He shook his head, helpless now. "Why are we talking about this?"

She laughed again. "You tell me."

"I don't think I can. I simply told you I wanted a Coke." He decided to dare a sort-of joke, if that was even what it was. "Maybe I should have asked for a coffee, after all."

"And drink something you already told me you don't like?" Lindy leaned a little forward. "Never."

Roger stared at her—the sparkle in her eyes, the smile still curving her lips, and felt a sensation similar to falling down a set of stairs. Startling, a bit painful, but also sort of thrilling. Was she toying with him? Teasing him? He couldn't credit any other possibility. "Coke it is, then," he said, his tone weirdly jolly, and thankfully, the waitress came to take their orders.

They both ordered Cokes—of course—and when the waitress left Roger felt the void of silence between them, a bottomless chasm he knew he could fall into and never climb out of.

"So," Lindy said. "You never managed to tell me if you grew up in Wychwood or not, because of the Great Dog Debacle."

The great…? It took Roger a second to realise what she was talking about—Poppy escaping, and the fact that he'd opened the kennel in the first place, which was something he would normally never, ever do. He was not a rule breaker, not remotely, not ever. "I did not grow up in Wychwood-on-Lea," he said.

"Where did you, then?"

"Swindon."

"But you live here now?"

"Yes, I moved here six months ago." When his mother had had her last diagnosis. *No further treatment possible.*

"And where did you live before that? Swindon?"

"No, Oxford." This was starting to feel like a rather laborious job interview. "What about you? I believe you're new to the village, as well?" he asked, trying to make this more of a conversation than an interrogation.

"Yes, I moved here from Manchester in June."

"To start a school of ballroom dancing."

"Yes, a bit daft, I know."

"Not at all."

Her mouth curved again, eyes alight. "You don't think so?"

"Certainly continuing in full-time employment as an accountant is the more fiscally responsible choice," he allowed.

"Indeed. I told myself I'd give it a year—I've got enough savings for that—and then I'd go back to accountancy." She sighed. "I'm not overly optimistic at the moment, to be honest. I was hoping for more pupils."

"Perhaps more will register."

"Perhaps." Her smile had slid off her face and she looked wistful for a moment, in a way that made Roger want to offer her some sort of comfort or encouragement. The problem was, he had no idea how to do either. "Anyway." She shrugged off her moment of melancholy like a dog shaking off water as she turned to face him with a purposeful air. "Tell me about yourself."

A more terrifying question Roger didn't think he had ever heard. Predictably, his mind blanked.

"Your mother lives in Wychwood," Lindy prompted.

"Yes."

"What about your dad? Siblings?"

"I'm an only child, and my father died when I was young. Twelve years old."

Her face softened in sympathy and sadness. "Oh, I'm sorry."

He nodded stiffly, because whenever he volunteered this particular bit of information, which was as rarely as possible, it created a certain awkwardness, on top of the awkwardness that was almost certainly already there, and he'd found the best way to deal with it was to simply move on. Then Lindy surprised him.

"My parents both died when I was young, as well," she said. "Although not as young as that. I was nineteen." She lapsed into silence as she glanced down at her hands lying flat on the table.

"I'm sorry," Roger said after a pause. He knew how inadequate those words were, just as he knew there weren't really any others.

"It was a car accident. They'd been visiting me at university and they were killed in a pile-up on the M6. At least it was quick."

Roger stared at her, aghast at such a matter-of-fact description of so devastating an event, yet knowing he did the same when it came to talking about his father. "That must have been very difficult," he said after a few seconds where he struggled to frame his thoughts and was only able to come up with such a massive understatement. "Do you have siblings?"

"No, just me." She gave a wry smile, touched with bittersweet whimsy. "It's been just me for a long time."

"I would have thought…" Roger paused. "You seem the sort of person to have many friends."

"Well, I do," Lindy allowed. "I've loads of acquaintances, colleagues, casual friends. Heaps and heaps." She let out a little laugh. "I'm very good at making friends, really."

"Yes." He certainly thought she was.

"But when it comes to family…you know people who know you inside and out?" She shook her head. "It really has just been me."

LINDY DIDN'T USUALLY talk about her parents' deaths. Fifteen years on and she wanted it to be old news, past history, even though she knew it never truly could be. Did anyone really ever get over the death of their parents? She was certainly trying.

And yet, for some strange reason, Roger Wentworth of all people felt like someone she could talk to—not just the usual chitchat, but the deeper stuff. Despite his stiffness, his somewhat awkward manner, she trusted him. She knew he was honest, and she'd just discovered he might understand, at least a little bit, of what she'd gone through.

"It must have been very difficult," he said again, the words seeming to be carefully chosen and touchingly heart-felt, "to be all alone in the world, at such a young age."

"Yes. It was." Something else she didn't really talk about. The waitress came with their Cokes then, and Lindy raised hers in a semi-mocking toast before taking a sip. "Really most refreshing," she said solemnly, and was rewarded with the very tiniest quirk of Roger's mouth. He could, she realised, make fun of himself, at least a little. The knowledge warmed her insides.

"Did you have relatives to help you, when your parents died?" he asked after a moment.

"Not really. My parents were older when they had me—their surprise blessing. My mother was forty-five, my dad fifty. Their parents had already passed away, and my dad had an older sister who was in a nursing home by the time he died. My mother had a brother, but he emigrated to Australia when I was a kid, and he didn't even come back for the funeral. I've completely lost touch with him." She shrugged. "I didn't really miss those kinds of relationships, because I'd never had them."

"I'm sorry." Roger shook his head, an expression of frustration flashing across his face. "I don't know what else to say."

"I'm not sure there is anything else," Lindy replied. She leaned her elbows on the table, gazing at him earnestly. "The thing is, in spite of all that, I had the most fantastic childhood." Roger raised his eyebrows, waiting for more. "My parents both took early retirement when I was six," Lindy explained. "They wanted to show me the world—and they did. We travelled all over the place, did everything. I saw the Northern Lights, Uluru, the Grand Canyon, the Taj Mahal…" She shook her head in wondering memory at all the adventures she'd shared with her mum and dad—memories she wouldn't trade for a more normal upbringing, or really, for anything, except perhaps to have them back again.

"We had so much fun. They homeschooled me until I was sixteen, but really they considered life the best education, and so it was. I don't regret any of it. Not one bit."

"Goodness." Roger looked both impressed and a bit startled by her words. Lindy knew her childhood had been utterly unconventional, and probably utterly unlike his, but she'd truly loved every moment of it. "And when you were sixteen?" he asked.

"We came back to our cottage in Derbyshire and I went to Sixth Form." She grimaced slightly. "After everything I'd experienced, I struggled to fit in and make friends. I suppose that was understandable, considering the circumstances, but it was a bit hard." Roger nodded in understanding, and Lindy let out a sudden, uncertain laugh. "I don't actually know why I'm telling you all this. I usually don't witter on about myself so much." She shook her head, deciding she really had rabbited on enough. Roger was looking a bit winded by her relentless download of information, and yet it had felt surprisingly good to say it all. She so rarely did. "Anyway, what about you? Were you very close to your dad?"

"Yes." He cleared his throat. "Although he was much like me, so we didn't actually talk all that much." Lindy smiled at that, and Roger continued, "He was the sort of person you could be silent with, and it didn't matter. You could just be."

She stared at him for a second, unable to speak. To just *be* with someone…not to have to explain or fill the silence or present your best self. She *ached* for that, she realised. "That's the best thing in the world," she said slowly, "to have someone like that in your life."

"Yes." Roger cleared his throat again, and Lindy thought he must have been struggling with a depth of emotion he didn't normally feel, just as she was. How odd, that they should experience it here, together. That they could bring it out in one another. "Yes, it is."

They were both quiet then, and while it wasn't quite the 'just be' type of silence they'd been talking about, it came close. Closer, at least, than anything Lindy had experienced in some time.

"You must be close to your mum," she said after a moment, wanting to keep the conversation going, for Roger had suddenly started to look as if he might drain the last of his Coke and scarper, "since you've agreed to the dancing lessons."

"Yes, we're close." Roger looked as if he was thinking of saying something more, but then decided not to. "Although whether we will still be close after I've stepped on her toes for two months running remains to be seen."

"It's the foxtrot this week," Lindy told him. "Nothing too scary."

"I have never been *scared* of dancing," Roger replied with dignity. "I'm simply not proficient in it."

"Which is the whole point of the class."

"Indeed." He gave a rather regal nod and Lindy smiled at him, liking the way his hair curled a bit by his ears, the warm brown of his eyes. He held himself stiffly but his body was powerful and for a scorching second Lindy wondered how it would feel pressed against hers…if she put her arms around him, if she kissed him.

She felt a blush begin to heat her face as she imagined it. Was she actually *crushing* on Roger Wentworth? It appeared she was. Rather badly. How absolutely odd, considering she didn't do crushes, and she hardly thought she'd have one on someone like Roger. And yet…

"I should get on," Roger said abruptly, pushing away his glass and rising in one sudden lurch.

"I suppose I should, too," Lindy said quickly, although there wasn't anything really to go back to. "Let me just pay for the Cokes and we can walk out together."

"I'll pay for the Cokes," Roger said firmly.

"But I'm the one who asked…"

"Even so." He was clearly not going to brook any argument whatsoever, and Lindy decided she rather liked the idea of him paying for their drinks. It made this feel more like a date.

"Thank you," she said when Roger had come back from the till, and they walked out into the early evening together, the town's busy high street now starting to empty out of day trippers. "Where are you parked?" Lindy asked. "I'm up at the top of the road…"

"I parked at the bottom, by the bridge."

They stared at each other; now was the time for goodbye. Lindy willed him to ask her out again. For dinner, or a movie…anything. She realised just how much she wanted him to, and why shouldn't he? They clearly got along. Well, sort of. And yet as he jangled his keys in his pocket, looking rather severe, she knew he wouldn't.

"This was fun," she said, and could not bring herself to add 'we should do it again,' fearing it would sound too desperate.

"Thank you for the invitation."

"You're welcome."

Another uneasy pause, accompanied by more jangling of keys. *Please say something*, Lindy thought silently. Yet what? Did she actually want him to ask her out? Of course, she could ask him out, on a proper date. She was a liberated woman; there was no reason not to, if it was what she wanted. Yet was it? She wasn't entirely sure. Roger could be kind, but he was also hard work. And she wasn't even sure he liked her. Besides, she wanted him to do something. To want to do something.

And he didn't.

"I suppose I shall see you on Monday, at class," he said, and she nodded. "You'll make an application with Blue

Cross?"

"Yes, as soon as I get home."

"Very good." He gave one more nod, another jangle, and then he started walking down the street, a stiff yet quick gait that made Lindy fear he couldn't get away fast enough. After the fizzy excitement and pleasure of the afternoon, she felt her mood tumbling down, down, down, so unlike her usual determined optimism, and yet she couldn't keep herself from it, although she tried.

It didn't really matter, she told herself as pragmatically as she could as she headed back up the high street towards her car. So what if he hadn't asked her out on a date? It wasn't the end of the world, far from it, considering how ambivalent she'd been feeling about the prospect. Hopefully she'd soon have Toby the greyhound, or another one of the rescue dogs, for companionship. She really didn't need Roger Wentworth to pay her attention.

And yet she couldn't keep from one last disconsolate look behind her to glimpse him walking down the street; he was no more than a speck in the distance, striding quickly and purposefully away.

Chapter Seven

L INDY GAVE HER reflection another quick and nervous glance—about the fifth one in the last ten minutes. It was Monday, and her students—including Roger—were about to arrive. Had she gone too overboard with her outfit? She loved to dress up for her dance classes, and the flowing ballgown in rusty-red satin—the same colour as fox fur—had seemed a perfect choice to introduce the foxtrot.

Yet now, as she glanced at herself yet again in the mirror, she wondered if she looked a bit too brazen. The V-neck of the gown was only just on the right side of plunging, and the cleavage on display was a bit more than she was used to or comfortable with. She didn't want to give Roger an eyeful, and yet…she sort of did.

He'd been in her thoughts a great deal in the forty-eight hours since she'd said goodbye to him in Burford. Too much, maybe. On Sunday she'd gone out to brunch in Witney with Emily and Olivia, and while it had been a very pleasant time, she'd been hopelessly distracted, wondering how Roger would act when she saw him again. Thinking about actually asking him out on a proper, honest-to-goodness date. Why not? What did she have to lose?

Well, her dignity, perhaps. Her pride, as well. Hopefully not more than that, if he refused. She liked him, despite or perhaps because of his quirkiness, but her heart was definitely not more dangerously engaged. Not yet. She wasn't even sure it ever would be. As quirkily charming as Roger could be, he was also sometimes pedantic, pompous, or just plain difficult.

And yet...she kept thinking about the warmth of his eyes, that little quirk of his smile, the heartfelt tone he'd used when he'd been talking about losing his dad. All of it made her want to ask him out—or preferably, for him to ask her out, but she had a rather decided feeling that wasn't going to happen.

In her thirty-five years, Lindy had had only a handful of dates and just one proper boyfriend. That relationship had only lasted a few months; in retrospect she didn't even know why it had begun, never mind ended. She and Philip had both more or less tolerated each other, but not much more than that.

He hadn't been interested in what she was interested in; she'd asked him to go dancing with her but he'd always refused. To be fair, he'd asked her to go to the rugby with him and she'd let herself be dragged along to one match before she'd started to make excuses he'd been more than happy to accept. They'd gone out to dinner once a week, if that, and had the occasional evening in but it had all felt rather damp squibby rather than being with the love of her life.

Would Roger be different? Did she want to take the risk to find out? Liking people was easy. Lindy was always more than happy and eager to do that. But *loving* people…actually letting them in to her life and her heart…that was harder. A lot harder.

But of course one date was hardly doing that. And the fact that she was still on the fence about dating at all surely made falling in love an even less likely possibility.

"Hello…?"

"Maureen!" Lindy whirled away from the mirror she'd been staring into unseeingly for the last five minutes to greet her first student. "Lovely to see you. How are you today?"

"My back's playing up," Maureen said as she hobbled into the room. "My knee, too."

"I'm sorry…"

"What can you do?" She shrugged pragmatically. "I know you'd find it hard to believe I was the Newcastle tango champion three years running—"

"I don't," Lindy assured her. Despite her obvious stiffness now, Maureen had an inherent grace that was still evident in her twisted and pain-racked body.

"In 1962, 1963, and 1965," Maureen stated proudly. "Tony slipped up in 1964, unfortunately." She shook her head sadly. "He was a good dancer, and an even better husband."

Lindy felt a pang of poignant sorrow at this simple statement as she gave the older woman a sympathetic smile. "That's the right way round, surely."

"I'm not sure I thought that in 1964." Maureen let out a cackle of rather wicked laughter. "But never mind. We stayed together to the end—eleven years ago now. Funny to think it's been that long."

"You must miss him."

"The way you'd miss your right hand, if it was cut off," Maureen said simply. "But you learn to make do. What about you, my girl? A nice, buxom woman like you." She eyed Lindy's cleavage with a nod of approval that made Lindy want to laugh—or blush. "You must have a man waiting in the wings, if not two or three."

Lindy did laugh then. "I'm afraid not."

"Well, you should. You've got the figure, certainly, but you're not getting any younger, are you?" She nodded shrewdly. "Best to get your skates on, dearie."

"I'll do my best," Lindy murmured. Maureen's advice was both brutal and well meant, but also timely. She would ask Roger out tonight, she decided. Why not? It was only a date, after all. It didn't have to mean anything.

"That's the ticket," Maureen approved.

The others were coming in now—Simon and Olivia looking shy and loved-up as usual, and then Roger and Ellen. Lindy's heart skipped an uneven beat at the sight of him. He wasn't wearing his usual stodgy suit, but rather a crisp blue button-down shirt, rolled up at the sleeves, and a pair of well-pressed khakis. The most boring clothes imaginable, and yet...he looked good in them. Really rather wonderful.

Lindy took a moment to admire his strong forearms, the brown column of throat where his shirt was unbuttoned—a sedate one button undone rather than a Casanova-ish two, the hair curling about his ears in the same way she'd noted on Saturday. She liked it all.

Then Roger noticed her, and his eyes widened almost comically at the sight of her in her get-up. She'd gone the whole kit and kaboodle tonight, with not just the dress but her hair piled on top of her head in an elegant updo, an extravagant use of eyeliner and a pair of gold heels that put her at a hairsbreadth under six foot three. Did she look ridiculous? Judging by Roger's rather shell-shocked expression, Lindy thought she probably did.

She'd always dressed up to go dancing, even as a little girl, waltzing along to the radio in the kitchen with her dad. Out came the organza and tulle, the shiny patent leather shoes and the satin hair bows. And later, when she'd gone to ballroom dancing evenings on her own, it had been a point of pride to get as gussied up as possible. Many ballroom dancing aficionados were the same. If you couldn't wear a ballgown while doing the samba, when could you?

There was, of course, the matter of her height. Next to her six-foot-five father and five-eleven mother, Lindy had never felt particularly tall, but after they'd died she'd become more conscious of the fact that she was a good half foot taller than most women, and topped most men by a few inches, as well. She had never wanted to let her height dictate her fashion choices—she loved high heels—but next to Maureen, who barely reached five feet, and Olivia not much taller, she felt truly Amazonian as Roger finally stopped goggling and looked away. Never mind. She straightened, throwing back her shoulders, giving Roger and Ellen and everyone else as dazzling a smile as she could.

"Great that you're here! I think we're ready to begin."

She spent the next twenty minutes teaching them all the basic steps of the foxtrot, which was, in her estimation, the easiest dance step to learn after the waltz with its basic quickstep, although it required a good deal more body contact, with both partners moving in close time to the other.

Although a far cry from the tango or rumba, it could still be quite a sexy, sensual dance, something she hadn't fully considered when she'd chosen to introduce it in just her third class for beginners.

As she set everyone to practising, partnering Maureen as usual, she couldn't keep from giving Ellen and Roger a glance—Ellen had her usual cheerful game face on, but Roger looked as if he were in agonies and trying unsuccessfully to suppress it. Lindy felt a stab of sympathy for him. The foxtrot, unlike the waltz, required a certain loose-limbed fluidity that seemed inherently contrary to Roger's nature.

With the brass notes of a big-band piece vibrating through the room, Lindy took Maureen through the basic steps. Arthritic though she was, the older woman caught on easily and seemed to enjoy it, despite the occasional creak or groan. Simon and Olivia, Lindy saw, were falling about laughing as they massacred the steps, and Roger…Roger looked as if he were in a straitjacket. Or perhaps he just wanted to be.

"You need to relax a little, darling," Ellen said patiently, and her son responded through gritted teeth, "I am *trying*."

Lindy didn't know whether she was taking pity on him or just wanting to be near him but as the first song came to an end, she clapped her hands and called out, "Let's switch partners now. Simon, with Ellen, please. Olivia with Maureen." She turned to Roger, who was staring at her with a neutral expression that still somehow reminded Lindy of Munch's painting *The Scream*. "Roger, I'll dance with you."

ROGER WATCHED LINDY come towards him with an expectant smile and felt his whole body freeze. He'd just about got the hang of the sedate waltz, but this foxtrot was something else entirely. And dancing it with Lindy, while she was looking so…so…*sexy* was a prospect that filled him with equal parts dread, terror, and deep, fizzing excitement.

"It's a basic box step, just like the waltz," she reminded

him as she came to stand next to him. In her heels they were almost eye level, which was most disconcerting as Roger was used to women coming up to his shoulder, or maybe his chin. There was no ignoring Lindy while she was gazing right into his eyes—no ignoring the faint, floral scent of her—or was it vanilla?—or the way a few tendrils of wavy golden-brown hair had fallen from her updo and were now tumbling down her shoulders. No ignoring the way her chest rose and fell with every breath, or the fact that if he glanced downwards he knew he would see the rather glorious display of her abundant cleavage, something he was determined *not* to do, because of course it would be obvious he was checking her out, and yet how could he not?

She was gorgeous. Vibrant and alive, earthy and sensual. Her dress gleamed every time she moved, her body swaying and undulating with graceful confidence as she'd shown them all the basic steps. He couldn't stop looking at her, and yet he had to stop, because he feared the expression on his face would be unguarded in its yearning.

He'd done his best not to think of her in the last forty-eight hours, and he'd managed somewhat successfully. He had comforted himself that he hadn't made too much of an idiot of himself while they'd had their drinks in Burford, and yet those moments outside the café while they'd said their goodbyes had been fairly excruciating. He hadn't been able to tell if she'd wanted him to ask her out, and he'd been too inherently risk-averse to take the chance and see. He'd been considered so unsuitable, he reminded himself—for what, he didn't know, but did it even matter? Just basic, general unsuitability. And he was afraid that the fact that he'd even been thinking about asking Lindy out was ridiculous, an absurdity that would become painfully apparent the second the words passed his lips. So they hadn't.

"Ready?" Lindy said, and Roger refocused on her face. She was very close. As close as she'd been when she'd turned to him in front of the kennel, and he'd bolted like a frightened horse.

"As ready as I'll ever be, I think," he answered stiffly, and she let out one of those breathy gurgles of laughter that electrified every nerve ending.

"I admire your spirit," she told him, and she clasped one hand with his and placed the other on his shoulder. Dutifully Roger placed his other hand on her waist, conscious of the curve of her hip under his fingers, the slippery satin of her dress, the warmth of her body. She was closer than the last time they'd danced, so her breasts were brushing his chest, her hips nearly nudging his. This could, Roger realised afresh, get *very* embarrassing.

The music began, and Lindy started to move, the folds of her dress seeming to envelop him, her thighs brushing his every time she moved. Roger did his best to mimic her steps with stiff, jerky movements, but he knew his performance was lamentable. He was the one supposed to be leading, after all, and instead he was following her as if he were a marionette, not a man.

"The thing with any dance," Lindy told him, her voice low and musical, "is you just have to let yourself *feel* it. Let it flow through you. It becomes intuitive—don't think which foot when, just feel the music, the movement."

Which might work for someone who had a modicum of rhythm, but for someone like him, Roger knew, the only thing he was going to feel was humiliation.

"I do not believe this is the sort of thing I can just feel," he stated, and Lindy pressed her body a little closer, so the entire length of her was very nearly against him, and she asked in a murmur, "So, what *do* you feel, Roger?"

That rather coy question was enough to make Roger experience that shocking and yet wonderful sense of short-circuiting both body and brain. What he felt was *desire*—heady, intoxicating, overwhelming. He had a gorgeous, lovely, interesting woman in his arms, and amazingly, it almost seemed as if she were flirting with him. As if she wanted him in the same way he knew he wanted her. But surely she couldn't. Surely he was reading the signals wrong, or she was just teasing him, or…something.

What was he going to *do*?

"That's the way, Roger," Lindy said in a voice full of warm approval, and he realised they had continued to move across the dance floor, and he'd managed the steps without having to think about them too much—because he was thinking about Lindy. How could he possibly think about anything else? And yet somehow he'd managed to keep dancing—until he didn't.

Roger wasn't sure what exactly happened at that moment—he became aware of the need to focus on the steps again, and he was *still* aware of Lindy so close to him, and that was simply too much awareness so somehow his legs got tangled with hers and he felt his balance shift and then falter.

The next thing he knew he was falling in an inelegant sprawl of limbs, unable to untangle himself from Lindy's embrace to break his fall. Lindy fell on top of him in a swirl of rust-red skirts as his cheekbone smacked into the floor hard enough for him to see dazzling pinpoints of light.

"Roger… *Roger!*"

A few seconds must have passed either in a blackout or simply a daze, for the next thing Roger knew was his mother was peering anxiously at him from above, the room was silent, and Lindy was still on top of him, her body most intimately entangled with his. And the entire side of his face was throbbing painfully.

"Are you all right?" Lindy propped herself on her elbows as Roger blinked her face into focus, just beneath his mother's. His brain felt as if it were full of cottony clouds. His face *hurt.* He felt too stunned to be embarrassed, but he knew that would most certainly come in time.

"Roger?" He thought he heard a thread of anxiety in Lindy's voice and he tried to pluck his thoughts from the clouds they'd snagged on.

"Yes…I'm all right. I believe my pride is more bruised than anything else."

"I think your face is going to be rather bruised, as well," Lindy said. "I'm so sorry."

"It was my fault."

"I don't know about that. Even the best dancers take a tumble once in a while."

"Are you hurt?" She was still sprawled on top of him, which, despite the pain in his cheek, felt quite delicious, but Roger was conscious they hadn't moved and everyone was watching as they lay tangled together on the floor.

"Yes, I'm fine." Lindy started to scramble up from him and, wincing, Roger managed to get himself into a seated position, conscious still of everyone's stares.

"You're going to have a nice shiner," Maureen pronounced, sounding rather pleased by the prospect. "And a swollen lip."

Roger put one hand gingerly to his face. How was he going to explain this to people at work? Although at this particular moment that felt like the least of his concerns.

"Let me help you get cleaned up," Lindy said, and took his hand. She helped to pull him up to his feet, and Roger, still somewhat dazed, allowed her to lead him out of the classroom, down the stairs, to the tiny kitchen at the back of the bakery.

It wasn't until she'd opened a first aid kid and the pungent smell of rubbing alcohol stung the air that Roger came to himself enough to say, "This isn't necessary. I'm perfectly capable of tending to my own injuries—"

"I know you are." Lindy gave him an impish smile as she held an alcohol-soaked piece of cotton wool. "But let me? I feel bad enough as it is. I think I tripped you up accidentally, and I'm meant to be the expert here."

He took in her teasing smile with a feeling of confusion. On top of his throbbing cheek and smarting eye, he couldn't process this conversation—or Lindy's intent. "As you said," he managed, "accidents happen."

"So they do." She leaned forward, close enough so he could breathe in her scent again—yes, it was vanilla—and feel the press of her breasts against his chest, the warmth of her breath on his face as she spoke. "This might sting a bit."

Roger found he could not respond, which was undoubtedly a blessing. He feared what he might blurt out in such a situation as this. He closed his eyes as she dabbed the cotton wool on the cut by his eyebrow, her body moving against his with every little dab of the wool. This was torture. Exquisite, unbelievable torture.

He must have drawn a decidedly unsteady breath, because she paused in her ministrations. "Does that hurt?"

"It's fine." His voice came out in something close to a snap. He pressed his lips together to keep from saying something he'd surely regret. Did she feel even an iota of what he was feeling?

Another dab. And then another. And then, with his eyes

still closed, he felt her fingertip gently trace the line of his eyebrow. The very air in the room seemed to tauten and shimmer from beneath his eyelids.

"You're definitely going to have a black eye," she said, and Roger opened his eyes.

Lindy was very close. Close enough to kiss, should he so dare. Her gaze locked on his and for a second neither of them spoke. Neither of them breathed.

He could kiss her right now. All he needed to do was move his head a few inches. Two, at most. It would be so easy...

And yet it felt like the most difficult thing he'd ever done. Impossible. What if he was reading the signals wrong? What if she was shocked, offended, or worse, incredulous?

What if she wasn't?

Did he even want to do this? Pursue some sort of relationship, begun with what most would see as a simple kiss? Heaven knew he'd kept himself from relationships before, and with good reason. They tended not to work out.

Besides, Lindy most likely didn't even want to kiss him. Flirting was undoubtedly an instinct with her, as a beautiful woman, and nothing more. It didn't *mean* anything.

They continued to stare at each other. Lindy's eyes widened a fraction. Her breath came out in an uneven rush. Without making a conscious decision about what he was actually going to do, Roger moved forward.

His head had been tilted backwards so she could access

his eye, and he straightened, intent on kissing her, or at least trying to kiss her, or maybe just seeing if she kissed him. Something. He wasn't sure what. Probably not kissing at all, actually. Probably just some sort of awkward hovering.

Except he hadn't realised there was a cupboard above his head and as he began moving in, he banged his head hard enough to see stars all over again.

With a muttered 'oof' he pressed one hand to the top of his now throbbing head and Lindy let out a smothered laugh.

"Oh, dear…"

"I seem to be accident prone." At least it had saved him from making a complete fool of himself. Lindy had stepped away, and was now briskly putting everything back into the first aid kit, and if there had even been a moment, which Roger was now doubting, it was surely broken now.

Roger ruefully rubbed his head as he heard his mother's wavery voice from the hall.

"Roger? Darling? Are you all right?"

Chapter Eight

"*L*INDY!"

With something between a laugh and a cry, Ellie ran towards Lindy and enveloped her in a tight hug. "I'm so sorry I haven't seen you more since you moved. I'm a bad friend."

"You're not a bad friend," Lindy assured her as she returned the tight embrace. This was only the second time she'd seen Ellie since moving to Wychwood-on-Lea three months ago, but that didn't matter now that they were finally together again. It was Saturday afternoon, nearly a week since the disastrous dancing class, and Lindy was still wincing inwardly at the whole black eye episode.

She wasn't sure what had happened, or who had tripped whom, but the sight of Roger's stunned face and emerging shiner had made Lindy feel wretched with guilt. And then there had been that exquisitely awkward and weirdly wonderful moment when she'd actually thought he might kiss her—she'd felt so tangled up inside, knowing she'd been flirting rather shamelessly and yet feeling so uncertain and even fearful. Did she want him to kiss her? Yes, she rather thought she did. And yet…what then? Did she want to date Roger Wentworth? Pursue some sort of romance? Lindy couldn't quite picture it, and yet in the moment, she'd ached for his kiss.

But Roger hadn't kissed her. He'd banged his head, and his mother had come in, looking worried, and Roger had been terse and monosyllabic, and then they'd all trooped back for the rest of the class, which he'd gone on with gamely enough, much to his credit. Lindy hadn't dared dance with him again. And she hadn't heard from or seen him since—she'd gone about her days, filled out her online application with Blue Cross for Toby, met with the head teacher of the primary about teaching Year Sixes, and had her junior class this morning, which had been brilliant.

Ollie had shown up in a tuxedo, while his dad Will had rolled his eyes good-naturedly. "We found it in a charity shop, can you believe? He was so excited to wear it for the class."

Lindy had been thrilled by her budding star, and she'd had a fantastic time teaching her three eager pupils how to waltz; Ollie had even said he was hoping to bring his best friend next week. As they'd all been leaving, Ishbel had asked if they could start a WhatsApp group for class parents, and Lindy had been pleased at how enthusiastic everyone had been at the prospect. Will had named it Twinkle Toes, and several messages had pinged in almost immediately, thanking her for the class and saying how thrilled their kids were with it. Lindy had felt buoyed by it all.

And now she was here with Ellie, so glad and grateful to see her friend, although Ellie looked a little tired, with violet shadows under her eyes.

"How are you?" Ellie exclaimed as the waitress gave them menus. They were in a restaurant in Witney on a rainy afternoon; the summery weather had turned, and there was more than a touch of autumn chill to the air.

"I'm doing well," Lindy answered, realising she meant it. Despite her constant wondering and dithering about Roger, she'd had a good week, and her school was starting to feel like it might actually, one day, be something of a success.

"You're not regretting moving to Wychwood?" Ellie asked anxiously. "I feel so badly, telling you to move down here and then basically never seeing you again."

"No, I don't regret it all, and you shouldn't feel badly about anything, Ellie. I know you're busy." Briefly Lindy touched her friend's hand. "Is everything okay?"

"Oh, it's all fine," Ellie said a bit dispiritedly, and then opened her menu. "What are you going to order?"

Lindy decided to take the rather heavy-handed hint and drop the subject for now. She scanned the menu with its upscale offerings—avocado toast and kale both featured heavily—and she decided on a burger and a Coke, of course. That made her think of Roger, which was silly, but that's where her mind had been going these last few days.

Had he been going to kiss her? Or had she been imagining—even willing—the whole thing? She'd certainly been flirting for England, if not the entirety of Europe. It wasn't like her, either. She didn't do breathy laughs or coy looks or standing a couple of inches closer than usual, and yet with Roger she seemed to lose her head and turn into some sort of weird, wannabe vamp. It was strange. And, Lindy acknowledged, if she thought it was strange, what on earth would Roger think?

He'd probably been horrified by her brazenness. Whoever he dated, it would be someone sensible—someone with a twinset and no-nonsense manner. Pearls, too. Not someone like her—scatty and impulsive and overwhelming and obvious.

The waitress came to take their orders, and once she'd left again, Lindy decided to level with her friend. "What's going on, Ellie?" she asked. "You seem a little down."

"I'm not..." Ellie protested, so half-heartedly that all Lindy had to do was raise an eyebrow. She sighed and her shoulders slumped. "It's nothing, really," she said. "I mean, nothing's *wrong*."

"But...?" Lindy prompted after a moment.

"You know Oliver's a viscount?" Ellie said and Lindy gave a little laugh.

"That's not something I'm likely to forget." She'd teased Ellie about being royalty now; she really had fallen into her own fairy tale.

"Well, I did, or at least I tried to," Ellie answered frankly. "I just wanted to live a normal life with my husband and daughter. That's been wonderful, but it's also been hard at times—Abby turning into a teenager, and Oliver's work has been demanding."

"So what happened with the viscount thingy?" Lindy asked, curious now, as well as concerned. Ellie's life had always seemed like a fairy tale to her, from afar. Charmed as well as charming.

"Oliver's father has become quite frail," Ellie said heavily. "Nothing serious, no diagnoses or anything, but he can't do as much as he used to and he wants Oliver to start taking up the slack. So we've been spending more time there—which shouldn't be difficult, the house is lovely, it's all lovely..." She sighed again, and to Lindy's alarm she saw that Ellie now looked near tears.

"What is it, Ellie?" she asked, reaching once more for her hand.

"Oliver's parents have never liked me particularly. They endure me, I suppose, and it hasn't been too bad because we see them so rarely. But now we're there every weekend, and I still get rattled by all the forks and spoons and things at dinner, and I'm hopeless at so many of the things Oliver seems to just take for granted..." Ellie shook her head slowly. "I feel like I'm not good enough for him. His parents have actually been all right about it all, but I feel it. Inside." Her face crumpled a bit before, with effort, she smoothed it out and tried for a smile.

"Oh, Ellie." Lindy's heart expanded with sympathy. "That's all got to be so very tough. But maybe you're just what the stodgy nobility need—a true breath of fresh air. I know Oliver adores you, and there's no way on God's green earth that he thinks you're not good enough for him. Absolutely not."

"I know that too," Ellie said quietly as Lindy squeezed her hand. "I really do. It's stupid to feel this way—it's just that this particular situation brings up a lot of old insecurities, and no matter how much I tell myself it's not like that, *I'm* not like that, I still feel it."

"Yes, I can see how easy that would be to do. We all fall into those traps, don't we?"

"Do you?" Ellie looked surprisingly sceptical. "Because you seem so confident all the time, Lindy. I really envy you that."

"Do you?" Lindy let out an uncertain laugh. "Well, I'm not sure how confident I am, really."

"You moved here to Wychwood on your own, didn't you?"

"So did you."

"And you started your own dancing school!" Ellie shook her head, marvelling. "You're amazing."

"Well, right back at you," Lindy replied with a smile.

"Anyway, enough about me," Ellie said firmly. "How are you doing? Have you met anyone? Any sweep-you-off-your-feet Casanovas who are waltzing with you?"

Lindy thought about Roger and suddenly couldn't keep from bursting into laughter. Ellie smiled, looking intrigued. "There's *so* a story there. Come on, tell me what it is."

"Well…" Lindy hesitated as she tried to organise her thoughts. "There is a man, but he's certainly not a Casanova, even if he did sweep me off my feet. Literally."

"What—"

Laughing a little, Lindy told her the story while Ellie listened avidly. "He sounds charming—"

"I don't know about charming," Lindy answered. "Quirky. Kind. Adorable." She blushed as Ellie let out a delighted laugh.

"You have it *bad*, don't you?"

"No, not really," Lindy quickly protested, although she wasn't sure why. She felt a need to protect herself, instinctive and elemental, even with Ellie. Even when Roger wasn't here. She didn't have it *bad*. Of course she didn't. She never did.

"So do you think he'll ask you out?"

Lindy thought of how quickly Roger had walked out of class on Monday night, without even looking at her. "Probably not," she admitted on a sigh.

"You could ask him out," Ellie suggested.

"I know—I was working myself up to do exactly that, and then we fell and he had a black eye and I couldn't find the right moment." Although perhaps she could have, when they'd been in the kitchen. When he'd maybe, almost kissed her. Or was she in fantasy land, even to hope that had been the case? *Did* she hope that was the case? Lindy wondered if she'd ever be able to make up her mind.

Their food came, and Lindy dug into her burger with appreciation. "Anyway, I don't know if I should ask him out, when I'm technically his teacher. I mean, isn't that some form of sexual harassment?"

"Surely not," Ellie exclaimed. "I mean, it's ballroom dancing, not Sixth Form."

Although sometimes she felt like she was in Sixth Form, a giggly girl making eyes at the cute boy. Lindy sighed, suddenly feeling childish. Perhaps she should just do her best to stop thinking about Roger that way. It was messing with her head. The last thing she wanted to be was obsessed about a man. About anyone. Fifteen years on, she'd become used to, and even a little protective of, her solitary existence.

"I think you should ask him out," Ellie said firmly. "Why not? You only live once."

"I know that." Lindy put her burger down and propped her chin in her hand as a sudden, unexpected melancholy descended on her like a fog. Why was she dithering so much? What might she miss out on, simply because she didn't want to take a risk? Or was it better to live the way she always had—friend to all, but never anything more?

"At the end of the day, it's just a date," Ellie told her pragmatically. "Not a ring or a vow or anything like that.

You could make it nonthreatening—an afternoon walk rather than a three-course meal at some Michelin-starred restaurant."

"That's true." As quickly as her melancholy had descended, it dissipated, clouds scattered by sunshine. An afternoon walk seemed a lot easier to handle than some big romantic endeavour. Surely, *surely* she could manage that. If she wanted to.

Lindy was still mulling over the prospect as she drove back to Willoughby Close. As she was heading towards her front door, Alice waved to her from the other side of the courtyard.

"I just slipped a note through your door," she called. "I wanted to invite you to Sunday lunch, although not for a few weeks as I'm afraid we've been terribly busy. In October— I'm doing a roast."

"Oh, that would be lovely," Lindy exclaimed. "Thanks."

She felt positively brimming with bonhomie as she unlocked her door and stepped inside her cottage. It had taken awhile, but she finally felt as if she were starting to make social strides here, proper ones. Seeing Ellie…Alice's invitation…planning a class for Year Sixes…even the WhatsApp group for the parents. It had all made her happy. Now all she needed to do now was call Roger…

She reached for her mobile, and was pleased to see a text had come through from Blue Cross, approving her application and asking her to ring to set up a home visit. It felt like a sign—if she had a dog, an afternoon walk made so much more sense, plus Roger had said Toby was his favourite. Perfect!

Before she could change her mind or lose her nerve, Lindy scrolled for his number and then pressed to make the call.

He answered on the second ring, his tone predictably terse. "Roger Wentworth speaking."

"Roger, it's Lindy." She paused, and when he did not reply, she added a bit uncertainly, "From ballroom dancing."

"Yes, I know. Your number is in my telephone."

"Right."

"Are you calling about the class? Is it cancelled?"

"No, it's not cancelled." And now she felt a bit foolish. Roger had spoken in the kind of tone that indicated there would be no other reason whatsoever to call him. "Far from it. I'm calling because…" She hesitated, then plunged. "Because I thought you might like to know that I've been approved by Blue Cross to adopt a dog. All I need to have now is the home visit."

"The home visit is quite important," Roger told her in that severe way of his. "There have been many clients who have had their applications denied at the home visit stage."

"Okay, well," Lindy answered with an uncertain laugh, "here's hoping mine won't be." She was starting to feel properly stupid now. *Why* had she called him again?

"Assuming your home and living situation are appropriate, I shouldn't think it would be," Roger said. "But as I said, the home visit is an important stage of the process that should not be dismissed."

"Well, fingers crossed."

An uncomfortable pause ensued, like a prickle along Lindy's skin. She could not think of a single thing to say that would make sense in this moment.

"Was that the only reason you called?" Roger finally asked.

Lindy bit her lip. Hard. "Yes, I suppose it was," she said, her voice pathetically small. "Sorry to disturb you."

"You didn't disturb me."

"Well, you don't sound particularly glad I rang," she retorted rather tartly. A girl could only take so much. How was it she'd told Ellie Roger was *adorable*?

"No, it's not—" Roger began, and then stopped abruptly. They were both wretchedly silent. "I apologise," he said after a pause. "I was merely surprised."

"Is it so surprising, that I'd ring you?"

"It is surprising to me—"

"It's just," she continued doggedly, determined to get it all out now, for better or worse, "I thought we were becoming friends."

"Friends," Roger repeated after a tiny, tense pause. "I suppose. Yes."

Which was hardly a ringing endorsement. Lindy told herself not to feel hurt. This was Roger, after all. This was how he conducted conversations. She needed to remember that.

"Well, if and when my application is approved," she said a bit recklessly, "and if I'm able to adopt Toby as I'm hoping to, perhaps you'd like to go for a walk with us one day? I know you said you were partial to him." And perhaps to her, as well, although right now that felt very much in doubt.

"There are quite a few variables in that equation," Roger said after another one of those pauses. "And you will need to spend time socialising Toby properly before you take him out for walks."

"Yes, that's true—"

"But if your application is approved," he cut across her, his tone as formal as ever, "and you do adopt Toby, then…yes. A walk would be…nice. Thank you."

"Great." Lindy realised she was grinning. "I'll keep you posted," she promised and she almost thought she heard a smile in Roger's voice as he answered, "Please do."

Chapter Nine

"HOW WAS YOUR weekend, Roger? Been to any raves?"

In the two years that his young associate Chris had been working at Hartley and Fein Accountants, Roger had been the recipient of this question nearly every Monday morning. The first time he'd been bewildered; he had not known what a rave was, and Chris had found his ignorance hilarious. The second time, thanks to some judicious Google research, Roger had replied quite seriously that no, he had not attended any raves, as he was not the type of person to enjoy loud, impromptu musical sessions. Chris had found this equally amusing.

Roger had realised then that the question was a joke, a gentle mockery, and he'd begun to answer in kind. It had become something of a challenge, similar to completing a sudoku puzzle, to consider what his reply would be on any given week. Sometimes he said he hadn't been *this* week, implying he had on some other occasion; other times he told Chris he'd only been to two or three. At other times he researched the latest rave online and mentioned salient details to an appreciative Chris.

Strangely enough, a bizarre camaraderie had sprung up between Roger and his young, over-gelled companion; their Monday morning banter had become something of a staple of both their working weeks, or so Roger liked to believe.

Now, as Roger made himself a cup of tea in the office kitchen, he considered this week's reply. "I'm afraid my raving days might finally be behind me," he said in the tone of someone making a grand pronouncement.

To his surprise, Chris let out a long, low whistle. "Is that where you got that shiner? Things got a little too wild during your last sesh?"

Embarrassed, Roger touched his eye and then winced. "No, that was a…domestic mishap."

Chris raised his eyebrows. "That sounds…interesting."

"I mean, an *accident*. I bumped into a cupboard." He was not about to explain about the ballroom dancing classes.

"Sure you did." Chris gave him a knowing wink. "Don't worry, I won't breathe a word about how rough it got."

"Nothing got *rough*—"

"Mr Wentworth is sounding mighty pleased with himself, though," he observed, which had Roger staring at him in bafflement. "I think dude's got himself a lady."

It took a few seconds for Roger to process that statement, and then he shook his head. "I'm afraid your assumption would be incorrect."

"Why are you looking so smug, then, despite the black eye?" Chris asked as he took a sip of his own sweet, milky coffee.

Smug? Was he? Admittedly, Roger had been feeling rather pleased with himself since Lindy's call on Saturday afternoon. While he could fully admit he hadn't handled their telephone conversation particularly well, the end result had been quite satisfactory.

"I am not smug," he told Chris, and then feeling that their three years of Monday morning banter deserved something more, he added, "But I admit, I do have some small hopes in that particular direction."

As soon as Roger had said the words, he wished he hadn't. He might have hopes—and he wasn't entirely sure he did yet—but he had no idea if Lindy shared them. Most likely she'd just been asking him on a walk for Toby's sake, not hers. Besides, it wasn't even a certainty yet. Far from it. There was the home visit, after all.

"Ooh, my man! Some hopes!" Chris crowed. "Who's the lucky lady? Tina from HR?"

"No, of course not." Roger stared at him, appalled. "It's no one at work. I would never be so imprudent."

"Of course not," Chris agreed, nodding.

"It's no one you know," he informed his colleague firmly. No one who someone like Chris, who lived in Oxford and frequented rowdy pubs and pulsing nightclubs, would ever know.

"Well, good luck, man," Chris said as he hefted his coffee mug in a toast. "We all need it."

Roger forced a small smile of acknowledgement. He knew full well that if he ever did decide to ask Lindy out, he would need all the luck he could get.

Lindy continued to prey on his mind all through his working day, which was extraordinary as Roger usually never lost focus at work. He was in his element when dealing with numbers and spreadsheets, things he understood and that didn't change. Yet in the middle of a meeting about one of their major accounts, he lost the thread of the conversation completely, and was caught out when his supervisor asked him a pointed question about last month's figures. Roger had gaped gormlessly for a second before he'd thankfully recovered himself.

This wouldn't do, he realised as he headed back home that evening. He drove from Wychwood to one of the park and rides on the outskirts of Oxford and then biked in, a commute that meant a bit of faff but at least got him exercising. On a Monday it also got him just in time for the ballroom dancing class, but when he came into his mother's cottage that evening he found her curled up on the settee with an old episode of *Inspector Morse* on the telly, looking remorseful.

"I'm sorry, darling. I just don't feel up for dancing tonight."

"Oh. Right." Roger tried valiantly to mask his unexpected disappointment; as much as he'd been dreading dancing, he'd been looking forward to seeing Lindy. "Well, never mind. I'll heat up some of the soup I made over the weekend and—"

"No, no," Ellen said with surprising vigour, considering her rather woebegone state. "I won't have you missing out. You go on without me."

"What?" Roger stared at her blankly. Such an idea had never occurred to him. "No, there's no need. You're the one who wanted lessons, not me. And besides, I don't want to leave you alone."

"Nonsense," Ellen declared briskly. "I don't mind being alone, and I know you enjoy the class, Rog. Secretly, deep down." She gave him a teasing smile. "Very deep down."

"Mum…"

"I insist." His mother sounded almost vehement. "There's no reason for you to stay here and babysit me. You know I don't like being mollycoddled."

"But—"

"Why don't you eat something quickly and then go change?" Ellen looked at him hopefully. "Wear your blue shirt. You look so nice in it."

Even someone as emotionally unastute as him was able to see what his mother was doing. She wanted to set him up with Lindy. The thought made Roger's insides squirm rather unpleasantly.

"Don't," he told his mum, and she raised her eyebrows,

the perfect picture of innocence.

"Don't what?"

"Don't meddle."

"I just want you to be happy, Rog. You're a good man and you deserve a woman who loves you for who you are—"

"I'm making supper now," Roger cut across her, unable to bear hearing his mother list all his supposedly wonderful attributes. They'd had this conversation before and it always made him feel a bit nauseous. A man of his age did *not* need to hear his mother telling him what a catch she thought he was.

With a sigh he headed into the kitchen to prepare them both the soup he'd made over the weekend. At moments like this he wondered how he'd got here—nearly forty, practically living with his mother, work being his entire life, no romantic prospects whatsoever.

A few years ago, after Laurel, he'd braved a dating site and that had been an unmitigated disaster. The three women who had responded to his profile had been either desperate or bossy, and the dates had been worse. Roger had suffered through two excruciating evenings of conversation that had come in uncomfortable fits and starts before he decided he was perhaps meant to be alone.

And then Lindy had come along and shook all that up…unless he was being ridiculous? She had said they were friends on the telephone, after all. Just friends.

And yet…surely he wasn't so clueless as to feel a spark

leaping between them when it wasn't there? On second thought, he probably was.

"Rog?" his mum called. "The class is in ten minutes."

"I know." Roger brought a bowl of soup and a slice of homemade bread to his mother, and she smiled at him gratefully.

"You're so good to me—"

"I know, I know." He waved her thanks aside with a quick smile. "I'll see you after the class," he promised her as he kissed her cheek.

He bolted a slice of bread as he headed back to his own house, a sixteenth-century terraced cottage on a side street he'd bought six months ago. It had a musty, unlived-in air, since he spent so much time at his mum's, and Roger glanced at the dusty surfaces with a slight grimace of distaste. He really needed to hire a housecleaner or get himself organised.

Upstairs he peeled off his suit, hesitating for a moment as he remembered his mother's entreaty for him to wear his blue shirt. It was washed and ironed, as he did all his work clothes on a Saturday, and yet he hesitated. *Did* he look nice in it? He had no idea. It was just a shirt, one he'd worn last week in fact. And last week Lindy had almost kissed him…

Well, maybe.

Roger reached for the shirt.

Five minutes later, in his usual off-duty uniform of button-down shirt and khakis, he headed out into the chilly autumn evening. It was the end of September and it felt like it—the leaves starting to turn, a crispness in the air that hadn't been there even just a week ago.

With a spring in his step, Roger headed towards Waggy Tails Bakery—and Lindy.

LINDY HAD DECIDED to dial it down for tonight's class. She couldn't help but remember her breathy laugh, the way she'd practically *caressed* Roger, last week without cringing inside. What must he have thought? After their phone call she was afraid she'd been friend-zoned, and she told herself that was just as well. She hardly wanted to jump into a relationship, did she? Not that that was even a possibility.

Tonight she'd chosen a pair of canary-yellow cigarette pants matched with a bright blue button-down shirt, and she'd pulled her hair back into a sleek ponytail. High heels were, as always, a must, and so she'd matched the outfit with a pair of bright blue open-toed sandals. Still, for her it was a bit lower key than usual, although Olivia didn't think so.

She and Simon were the first to arrive, and she let out a delighted laugh as she took in Lindy's ensemble.

"You always look so fabulous, Lindy. Where do you get your clothes?"

"Charity shops, mostly. Also from my grandmother."

"Your grandmother? How wonderful."

"I never met her, but my dad always told me she was a

pistol." Nearly as tall as Lindy herself, with a lot of attitude, Rosalind Jamison had seemed like a force to be reckoned with. Lindy wished she'd had a chance to meet her; Rosalind had died five years before Lindy was born, another person in her life she'd never had a chance to love.

At times, mostly when she was feeling a bit low, she longed for the sprawling web of relatives that so many people had—grandparents, aunts and uncles, cousins. It was all so beyond her experience, and usually that was fine. She made herself not mind, because she'd had so many blessings already.

"Listen, you two," Lindy told Simon and Olivia with semi-mock sternness, pushing away her melancholy thoughts, "I need to give you a bit of a talking-to."

"You do?" Simon raised shaggy eyebrows with an expression of teasing alarm. "Uh-oh."

"I know you're having a laugh and a half, falling over each other every class, but you told me you were taking this class so you could wow people at your wedding, and I have to tell you, the way you're going, that's not going to happen."

Simon grinned but Olivia looked shamefaced. "It's just we're both so clumsy…"

"I don't care about clumsy. Even the most awkward person can learn how to dance. But you've got to put the effort in." She wagged a finger at them. "Try harder."

"We will, Miss Jamison," Simon said solemnly, and

Lindy rolled her eyes.

"We're reviewing the waltz and the foxtrot today, and I want to see some dedication, okay?"

"Aye aye, Captain."

Maureen came in then, hobbling a bit more than usual, although she was as sparky as ever. "It's my hip today," she told Lindy. "And my ankle. It's always something."

"Are you going to be all right to dance?" Lindy asked.

Maureen gave her a severe look. "I'm always all right to dance, missy. Now what about you and your man?"

Lindy clocked Olivia's interested look as she looked at Maureen in exasperated confusion. "What man?"

"The stuffed shirt who comes along to the classes," Maureen declared in a voice loud enough for everyone within a five-hundred-foot radius to hear. "You couldn't keep your eyes off each other last week, I noticed. Or your hands, for that matter. *That's* the way to do the foxtrot."

"Maureen…" Lindy could only goggle helplessly as the older woman let out one of her dirty cackles and Simon and Olivia pretended to be very interested in studying the *Strictly Ballroom* poster. "There's nothing like that between us," she informed Maureen rather sternly, only to have Roger walk through the door. Judging from the colour touching his cheekbones, it was likely he'd heard the whole conversation. Perfect.

Lindy quickly looked away, busying herself with setting up the speaker, conscious of Roger's presence like a force field drawing her towards him. After several minutes of pointless fussing with her phone, she turned back to him—and noticed he was alone.

"Where's Ellen?" she exclaimed, and Roger gave a little shrug.

"She's a bit tired tonight, so she decided to stay home and rest."

"Oh…" But he'd come anyway? Lindy was pleased, of course, but as she absorbed the news she realised it meant she'd have no reason to dance with Roger. There would be four students in the class. They could all dance with each other while she watched and instructed. The knowledge brought a pang of disappointment, which she firmly pushed away.

It was just as well, she told herself. She really didn't need to be embarrassing herself again.

"Right, then," she called out. "Let's get started."

Over the next hour, Simon and Olivia applied them-selves remarkably well, and Maureen gave Roger what-for, telling him to stop being so stiff and actually *move*.

"Or else I'll have to ask Lindy to come and show you how it's done," she said with a cackle, "and I know how much you'd like that."

Roger's expression was completely unreadable, but Lindy *felt* his embarrassment. Or maybe she just felt her own. Maureen's lack of inhibition when it came to commenting on their love lives or lack thereof was a decided danger to the class dynamic, as well as to Lindy's own mental wellbeing.

"Shall I help you get the teas?" Olivia asked with a sympathetic smile during the break. "Maureen doesn't know when to stop, does she?" she said with a little laugh once they were safely ensconced in the kitchen. "Poor Roger."

"And poor me," Lindy said with a feeling. "Honestly…"

"But he is a lovely man, you know," Olivia said as she switched on the kettle. "I know he can be a bit—well—wooden, I suppose, but he's got a heart of gold. Truly."

"I didn't realise you knew him so well," Lindy said after a moment, startled by Olivia's assessment, and very stupidly, the tiniest bit jealous.

"Just through the bakery. He comes in a couple of times a week to buy scones for his mum."

"Ah yes, cheese scones." She remembered the scene from a few weeks ago with a twinge of discomfort. She still hadn't apologised for that whole unsuitable remark.

"He moved to Wychwood-on-Lea to take care of her," Olivia explained. "She has cancer."

"She does?" Lindy looked at Olivia in surprise. "I had no idea." Admittedly Ellen had always seemed a bit frail, but Lindy had just thought it had been because of her age.

"Yes, and from what I gather, the diagnosis isn't all that encouraging, although Roger has never said as much. It's more just a feeling I have than anything else."

"Oh…" Why hadn't Roger told her? There surely had been opportunity during their various chats.

"Anyway, all this to say I think he's a great guy. I know he comes across as odd sometimes—Harriet certainly thought so—but I really do think there's more going on beneath the surface."

"So what are you saying?" Lindy asked with a small smile. "I should give him a chance?"

"Well." Olivia gave an abashed laugh. "Yes, I suppose so."

"I'm not even sure he's interested in me," she stated baldly, deciding to be reckless with her confidences. "He's a very hard man to read."

"Oh Lindy," Olivia exclaimed with a laugh, "do you honestly think Roger would come to this class without his mother if he wasn't interested in you? I think he'd rather have his eye gouged out with—with an oyster fork!"

"Ouch." Lindy winced at the mental image even as pleasure unfurled in her at the realisation. Judging from how painful Roger had found some of the dance lessons, she thought Olivia might be right.

And if so…then what was she going to do with that information? Just the nameless, barely formed possibilities made everything in her fizz with excitement and fear. Lindy was still battling both emotions as she headed back upstairs with a tray of teas, only to stop in surprise at the sight of a pretty, shy-looking young woman standing by the door, chatting to Roger.

"Oh!" The syllable seemed to explode out of her, tea

slopped from the cups onto the tray, and the woman turned to her with a questioning smile.

"You must be Belinda Jamison?"

"Please call me Lindy." She glanced enquiringly at Roger, who was as blank-faced as usual. "And you are…?"

"Helena Winter. I'm so sorry I'm late. I had to cycle in from Witney. I was hoping you had space in the class…?"

"You wish to register for the Monday class for beginners?" Lindy said a bit stupidly, belatedly realising she sounded rather like Roger in her wooden formality.

"Yes…if that's okay?" The woman smiled at her encouragingly, while Lindy just stared, her mind spinning.

Why was she feeling so wrong-footed? Perhaps it was the way Helena had seemed to chat so easily to Roger, as if they already knew each other. Did they? Had he invited her? Was that why he'd come alone tonight, wearing the blue shirt he looked so nice in? He seemed to have taken extra care with his appearance, and now Lindy thought she knew why.

Helena was young and shy-looking, but also lovely, with wheat-blonde hair that brushed her shoulders and wide, blue eyes. She looked like a gentle Barbie.

"Yes, of course it's okay," Lindy said as brightly as she could. "Let me just put this tray down and then I'll get you a registration form."

The next few moments seemed to pass in a blur as Olivia handed out cups of tea and Lindy found a form for Helena to fill out.

"How did you hear about the class?" she asked as Helena began writing, her blonde hair swinging down to hide her face.

"I saw a leaflet in the post office. My auntie lives in Wychwood and so I come here often enough."

"I see…"

"I had no idea Roger was taking the class," Helena added with a laugh. She shot Roger a smiling look that seemed both secretive and knowing, and made Lindy ridiculously feel like hissing.

"Helena and I work together," Roger explained stiffly. "At Hartley and Fein Accountants."

"Do you?" Lindy tried not to reel from this unexpected information. "How lovely."

She let the conversation drift over as she sipped her tea; Helena was quite chatty. She worked as a receptionist where Roger was a senior CPA. She'd been there for eighteen months, and judging by the looks she kept shooting at a straight-faced Roger, she had something of a crush.

Lindy thought Helena couldn't be more than twenty-one or twenty-two, but perhaps Roger didn't mind the age difference. She had lovely hair and skin, a willowy figure, and a tinkling laugh. All of it made Lindy fight an urge to clench her hands into claw-like fists.

As they all finished their tea, a weird pettishness took over her, like some sort of OCD alien invading her body; she heard herself asking Helena to put the cup on the tray rather than the counter, and wondered what on earth had got into her. She wasn't like this. She didn't do passive-aggressive or snippy; she hated veiled barbs. And yet here she was, rocking all three. This had to stop.

Lindy realised, as she took the tray of empty cups back to the kitchen, that she'd never actually thought she'd have to compete for Roger's attention. She'd never expected to feel jealous, and it was an emotion she didn't like at all—prickly and unpleasant, like a rash spreading over her skin, making her want to scratch viciously. It was a wake-up call to the reality of relationships, and all the messy, tangled feelings they created and exposed in her. She hated every single one.

Things only got more complicated when they started up with the foxtrot—Maureen insisted on dancing with Lindy, because 'it helped her hip' and so Helena was partnered with Roger. She only came up to his shoulder, and she looked tiny and delicate next to him, and made Lindy feel like a lumbering giantess.

She tried to lift her dark mood as she foxtrotted with Maureen, whose hip, for once, seemed fine. It really wasn't like her to feel this way—grumpy and jealous and fierce. Every so often she couldn't keep from glancing at Roger and Helena, and noticing how awkwardly they moved around the dance floor; it would have given her an absurd and savage sort of pleasure, except for the fact that Helena didn't seem to mind at all.

She was chatting nineteen to the dozen, and every time

her tinkling little laugh floated through the room Lindy felt herself tense. This was so not good. This was so not *her*.

"You'd better scoop him up fast," Maureen said, fortunately in a quieter voice than usual. "Before that young one takes him. She's got the looks for it, you know."

Lindy bit the inside of her cheek and did not reply.

The evening felt endless by the time everyone was saying their goodbyes, Helena lingering by the door, as if waiting for Roger.

"Do you have to cycle all the way back to Witney?" Lindy asked, trying to sound concerned rather than waspish. What she really wanted to say was, *Hadn't you better get going?*

What was *wrong* with her?

"Yes," Helena said on a sigh. "And it's getting so dark in the evenings now." She glanced at Roger, who was thankfully not taking the hint.

"I can run you back," Simon offered. "I've got the car parked out front. I don't mind."

"Oh…" Helena looked torn, and Roger was still silent. "Thanks," she finally said, "but there's no need. The exercise is good for me."

At last they were all gone, Roger included, and Lindy locked up, doing her best not to feel utterly disconsolate. She had another student, so that was something. And if Roger preferred Helena, then so be it. Perhaps it was better that way. She certainly didn't enjoy feeling so tangled up inside, and hopefully she wouldn't, if she and Roger stayed just friends.

Maybe that was how it should be—friends, and nothing more. No what-ifs, no possibility, just another person to smile and chat to. She hated feeling so out of control, being snappish instead of sunny. Maybe, Lindy thought, she wasn't cut out for romantic relationships. The jealousy she felt was most unsettling, especially because she'd never experienced it before. She certainly hadn't felt it with Philip. She didn't want to feel it now. Friends it was, then. *Good.*

So why did that thought make her feel even worse?

Chapter Ten

SOMETHING HAD GONE wrong. It was a Tuesday morning in mid-October, two weeks after Roger had shown up to dance class in his blue shirt, feeling fine. Feeling hopeful. And since then everything had gone depressingly downhill.

The kettle in the office kitchen switched off, and morosely Roger poured boiling water over his limp-looking teabag. What *had* gone wrong? Maybe he'd just been misreading the signals all along, something he knew was perfectly possible, even likely. Or Lindy had gone off him, if she'd even been *on* him in the first place. Whatever it was, the last two weeks she'd done her best to be a cheerful, chirpy dance instructor and nothing more.

At first Roger had wondered if it had to do with Helena showing up, something that had rather blindsided him. He hadn't even recognised her from the office, and yet Helena had acted as if they were far friendlier than they were. She'd kept looking at him as if he had the answers to the universe, and Roger hadn't known how to act—not an unusual occurrence, admittedly. Helena hadn't been flirting with him, as far as he could tell, but she'd been looking at him like she wanted something from him and he had no idea what it was.

She'd kept by his side the whole evening, and she hadn't seemed to mind that he had absolutely no response when she'd mentioned she was taking her A levels, because she'd missed out on them when she was younger. Roger had stared at her in something like bafflement; he'd taken his A levels twenty years ago.

While Helena had continued to stay near him, Lindy had continued to treat him as if he were the same as Maureen, and if he'd had more reason to hope, he would have thought she was jealous. As it was, he was pretty sure she'd simply had enough of him.

On Saturday he'd volunteered at Blue Cross and noticed Lindy had had her home visit and was officially approved to adopt a pet. She was picking up Toby on Thursday, and she hadn't even told him.

"Roger, my man!" Chris came into the kitchen with his usual waft of Lynx Africa and Polo mints. "How's it going?"

"Fine, thank you," Roger returned as he dunked his teabag. Yesterday they'd had their usual rave exchange and Roger's reply that he was thinking of starting his own had been decidedly lacklustre. He simply hadn't been able to put his heart into the usual banter, not that Chris would even realise he had been doing that all along.

"You're looking a bit down, Rog," Chris said in his overly familiar way. "How's your lady friend?"

Roger hesitated and then, deciding on honesty, said, "Not very well, I'm afraid."

Chris staggered back, looking comically shocked. "What? No..."

"She seems to have cooled in her affections," Roger said stiffly as he reached for the milk. "At least, that is my best estimation."

"What happened?"

He gave a little shrug. "Nothing. I suspect it was all wishful conjecture on my part, nothing more."

"She must have given you some hints to how she was feeling," Chris pressed, and briefly Roger thought of Lindy doing the foxtrot with him, her body pressed against his. He remembered their time in the kitchen, her fingers tracing his eyebrow...

"I believed she did," he allowed. "But it appears I was mistaken."

"She's changed her tune?" Chris shook his head sorrowfully. "It happens, man. These women...they don't know their own minds."

"I believe the lady in question knows her own mind very well indeed," Roger replied. "I am quite sure the misconception was entirely my fault."

Chris cocked an eyebrow. "You don't seem like the kind of bloke who would go around thinking a woman had the hots for him when she didn't, you know what I'm saying?"

"I believe I do," Roger answered after a pause. He wouldn't have phrased it that way, certainly.

"She must have changed her mind. Did you do something to put her off? Forget to send her flowers?"

"I have never sent her flowers," Roger replied, scandalised. "Our relationship had not remotely reached that stage."

"Ah." Chris nodded knowingly and Roger wondered what on earth he was doing, talking about his love life with this gel-haired twenty-three-year-old. "So do you think you've been friend-zoned?" he asked, and Roger stared at him for a moment.

Friend-zoned. He had not heard the term before but he could guess what it meant, and as he stared at Chris, idly wondering just how much gel he had to use to get his hair to stick up in such stiff points, he realised that had to be exactly what had happened.

Lindy had friend-zoned him. Completely and utterly. He didn't know why, but did it even matter? And really, wasn't it just as well? If things had gone any further, he would have undoubtedly made a mess of their fledgling relationship, disappointed or even hurt Lindy, and frustrated himself in the process. Really, this was better.

Even if it didn't feel like it.

"What you've got to do," Chris says, "is really wow her. Make her look at you differently."

Roger gazed at him, nonplussed. "I'm not sure I'm capable of wowing anybody," he said matter-of-factly, and Chris let out a sympathetic laugh.

"Come on, Rog, you've got your pluses. The ladies love tall guys."

"So you are implying my height is my only advantage?"

"Well, it's one of them." Chris rubbed his spotty chin. "You've got to make her see you as something other than a mate."

That, Roger thought, was obvious even to someone like him. "Thank you," he answered as he took his tea back to his desk. "I'll bear it in mind."

ALL DAY LONG Roger did his best not to think about Lindy, which wasn't too difficult because work took up all his mental energies, as it so often did. When he was gazing at a spreadsheet, he felt consumed. It was an emotion he suspected most people would not understand.

Still, despite his focus on figures, Lindy remained on the edges of his mind, the periphery of his vision, just out of reach and yet still most definitely there. And even when he absolutely wasn't, it still felt as if he were thinking about her.

It wasn't until he'd got back to Wychwood that he decided to do something about it. So he'd been friend-zoned, he thought as he checked on his mum, who seemed cheerful, and then headed back to his own cottage. He'd stay in that zone, then. He didn't mind, not really. He could use a friend, heaven knew, and he realised he *liked* Lindy. As a person. He would like to spend time with her.

And if he really was just a friend, then surely it would be a fairly normal thing to do, to ring Lindy and ask her how the adoption process was going. Of course, he already knew how it was going, and he wasn't good at prevarication. Still, it was a reason to call.

Roger waited until he'd changed out of his suit, put a load of laundry in, and heated up the shepherd's pie he'd made over the weekend, before he called Lindy. He cracked open a beer for a bit of Dutch courage and then swiped his phone to dial her number.

Ring. Ring.

What should he say his first? How should he sound?

Ring.

Hey, I was just calling to see how it was going with Toby. That sounded okay, didn't it?

"Roger?" The sound of her voice, so warm and vibrant, shocked him into a moment of stupefied silence that stretched on uncomfortably. *"Roger?"* she said again, sounding concerned.

"Yes, um, hello." He cleared his throat, conscious he'd already messed up.

"Is everything all right?"

"Yes, fine. Er…I was just wondering if you'd managed to pick up Toby yet."

"Oh. No, not yet. But I've been approved. Did you

know, from your volunteering…?"

"Yes, I did see your application. Well, it's good news."

"Yes, I'm very excited. I pick him up on Thursday."

Which he already knew. "Right-o, very good," he said, sounding, he thought, a bit like he imagined Colonel Mustard would.

"What have you been up to?" Lindy asked, and again Roger's mind blanked.

"Work," he said after a moment. "Mainly."

"Right."

Another one of those awful, sticky silences where his mind felt as if it had spun itself into a web and he had no idea what to say.

"And you?" he finally forced out, and Lindy gave a little laugh.

"Work, too, I suppose. I've started teaching a class of Year Sixes at the primary, and I've got four in my junior class. Twinkle Toes, it's called now."

"Oh. Good."

"Yes, slowly but surely, I suppose."

Silence. This was horrible. This was not at all how Roger wanted this conversation to go. "Well," Roger said, to no purpose.

"Are you…are you still up for walking Toby with me?" Lindy asked after a moment, sounding uncertain. "Maybe on Saturday?"

Relief rushed through him, along with a frustration that

he had not been able to ask her himself. "Yes, that would be…" He paused, trying to think of a word, and ended up saying, "Acceptable."

Right.

"Oh, okay, then." Lindy sounded a bit startled. "How about two o'clock?"

"Yes, that should be fine."

"All right. See you then."

"Okay. Yes. Bye." Roger swiped to end the call and then let out a huge exhalation of relief. That had been painful, but he'd got the result he wanted. They were going on a walk.

LINDY WAS IN love. Completely and utterly.

From the moment the staff member at Blue Cross had opened the door to Toby's kennel and the sleek, trembling greyhound had cautiously ventured out, stubby tail wagging, her heart had been taken. Forget romantic relationships; here was what she needed.

"Hey, Toby." Her voice had dropped to a soft, encouraging whisper as she stroked the dog's narrow head. "Aren't you a sweet boy."

It had only taken a couple of weeks for her to be approved for adoption, and it still felt surreal to walk out of Blue Cross having signed a few forms and paid a bit of cash, with a dog. Her very own dog.

She'd kept glancing at Toby curled up in the back seat of

her car, his thin body trembling with nerves, amazed he was actually hers. She had a faithful companion, a partner in crime. Never mind that he couldn't actually talk; his eyes, like melting chocolate buttons, spoke volumes. Why had she never thought of getting a dog before?

Of course, she knew the answer to that—she hadn't had the time or space or opportunity. But now she had all three, and she was so very happy.

The first night in her home, Toby had started in his fleece-lined bed downstairs. But it had only taken a few seconds of mournful whimpering for Lindy to bring him up to bed with her. All the rules about being a strict and responsible dog owner went right out the window. Why shouldn't Toby sleep in her bedroom? No one else was.

He settled onto the sheepskin rug at the foot of her bed like he was made for it.

Of course there had been some growing pains—Toby could be clingy, and when he was nervous he tended to wee, which was challenging as he was nervous about ninety per cent of the time. Plus he liked to chew, but a boxful of squeaky toys and a few treats from Waggy Tails had helped to solve that particular problem.

"You'll have to bring him in to say hello," Monica said when Lindy had stopped by to purchase a few dog biscuits. "He sounds like a sweetheart."

"He is. I'm not taking him out into public places too much yet, because he's nervous and apparently he has to learn to socialise slowly." She had a raft of literature from Blue Cross, and she'd also been spending some time on a website for greyhound owners called Gaga for Greyhounds, which had plenty of advice for newbies like her.

"Well, when he's ready," Monica answered. She leaned her elbows on the counter, looking curious. "How is everything going, anyway? I've hardly seen you since you've opened Take a Twirl. It's going well, I hope?"

"It is." Monica had usually locked up by the time Lindy came for her Monday evening classes, and on Saturday a young girl named Pip worked the counter. She'd hardly seen Monica at all since she'd had the floors done back in August, which was already feeling like a lifetime ago. "It's all going well," Lindy reaffirmed. "Really well."

And it *was*, although occasionally Lindy felt a strange, niggling restlessness that she did her best to ignore. She'd managed not to feel it for fifteen years, so why start now?

And yet Lindy knew she did feel it, and that was in part due to Roger. After the appearance of Helena—who was, Lindy discovered, a lovely, shy young woman—she'd decided, quite firmly, to drop any romantic notions towards him. It simply wasn't worth the aggro—or the heartache. She'd done fine with friends before, and she could do so again. And so she'd done her chipper, chirpy best to be his friend, and it seemed to be working, but it was still leaving her feeling a little flat, even if she was trying not to let it.

But never mind, Lindy told herself as she left Waggy

Tails. There were worse things, surely, and in any case it would be good to be Roger's friend. They were taking that walk tomorrow and Lindy hoped it would be a fun and relaxed time—although when she thought about it fun and relaxed were not words she really associated with Roger. Still, she hoped it was...*acceptable.*

The weather outdid itself, which was a plus; a rain-washed blue sky, everything damp and fresh, but with the sun out in full force and an autumnal crispness in the air that made you feel like taking a deep breath and drinking it in.

Toby was eager, if a bit skittish for his walk; Lindy had arranged to meet Roger by the gazebo on the village green. They'd walk up the high street to help Toby socialise, and then stroll along the Lea River, which was a bit more quiet.

She was feeling almost as skittish as Toby as she walked towards the village green, Toby glued to her side, his ears flattened back with nervousness. She'd been keeping her distance from Roger for the last two weeks, although she wasn't sure if he'd even have noticed. She certainly hadn't been flirting any longer. But now she wondered how they would get on, just the two of them.

As she came towards the gazebo, she saw his tall, solitary figure standing by it; he was dressed in his usual uniform of khakis and a button-down shirt, and wore a sturdy pair of work boots as well as a weatherproof parka.

"You look prepared to hike Everest," Lindy teased as she came up to him. She realised she was glad to see him, and it didn't feel weird. At least, not *too* weird.

"I prefer to be prepared for all eventualities," Roger answered. He glanced up at the cloudless sky. "Although perhaps the waterproof wasn't necessary."

"You never know," Lindy answered. "The weather can change on a sixpence, after all." But she didn't want to natter on about the weather. "So here's Toby."

"Hey, boy." Roger crouched down to stroke Toby's narrow head and Lindy smiled at the sight, while Toby quivered and pressed closer to Roger.

"He knows you."

"I should hope so." Roger glanced up at her, his eyes crinkling at the corners, and Lindy had to catch her breath. She was not going to react that way, she reminded herself sternly. They were friends. Friends only. Better—and safer— all around.

"Shall we walk?" she asked as Roger straightened. "I thought we could go up the high street to help him get used to people, and then along the river."

"That sounds like a well-thought-out plan."

"Thank you." She couldn't keep from giving him a teasing smile—which was not flirting—and was rewarded with the tiniest quirk back. "Have you explored much of the area?" she asked as they headed up the high street, past Waggy Tails, and then Tea on the Lea.

"No, I've been too busy with work and—" He stopped abruptly, and Lindy filled in gently, "Caring for your mother?" Roger gave her a quick, startled glance, and she explained, "Olivia told me she has cancer. I hope that was okay for her to—"

"Yes, I suppose it's fairly common knowledge by now."

"I'm so sorry, Roger." He gave a terse nod. "That's why you moved to Wychwood? To take care of her?"

"Yes. She only moved here a year ago, when she retired from teaching. She didn't know that many people and..." He blew out a breath. "It's been just us since I was twelve."

"I understand that."

"Yes, I imagine you do. The joys as well as the sorrows of being close to your parents."

"Yes." Lindy glanced down at Toby, trotting happily between them. "It's wonderful, but when it's gone..."

"It's gone." He spoke flatly, but Lindy sensed the ocean of grief seething beneath, and it made her ache.

"Her prognosis?" she asked after a moment, and Roger shrugged.

"She had several rounds of chemo but the consultant was never optimistic. Pancreatic cancer has one of the worst five-year survival rates—only seven per cent. She was diagnosed a year ago, and six months later they said there was no further treatment possible."

"So..."

"We're just waiting."

"Oh, Roger." His expression was so bleak that Lindy couldn't keep from putting a hand on his arm.

He turned to her with a set expression. "In some ways it's a mercy to know. There's been time for her to get her affairs in order, which is very important."

"Ever the accountant."

"Numbers don't change."

"That's what attracted me to them, as well," she replied with a little, sorrowful laugh. "You can *depend* on them. You can move them around. You know just where you are with a stack of figures." And they never died.

"Yes, exactly."

They shared a quick, complicit smile that made something in Lindy settle rather than fizz. Yes, she was Roger's friend—and she was glad of it.

Chapter Eleven

"COME IN, COME in!"

Henry Trent, the Earl of Stokeley, was full of gracious bonhomie as he opened the door of Willoughby Manor and ushered Lindy in. She handed him her six-pound bottle of wine and box of chocolates from M&S with a slightly shamefaced smile; for anyone else they would have felt appropriate and even generous but here she couldn't quite shake the feeling that she should have come with a bottle of Dom Perignon and a hamper from Fortnum and Mason.

Henry, however, took both with apparent pleasure. "How delicious! You didn't have to bring anything though, you know. Come through to the kitchen—I won't stand on ceremony, and in any case it's still the most comfortable room in the house."

As Lindy followed Henry past several elegant and grand reception rooms, she wondered at that, but she was as happy as he was to stay in the kitchen. She knew from Alice that they'd been doing the manor up slowly, room by room, in preparation to offer holidays to foster children. They'd been able to offer their first week at the end of July, and it had been a success, although Alice had admitted ruefully there was still plenty of room for improvement.

Lindy felt a bit awed to be in the house at all; this was only her second time inside, the first being a drinks party for all the Willoughby Close residents back in June, when she'd only just arrived.

The kitchen was as welcoming a room as Henry had promised, with a big, rectangular table and an enormous Aga taking up most of the space. A soft grey cat was curled up on an armchair, and the windowsill was cluttered with house-plants and cookbooks.

The cosy clutter reminded Lindy so much of her home growing up that for a second she could only stand in the doorway and stare, trying desperately to rein in the emotion she hadn't expected to feel.

"Sorry, it's all a bit of a mess," Alice said as she turned from the Aga where various pots were boiling and bubbling away.

"It's lovely," Lindy answered, because it was. The lovable mess, the chaotic warmth…it was all so similar to the home she'd left when her parents had died. It had been lovely like this, as well. So very lovely.

In the fifteen years since she'd lost her parents, she'd kept to comfortable but fairly utilitarian flats, never wanting to attempt to replicate the crowded clutter of the home she'd absolutely adored—and still owned, since she'd inherited it when her parents had died. She hadn't been able to bear either visiting it or selling it, and so she'd kept it as it was, looked after by a neighbour, the heating and electricity bills paid regularly to keep it all going. For what purpose, Lindy didn't even know, but she liked simply knowing it was there. Perhaps she'd go visit it again at some point, she thought, knowing that she wouldn't actually.

"Come, sit down, make yourself comfortable," Henry entreated. "What can I get you? White? Red? Gin? Vodka?"

Lindy laughed at that. "A glass of red would be lovely."

She settled herself at the table as Henry opened a bottle of wine and Alice turned back to the Aga to stir something that smelled delicious. Outside the sky had turned to slate grey, the brilliant weather from yesterday having turned, after all. Already it was feeling closer to winter than summer; there had been frost on the ground this morning, every blade of grass tipped with glittering white.

"So how are you finding Willoughby Close?" Henry asked as he handed her a glass of wine. "And Wychwood-on-Lea?"

"I'm finding both very friendly," Lindy replied with a smile. "It already feels as if I've been here for ages."

"Willoughby Close has that effect on people," Alice chimed in. "I enjoyed my time in number four."

"But I'm glad it was brief," Henry interjected with a loved-up look for his wife. "I'm just going to check on the fire in the sitting room. I'm hoping to have a roaring blaze going by the time we've finished dinner."

As he left, Lindy gave Alice a smiling look. "You two seem very happy."

"We are." Alice blushed and ducked her head. "I still feel like a newlywed even though we've been married for nearly two years," she confessed. "Some days I still have to pinch myself."

The words were genuine, and yet as Lindy watched Alice fuss about the stove, she couldn't help but feel there was something slightly brittle about her smile, and she wondered why.

Alice had everything—the huge house, the lovely husband, rewarding work. She was, quite literally, living the fairy tale; the only thing missing, perhaps, was a baby or two...but surely that would come in time, if they wanted them to?

"What about you?" Alice asked as she poured herself a glass of wine and joined her at the table. "Any possibilities here in Wychwood?"

"For romance? No." Lindy spoke as firmly as she could while remaining upbeat.

"Are you sure?" Alice asked teasingly. "A little bird told me she saw you walking with someone up the high street, and the two of you looked very cosy."

"Wha—what?" Lindy stammered, surprised and yet knowing she shouldn't be. After fifteen years in a big city, village life still took some getting used to, but she should have known you couldn't parade down the high street with a man and a dog without people assuming intentions had been declared, vows spoken.

"Sorry, I'm being nosy," Alice said, only slightly abashed. "I just wondered…"

"We're friends," Lindy answered. "He's from my dance class."

Alice's eyebrows rose. "Wait—the man who was so unsuitable?"

Lindy flushed at the memory of that unfortunate conversation. She still hadn't figured out a way to apologise to Roger about that, and she hoped it was no longer necessary.

"He's not unsuitable," she protested, conscious of how hot her cheeks felt. "I shouldn't have said that."

"But you're just friends?" Alice said, looking unconvinced.

"Yes."

Alice gave her another searching look before she threw up her hands with a laugh. "Okay, I give up," she said. "Sounds interestingly complicated."

"It really isn't," Lindy answered with a smile. At least, she didn't want it to be. Yesterday had been lovely; she and Roger had managed to chat all the way up the high street and then while ambling along the Lea River, the conversation surprisingly easy. After that brief heart-to-heart about his mum, they'd chatted about accountancy, and Lindy liked to think there had been some low-grade banter involved. Then they'd talk about travelling—she'd told him some of her highlights over the years and he'd mentioned always wanting to go to Alaska, because, he'd told her matter-of-factly, it had beautiful scenery and no native snakes.

"Snakes!" Lindy exclaimed. "Are you scared of snakes, Roger?"

He'd given her a serious look. "I have a healthy and in-formed wariness of them, especially poisonous ones."

Which had made her smile. In fact, she'd smiled quite a lot yesterday, which had obviously made the little bird Alice had mentioned notice. She wondered how many other little birds were twittering around Wychwood.

Henry came back into the kitchen, and the next few moments were taken up with getting the food to the table, all of which looked delicious—roast lamb with mint sauce, roast potatoes deliciously golden and crispy, fluffy Yorkshire puddings, green beans, and a sherry trifle for pudding with masses of whipped cream. Lindy couldn't remember the last time she'd eaten so much or so well.

Fortunately Henry and Alice kept the conversation easy and light as they ate, with no more talk of romance, at least not Lindy's. She asked questions about the charity they'd formed, Willoughby Holidays, and the hopes they had to run a full season of week-long camps next summer.

"And I have to tell you about our Christmas ball," Alice said when they'd started on the trifle. "You're invited, of course. Everyone is."

"Sounds fab," Lindy replied as she licked her spoon. "Is it another charity fundraiser?"

"No, this time it's just for fun. A thank you to all our friends and neighbours, and really, this house is built for a ball. Have you seen the ballroom?"

Lindy shook her head.

"I'll show you," Alice said. "It's amazing."

While Henry made their coffees, Alice took Lindy through the house to show her the room in question, which was every bit as grand as Lindy could have imagined, with frescoed walls interspersed with wall-length mirrors, and floor-to-ceiling windows overlooking a stunning terrace and the landscaped gardens.

"I should have had my lessons in here," she joked, only to have Alice beam at her.

"But that's a brilliant idea! I don't know why I didn't even think of it. You must have them here. It would be perfect."

"I've already signed a lease on the room above Waggy Tails for the year," Lindy told her, a bit taken aback at Alice's enthusiasm, but also touched by the offer. "But if the school is a success, I'll keep this in mind, I promise." She looked around the room again. "Teaching a class in here would be absolutely amazing."

"If you can't teach a class, what about a performance?" Alice suggested, and Lindy glanced at her, nonplussed.

"What do you mean?"

"A performance," Alice repeated, clearly warming to the idea. "At the Christmas ball! That would be perfect!"

"A performance…"

"Of all your pupils. An extravaganza!" She gestured expansively, to encompass the ballroom, or even the whole manor. "We could open the dancing with it—or perhaps we should have it in the middle. Either way, it would be so much fun and it would be a fabulous advertisement for your dancing school. All your pupils could perform for everyone."

"True…" Lindy's mind was racing as she pictured the possibilities. While she absolutely thrilled to the idea of putting on a performance in this gorgeous room, when she considered her small, motley crew of pupils she wasn't so sure. Roger would have a conniption at the thought of dancing in public, and Simon and Olivia still preferred to fall over each other laughing rather than actually dance. Maureen had the will if not the body, and Helena was very much a beginner; Lindy had started to suspect she kept coming simply to see Roger rather than to learn the box step.

And what about her juniors? Ollie would love it, she was sure, and she thought the other three would as well, but they were all *six*. Which made her think of her Year Sixes… She'd only had two sessions with them so far, and while there were many lovely pupils, there were also several who skulked about the corners, looking determinedly bored.

And yet. And yet…

"What do you think?" Alice asked, looking at her hopefully.

"I think I love the idea," Lindy said honestly. "It's really just a matter of whether I can convince all my pupils."

SHE DECIDED TO broach the topic the very next evening, at her beginners' class. Tonight they were learning the samba, which required a bit more of bounce and hip wiggle than anything else they'd learned so far, but was otherwise fairly sedate. She hoped her students were up for it, especially Roger, who was still approaching the lessons with an attitude of sorely tested forbearance.

Helena was the first to arrive, surprising Lindy since she usually was a good fifteen minutes late, thanks to having to bike.

"Helena! Did you get off work early?"

"I had a dentist appointment this afternoon," Helena answered with a grimace. "Two fillings. I took the rest of the afternoon off."

"And rightly so," Lindy agreed with a commiserating smile. "Are you ready to samba?"

"As ready as I'll ever be, I suppose."

Lindy couldn't help but notice how dejected the young woman looked, and she didn't think it had to do with her dentistry. "Is everything all right?" she asked gently. The waspish jealousy she'd first felt upon meeting Helena had thankfully subsided to sudden pulses of anxiety that she did her best to suppress. Roger hadn't responded to Helena's overt friendliness, which Lindy was honest enough to admit was a relief, and she was still determined that they were friends and friends only. But she didn't enjoy seeing Helena look so flat.

"Yes, it's all fine," Helena said on a sigh. She picked at a ragged thumbnail before giving Lindy a guiltily embarrassed look. "I think I've just been a bit of an idiot, is all."

Lindy tensed even as she tried to relax. "I think we've all been that once or twice," she answered lightly. "Do you want to tell me about it?"

Helena paused, and then said slowly, "You know Roger?"

"Yes." Of course she knew Roger. Lindy focused on setting up the speaker for the music, conscious of the need to give Helena a little space, and also not trusting the expression on her face.

"Well, I came to this class because of him," Helena confessed in a rush. "Which is so stupid, I know. I've tried talking to him but I think I just annoy him."

"I'm sure you don't," Lindy said, refraining from adding that Roger could sometimes seem as if everyone annoyed him.

"I probably do. I seem young and silly to him, I'm sure. I told him about my A levels and he looked at me as if I were crazy."

A levels? She had to be younger than Lindy had thought.

"Well, there is quite an age gap," Lindy allowed, and Helena gave her the most incredulous look she'd ever received.

"Well, of *course* there is."

Lindy stared at her in wary confusion. "So…"

The penny dropped for Helena first, and she started to laugh, covering her mouth to suppress her giggles. "Wait…did you think I was *interested* in Roger? Like, romantically?"

"Er…" Lindy had a feeling she was about to be embarrassed, and she'd been the one trying to act like the mature, listening ear. "I suppose?" she hazarded and still laughing, Helena shook her head.

"No way. I mean, he's ancient." She bit her lip. "Sorry…"

"He's older than me, so don't worry," Lindy said a bit tartly. Roger had let it slip on their walk that he was thirty-eight, hardly *ancient*. "So if you aren't interested in him that way," she asked, "why were you coming to the class just to see him?" She felt as if she'd definitely missed something there.

"Because he reminds me of my dad," Helena said, and for a few seconds Lindy could only goggle.

"Your *dad*…?"

"He left when I was fifteen." Helena pressed her lips together and Lindy experienced a shaft of sympathy for the pain she knew the younger woman was struggling to contain. "Right before my GCSEs. I flubbed them all, and decided not to do A levels. I'm taking them now, but..." She drew a ragged breath. "For a while it really sent me spinning. He just upped and left. Found a new wife, a new family. Didn't care to maintain any contact, or at least not much. I see him once a year, if that."

"Helena, I'm so sorry." Lindy touched her arm. "I can't imagine how difficult that all must have been. But...Roger reminds you of him?" Lindy couldn't imagine someone less likely to remind someone of such a tosser.

"He wears the same sort of clothes," Helena explained, "and has the same aftershave. I don't know, when I saw him at work, it brought it right back. *My dad.* And I just, sort of, liked to pretend..." She let out a sniff, and it felt entirely right and natural for Lindy to put her arms around her while Helena tried not to cry.

"I'm so sorry," she murmured. "So sorry."

She knew what it was like to lose a parent, but in some ways, Lindy thought, Helena's experience felt worse than her own. At least her mum and dad hadn't chosen to leave her.

"Hello..." Ellen called out cheerily, only to falter as she saw Helena enfolded in Lindy's arms.

Helena immediately bolted, scurrying to the bathroom downstairs, and Ellen gave Lindy a conciliatory look. "I'm sorry. Was I interrupting something?"

"No, don't worry. It's fine." Lindy smiled reassuringly at her. "Just a bit of a moment, that's all." She glanced at Roger, who was looking severe, which Lindy was starting to realise was how he looked whenever he was unsure about a social situation, which was pretty much every single one.

Ellen looked wan, her wrists poking out of her jumper seeming like twigs. Roger had told Lindy during their Saturday walk about how Ellen wouldn't eat, and how he tried to buy or make whatever she fancied.

"Like four cheese scones?" Lindy had surmised, and flushing slightly, Roger had nodded. It would have been the perfect time to apologise for that dratted unsuitable comment, which she was almost certain he'd heard, but the words had bottled in her throat. They were having such a lovely time, and she didn't want to ruin it.

"So, I have some exciting news," Lindy told Ellen and Roger now, figuring she should give Roger at least a heads-up before she dropped her bombshell on the class. "And I know at least one of you will be pretty thrilled by it."

"Ooh, goody," Ellen said, rubbing her hands together, while Roger gave Lindy one of his no-nonsense looks.

"I presume I am the person who will not be so thrilled," he stated, and Ellen let out a laugh.

"Of course you won't be, Roger, but I'm sure it will be something that's good for you."

"Vitamins," Roger replied, "are good for me."

It sounded as if they'd had this exact discussion before, and it filled Lindy with affection for them both. "It's the possibility of a performance," she stated. "At Willoughby Manor, during the Christmas ball."

"Ooh…" Ellen squealed, while Roger stared at her as if she were speaking a foreign language. She probably was.

"What's this I hear about a performance?" Maureen barked as she came into the room, and Lindy explained again. "As long as it's the tango," Maureen stated, "it'll be worth the pain."

Helena returned then, slightly red-eyed, and then Simon and Olivia came in, holding hands. Lindy explained it all over again, and to her surprise everyone was more or less on board—except Roger. She should have known. She *had* known.

"Absolutely not," he stated flatly. "One hundred per cent no." He glanced at his mother, looking apologetic and yet completely implacable. "I'm sorry, but I simply cannot do it. This is as far as I go."

"You've done so much already, Roger," Ellen murmured, but she looked crestfallen. Lindy knew it meant a lot to her, just as she knew a public performance had to be Roger's worst nightmare. She decided to leave it, at least for now.

"Let's start the class," she told everyone. "And we'll discuss a possible performance during our tea break." She glanced at Roger, who was looking stony-faced. "Not everyone has to be involved, of course," she added diplomatically, although she still hoped Roger would be, even if his mother had to guilt-trip him into it.

With a swirl of her scarlet skirts—she always wore red to do the samba—Lindy went to switch on the music and then show her class the first steps.

"It's all about the knees," she said as she partnered an imaginary man. "Bending the knees."

"This isn't going to be good," Maureen stated with relish. Lindy knew she loved a challenge; they would all hear the creak of her joints as she shimmied.

She glanced again at Roger, who had taken position with his mother. Ellen was doing her best to bend and wiggle, and Roger was moving around the floor like he was a statue being pushed. Lindy suppressed a sigh.

She wanted Roger to take part in the Take a Twirl Extravaganza, and she knew Ellen did, as well. It was just a matter of how they could get him to agree.

Chapter Twelve

I T WAS—WELL, ALMOST—A go. Lindy had, a bit nervous-ly, proposed the idea of the performance at the Christmas ball to the primary school's head teacher, a lovely man in his forties named Dan Rhodes, and he'd agreed in principle, assuming that all the safeguarding assessments and forms could be completed.

When Lindy mentioned the possibility to her twenty-eight Year Sixes, the majority of them had looked thrilled. A few had seemed quietly appalled and several had guffawed incredulously, but Lindy had assured them that no one who didn't want to had to take part. She'd said as much to Roger on Monday, and he'd taken her at her word. When she'd cautiously broached the topic again during their tea break, he had remained immovable.

"You have most likely realised that attending this class was something I did with great reluctance," he informed her stiffly. "And I continue to do it, for my mother's sake, because she has always wanted to learn how to dance. But I cannot perform publicly." He stated it as immutable fact.

"It would be in a group—"

"I cannot," he repeated, his tone utterly final, and Lindy fell silent. When she looked at Roger's steely expression, she felt she had no choice but to drop it. And yet she was still hoping she could talk him around somehow, in time.

The idea of the extravaganza had taken hold and fired her with purpose. She loved the prospect of so many people of different ages and different abilities coming together to strut their stuff. She'd put feelers out on the WhatsApp group for the Twinkle Toes parents, and had been rewarded with four exuberant thumbs-up emojis, as well as a request for them all to go out for drinks. *Can Ollie wear his tuxedo?* Will had texted, and laughing, Lindy had texted back, *I'm counting on it.*

Over the next two weeks she spent countless hours planning routines for her different classes, picking music, watching videos for inspiration, and generally feeling both optimistic and daunted. It was only two months until the Christmas ball, just before the actual holiday—really, not long at all to get a bunch of beginners up to performance standard.

The weather had turned colder and crisper, winter closing in as November loomed. Despite Roger's continued reluctance, Lindy was feeling determinedly buoyant. Toby had settled in well, the behaviour specialist who had come to assess him four weeks after she'd picked him up from Blue Cross was happy, and life felt good.

She'd gone out for drinks with the whole Willoughby Close gang save Ellie—Harriet, Ava, Alice, Olivia, and Emily—and had a riotous time and fortunately no nosy questions about Roger and his supposed unsuitability.

At the end of the month, she went on another walk with Roger and Toby; she'd texted to ask him and he'd agreed with pleasing alacrity. They walked along the river path, the yellowing leaves gathering in drifts, and Lindy managed not to talk about the performance, as much as she wanted to, at least until the walk was almost over.

"Would anything make you consider it?" she asked a bit desperately, pausing in their walk as they came to the quaint little wooden bridge that crossed the Lea River. Roger sighed as he gazed out at the pretty, pastoral scene, his hands deep in the pockets of his parka, his eyes narrowed against the late afternoon sunshine. It was only four o'clock but the sun was already sinking towards the horizon, sending long, golden rays along the meadows bordering the river.

"This is not about me being stubborn," he said, and Lindy raised an eyebrow.

"Are you sure about that?"

"I wouldn't have said it otherwise."

"Then what is it about?" She realised she was curious; Roger seemed very sure of himself in this. Very…resigned.

He sighed again and then kept walking, leaving her no choice but to follow him over the little wooden bridge, the river burbling with cheerful fury below them.

"I know my mother wants me to do it," he said at last. "I am well aware of her wishes in this matter, although she's tried not to push me into anything. And if it were simply an issue of going along with what she wants and in so doing make her happy, then I would do it. Of course I would. In a heartbeat." He turned to look at her, his expression so grimly sincere that Lindy had to believe him.

"So what is the problem?" she asked after a moment, her tone gentle. She sensed Roger was struggling with something, but she didn't know what it was. He remained silent for a long moment; they'd crossed the bridge and were walking the narrow, wooded path through the forest, a carpet of damp, mulchy leaves beneath their boots as they headed back to Willoughby Manor.

"The problem," he finally said, "is that it won't make my mother happy in the least. Quite the opposite, in fact. It will make her feel worse."

"How?"

He gave her a look of exasperation, as if she should be getting it; he shouldn't have to spell it out for her.

"I'm sorry," Lindy said with an apologetic grimace. "I'm not taking your meaning here."

"I think it would be obvious enough," he replied, and Lindy shook her head slowly.

"Not really."

"My mother has certain…aspirations for me. She always has, since I was a child, although of course they've changed over the years. Even though I'm nearing forty, she's still hopeful that I'll find a wife, have children, settle down. All that."

Lindy's heart felt as if it were bumping in her chest. "That's a fairly normal aspiration for a mum to have," she pointed out reasonably, trying not to imagine little Rogers running around, or his arm around a lovely young woman who found him as endearing as she did.

"Yes, of course it is, but it must be obvious now that I'm not normal." He spoke matter-of-factly, but Lindy was still startled by his tone, as well as his words.

"Roger," she said with an uncertain, little laugh, "you're normal, as normal as anyone is."

"I'm not completely off the radar in terms of normality, I grant you," he stated in that same matter-of-fact voice. "I am employed in a position of responsibility; I am able to make social niceties on occasion; I own a house." He ticked them all off on his fingers as if there was a checklist as to what comprised a normal person. Perhaps for him there was. "I am indeed a functioning member of society in all those respects."

Lindy smothered a laugh that she knew would not be helpful in this situation. She wanted to believe Roger was joking, but she sensed he was as deadly serious as he always was, and it tore at her heart. "Surely you can aim a little higher than that," she protested.

"Can I?" Roger gave her a questioning look. "I'm not

sure that is an accurate statement. For example, I don't really have friends."

"I'm your friend," Lindy returned quickly.

Roger nodded his agreement. "You are indeed an anomaly."

She hesitated, feeling her way through the words. "Why do you think you don't have any friends?"

"I assume you are asking the reason for the lack of friendship in my life, rather than why I feel as if I don't, considering the factual reality is surely obvious."

"Yes, I suppose…"

He shrugged. "I've always had trouble making them. School, frankly, was a nightmare. I was bullied until Sixth Form, and then I just studied hard and kept to myself."

Lindy's heart ached at this brutal assessment, yet she realised she'd been much the same. She hadn't had any friends growing up save for her parents and the strangers they encountered on their travels, and Sixth Form had pretty much been a nightmare for her, as well. "Why were you bullied?" she asked.

He gave her an incredulous look. "Why do you think? I have a habit of blurting out awkward statements, that while factually true, tend to be inappropriate in the moment, something that unfortunately doesn't occur to me until after it has passed." Lindy was silent for a moment, absorbing that information, and Roger gave her a shrewd look. "What? You didn't think I was aware of this unfortunate quirk of my personality?"

"Well…not really. But I suppose that goes to show how normal you are."

"Being aware of one's abnormality does not make it less so."

"Still, it's not…it's not a game changer, is it?" They'd left the wooded path and had come out onto a pristine green lawn that led to the lane back to Willoughby Close. Shadows were lengthening, night drawing in. Toby tugged at his lead, eager to get back to the warmth of his home and bed.

"I suppose," Roger answered, "it depends on what game you're playing."

"All I mean is," Lindy insisted, warming to her theme, "is that everyone has got something."

He glanced at her, one eyebrow raised. "Such as?"

"No one's *normal*, Roger. We're all just different versions of weird. Some people hide it better than others."

He was silent for a moment, and Lindy let herself believe she'd convinced him. "The definition of normal," he stated as they crossed the wide lawn and headed down the lane towards Willoughby Close, "is 'conforming to a standard, usual, typical, or expected.' That is the adjective, and I am not any of those things."

"Neither am I," Lindy retorted. "And I wouldn't want to be."

He smiled at that, if only a little, before shaking his head. "Stop arguing with me."

"I just don't see why you have to pigeonhole yourself so much."

"I'm merely being realistic."

"Says every cynic, ever."

"Why do you care so much?" Roger challenged. "Is it just because of this performance?"

Lindy had completely forgotten about the performance. "So what does this have to do with that?" she asked. She scrolled back through the conversation to its prickly starting point. "You said your mum had aspirations for you, and so I'm guessing those are somehow tied up with the performance?"

"My mother is hoping I'll dance in this extravaganza of yours and somehow show myself to be a misunderstood Fred Astaire," Roger explained wearily. "She has it all mapped out in her head—how I'll stun the crowds, how everyone will suddenly see me differently, the way she thinks I really am, and of course the love of my life will fall into my arms."

"Of course," Lindy agreed, and he gave her a narrowed look.

"I'm not exaggerating."

"I doubt you're capable of exaggeration."

They'd reached Willoughby Close, and Lindy hesitated in the courtyard. Twilight had started to fall, the sky a livid violet, like the colour of a bruise. "Would you like to come in for a refreshing drink?" she asked, daring to tease a little, and she was rewarded with a smile.

"Thank you, I will."

ROGER FOLLOWED LINDY into her cottage, half-wishing this conversation had never started, even though some strange part of him was glad he'd said what he had. He'd never had a close enough friend to say it to before, a fact that felt both depressing and exhilarating, because it seemed he did now.

He glanced around Lindy's living area as she shed her coat and boots; it was comfortable enough with a love seat and squashy armchair, a table for four by the French windows, but somehow he'd expected her home to have more personality—posters of ballroom dancers, or vivid-coloured flowers, or a hat stand adorned with wildly patterned scarves. Something to indicate the kind of vibrant person she was, but everything looked fairly bland and standard, like an upscale Airbnb, pleasant but a little boring. It surprised him—the lack of pizzazz.

"I have Coke, of course," Lindy said as she headed towards the kitchen area and Roger took off his coat. "Or tea. Or coffee, but I know you don't like that."

"Tea would be pleasant, thank you." He hung up his coat by the hook on the door, trying not to notice how womanly and warm Lindy looked in her snug-fitting jeans and cranberry-coloured jumper. He'd told himself he was fine with being friend-zoned, that in fact it was better for both of them. He knew he could certainly use a friend, as this afternoon's conversation had testified to.

Lindy went to fill the kettle, and Roger crouched down to scratch Toby behind the ears; the dog had flopped onto his fleece-lined bed by the wood burner, and looked happy to stay there for the duration, his eyes rolling back as Roger continued to scratch.

"So," Lindy said in a no-nonsense way that Roger knew meant she was intent on continuing the conversation, something he'd rather not do, even though he really had come to terms with who he was over the years. Still, spelling it out to somebody he cared about wasn't doing his ego any favours.

"I think you're underestimating your mum," she said, and Roger straightened so he could give her what was meant to be a level look.

"How did you reach that conclusion?"

"Your mum seems to me like a very grounded person. She's not away with the fairies, and I think she sees things the way they are, her son included."

If Roger was an eye-roller, this would have been the perfect moment. As it was he just gave her a rather wooden look. "How do you think she sees me, then?"

"As someone who can be a bit standoffish, a little awkward, sometimes plain rude." A blush touched Lindy's cheeks but she held his gaze. "And someone who is lovely and kind, with a good heart and a surprisingly gentle manner when it counts."

Roger realised he was blushing, too. Was Lindy talking about how his mother saw him—or how she did? Was he crazy to suddenly hope, wildly, that it was the latter—and that somehow it mattered? It changed things between them?

He cleared his throat, a necessary action. "Thank you for saying so."

"I mean it." She was still holding his gaze, and Roger found he couldn't look away, although part of him was desperate to. Another part of him was desperate to kiss her. Friends, he reminded himself rather frantically. They were friends. And kissing her now would undoubtedly be a bad idea, not that he would actually be able to work up the nerve to do it.

"I'm not quite sure how this relates to the possibility of me humiliating myself in a public performance," he said after a moment. The kettle started to whistle, and then clicked off.

"I don't think she believes you're suddenly going to turn into Fred Astaire," Lindy said as she poured boiling water into two mugs with teabags. "I think she's got more emotional intelligence than that."

"Perhaps," Roger answered doubtfully. He thought his mother was sensible, but like everyone, she still hoped. Still dreamed.

"I think she hopes that you're going to surprise yourself," Lindy continued as she fetched the milk from the fridge. "That even if you fall flat on your face, you'll find you haven't humiliated yourself, after all. People will be supportive and encouraging, and you'll discover they've got your back." She paused in pouring the milk to give him an earnest, sincere look, and Roger found he had no idea what to say, or even how to feel.

No, he knew how he felt. Yearning and hopeful, longing for something nebulous and nameless and yet unable to articulate it, even to himself. And Lindy's soft, sincere look was making it harder to act *normal*, if he even could.

"You seem very sure of all that," he said after a moment when the silence seemed to spin on between them, a golden thread Roger was afraid to tug.

"I am, at least as sure as I can be of anything." She paused, seeming to struggle with herself for a moment, and then added, "You know, I had a similar school experience to you. I wasn't bullied, exactly, but I didn't really have any friends, because we travelled so much, and Sixth Form was just something to be endured." Another pause while he struggled to fill the silence, and then she continued, "And even now I don't know that I have a lot of friends. Real friends, anyway. I've got plenty of acquaintances and people to have coffee with, go out for dancing or drinks, but the kind of friend you can call in the middle of the night and just say 'help'?" She gave him an honest, almost bleak look. "Not so much. No one, in fact, except maybe Ellie, and she's so busy now with her own life..." She shrugged. "So yeah, no one."

Roger simply stared, words bottling in his throat. Words

he longed to say—how he didn't have that person, either, and how he could be a friend like that for Lindy. He wanted to be that person, and he wanted to be able to say it. Yet despite the intensity of his feelings, the words wouldn't come. They felt physically impossible to verbalise, a pressure in his chest that wouldn't be moved, and so he simply stared.

Lindy smiled wryly and handed him a mug.

"Thanks for the tea," Roger finally managed to say, wishing he was saying so much more, and yet knowing that he couldn't. He only wished he could.

Chapter Thirteen

"WHAT WE REALLY need to be thinking about now, is palliative care."

The words seemed to fall in the unhappy stillness of the consulting room and then evaporate into nothingness. At least, that was how it felt to Roger. He certainly didn't absorb their meaning, for he was still staring dumbly at the consultant, a kindly looking woman in her fifties with frizzy grey hair who had been seeing his mum from the start, with a look of blank incomprehension.

"Roger?" Ellen prompted gently, and he realised his mother must have said something, and he hadn't heard.

"Sorry…what were you saying?" He turned to her, trying to focus on her face yet for some reason it blurred in front of him. Still, he knew it so well. A neat grey bob. Faded blue eyes. Skin that was wrinkly and yet soft, a smile that curled up at the corners.

"I was asking Ms Weston if I should look into hospice care," Ellen said, her tone soft and full of sympathy…for him. She was the one with cancer, and yet she was treating him as if he were the one in need of care and support.

"No, of course not," Roger answered swiftly. "There's no need for that. I moved to Wychwood to take care of you, and that's what I'm going to do." Belatedly he realised how aggressive he sounded.

Ellen laid a hand on his arm. "Roger...the burden might be too much for you. And the last thing I want is to be a burden, to you or to anyone."

"There is a very good hospice locally," the consultant supplied. "A very welcoming and homely place."

Was that supposed to make him feel *better*? "I don't understand why we're talking about hospices," Roger declared. He still sounded aggressive.

"Because it's time, Roger," Ellen said gently. He couldn't stand the fact that she felt the need to comfort him.

"But you're perfectly healthy. I mean, you *seem* perfectly healthy. I know that is not actually the case, but..." His mum was *fine*. Yes, she was thin and frail and tired, and she often fell asleep on the sofa several times a day, and going to the ballroom dancing class was just about the only thing she could do all week, but *still*. She didn't need to go into a hospice. Not yet.

"Of course, Ellen, you don't need to go into hospice at this very moment," the consultant said in a strangely jolly tone. Talk about inappropriate. "I think perhaps after Christmas, maybe January or February would be the time to make that transition. But it's important to be prepared, and also to contact the hospice in question, to make sure there is space."

"Book a room like in a hotel?" Roger filled in bitterly. The notion was offensive to him, but the consultant gave him a level look.

"Yes, more or less, I'm afraid."

"Roger," Ellen said softly. "We knew this was coming."

Yes, they did, especially when, six months ago, the consultant had advised no further treatment. But there was, Roger realised, knowing something in theory, in his head, and knowing it in reality, in his heart. The two were worlds apart, and it was the second kind of knowledge—immediate, overwhelming—that was hammering him now.

"We will discuss it, of course," he said, his voice colder than he intended, considering he was talking to his mother. "But I believe it is rather precipitous, to be talking about matters relating to hospices and palliative care at this stage in your illness."

"Like I said, it's important to plan ahead," the consultant reminded him as she gave Ellen a sympathetic smile. "But I think there is some discussion that needs to happen between you two, so perhaps I should leave you to it? Unless you have any further questions, Ellen?"

"No, thank you, Gina," Ellen replied warmly. "You've been brilliant. I don't have any questions."

Roger said nothing.

Neither of them spoke again until they were out in the

hospital car park, under a steely late-October sky.

"It's not her fault, you know, Roger," Ellen said gently. "You need to stop blaming Ms Weston for the fact I have cancer."

"Of course I don't blame your oncology consultant for your cancer diagnosis," Roger said, stumbling only slightly over the dreaded C-word. "The idea is completely nonsensical."

"Feelings are sometimes nonsensical, Roger," Ellen answered. "Even for you."

"I don't blame Ms Weston," Roger insisted.

"It's tempting to blame someone, though, isn't it?" Ellen said on a sigh. "Heaven knows I'd like to sometimes."

"I simply don't believe it is necessary to discuss palliative care at this precise moment," Roger said, sidestepping the whole uncomfortable blame conversation, which he definitely did not have the emotional capacity to think about.

"If my consultant thinks it's necessary, it most likely is."

Roger unlocked the car and opened the passenger door for his mother before he headed around to the driver's side. "She sees you once every six weeks," he stated as matter-of-factly as he could. "Granted she has the expertise, but she does not see you day in and day out the way I do, and so she does not have the familiarity with your situation that I have."

"Which I believe is exactly the point. You see me every day, Roger, and so you don't notice. It's the same with children—you don't realise they're growing until you look back and see a photo of them seeming so much smaller, or their trousers are suddenly three inches too short. You always grew out of them so quickly."

"What is the point you are making?"

"That I have been growing weaker," Ellen stated quietly. "That I've been feeling…like I'm fading. Every day I feel a little less here than I used to. It's an extraordinary feeling…but it's also a good one. When I die, it won't be a wrench. It will be a slipping away."

Roger's throat was too tight to speak, and so he simply concentrated on navigating out of the car park at the John Radcliffe. He didn't want to think about his mother *fading*. She was only sixty-six.

"I'm sorry, Roger," Ellen said. "I know this is hard on you."

He shook his head, an instinctive movement. "It's harder on you."

"I don't think it is. I know where I'm going." His mother had been a devout churchgoer all her life. Roger did his best to attend with her most Sundays. "You're the one who is going to be left alone."

He didn't need reminding of that. "Still," he managed.

"It's why I've hoped to see you settled," Ellen said on a soft sigh. "I know you get impatient with me and my obvious attempts, but you're a good man, Roger. You'd make a lucky woman a wonderful husband."

Debatable in the extreme. Roger stayed silent.

"I was hoping something might have happened with Lindy," Ellen confessed. This seemed to be the time for honesty, but Roger couldn't rise to his mother's heartfelt level.

"We're just friends."

"That's a good basis for more—"

"I don't think there's going to be more, Mum. Sorry." Despite—or perhaps because of—their heartfelt conversation a few days ago. He'd talked far more honestly with Lindy than he had with anyone else in his entire life, and he'd felt, or at least hoped, that it had been the same for her, based on what she'd said.

And yet despite that, they were still clearly friends. Just friends. They'd had a lovely time drinking tea and chatting once that brief intensity had passed, but Roger knew he was still firmly in the friend zone, and he definitely didn't have either the expertise or confidence to attempt to remove himself from that area.

"Well, you never know," Ellen said with a firm upbeatness that was her trademark tone. "Don't give up hope quite yet, sweetheart."

The fact that his mother knew he had any hope was humiliating, although unsurprising. Once again Roger didn't reply.

HE COULD HAVE gone back to work after the appointment,

and in fact he'd been intending to, but by the time Ellen was settled back in Wychwood, Roger knew he didn't feel like logging a few hours at the office, crunching numbers. The reality of his mother's situation was starting to penetrate the dazed numbness he'd been feeling since Ms Weston had delivered the news about palliative care—and it was being replaced with a swamping sense of desolation he couldn't bear to acknowledge, never mind actually feel.

And yet he did feel it—it permeated every pore, took over every sense. It was like a fog surrounding him, claiming him, no matter how he tried to fight against it. A man his age shouldn't feel this devastated, he told himself, to no avail. Losing one's parents as an adult was the expected course of events. It was natural, more natural than the reverse, at least.

And yet everything about it felt wrong.

"You don't have to fuss over me," Ellen chided him as he tried to push a cheese scone on her for the third time that afternoon. "Really, Roger, I'm all right. I think I'd just like to sleep."

Which he was keeping her from. "Okay," he said reluctantly. "But call me if you need anything."

"I will, I promise."

It was four o'clock on a chilly, grey afternoon, and Roger had nothing to do. He left his mother's cottage and walked down Wychwood's high street, feeling at a loss. He was caught up on housework and cooking, laundry and ironing, and the weather wasn't welcoming for a walk. Besides, wandering alone through the woods or along the river would just remind him of Lindy, and in the state he was in, he couldn't bear to think about her—her friendliness, his mother's wishes. His own hopes, because yes, he hoped, even though he had no real reason to.

He kept walking down the street, with nowhere to go, feeling lost in a way that had nothing to do with his physical location. His gaze blurred as he took in the quaint shops, the people hurrying to and fro, the sun blotted behind thick grey cloud. Then he focused on the Tudor-looking building in front of him—The Three Pennies, Wychwood's remaining pub.

Roger had never been inside; he wasn't particularly a pub man, although he occasionally made himself go out with some co-workers in Oxford when they went to the effort of asking him. Yet now he headed into The Three Pennies, resolute and on his own. He needed a drink.

"IT'S NOT EVEN five," Emily protested laughingly as the four women headed into The Three Pennies on a wave of reckless bonhomie, with Lindy taking up the rear.

"It'll be five by the time we get our drinks," Ava answered blithely. "Or almost. And I'm not even drinking, so the rest of you lot better be, so I can at least watch."

"That sounds a bit weird," Alice teased.

It had been Ava's idea to go out to the pub at four

o'clock on a Wednesday afternoon; Lindy had been doing some paperwork at home when Ava had marched up to her door.

"I'm summoning the troops," she'd announced. "I've got baby brain and swollen ankles and stretch marks, and I need sympathy."

"Okay," Lindy had said gamely enough. She didn't know Ava all that well, having only socialised with her in groups, and frankly she was still a bit intimidated by her oozing sensuality and confidence, even when she was six months pregnant, but she was determined to accept any and all invitations, especially after her unexpected confession to Roger that she didn't really have good friends.

It hadn't surprised her, really, and yet somehow saying it out loud had been a shock. *I don't have good friends.* The kind whom you called for help and they came running.

It was clearly time to start making some deeper connections, and so she'd said yes to the pub at four o'clock on a Wednesday afternoon, although judging by Ava's breezy attitude, Lindy didn't think this was going to be a time of deep sharing. Still, a glass of wine—or two—wouldn't go amiss.

"So what's everyone having?" Ava asked when they were all settled in a booth in the back. The pub was nearly empty at this time of day, with just a few people at tables scattered around, and a few old guys hunched over the bar. "I'll do the first round."

"Is there going to be more than one?" Alice asked dubiously.

"There better be," Ava replied grandly, and then took everyone's orders. Lindy settled for a boring white wine, but with a laugh, Emily had agreed to push the boat out and had ordered a passionfruit martini. Alice had gone with a fairly sedate G&T.

"So, how are the plans for your performance going?" Alice asked eagerly. It had been two weeks since she'd floated the idea, and Lindy had been busy making preparations.

"They're going well, although we're going to be hard pressed for time." She'd only just started choreographing routines for each of her classes, and teaching and then perfecting it within two months would be challenging indeed, but one Lindy thought she was up for. It was good to have focus, as well as something to aim for.

"I think it all sounds amazing," Emily said. "And who knows, maybe I can convince Owen to sign up for classes. He insists he has two left feet, but I think he could be a smooth operator if he tried."

"All are welcome, no matter what the ability," Lindy answered. "In fact, the less ability the better—I love seeing people find their groove."

"Isn't that one of your students at the bar?" Ava chimed in as she came back with a tray of drinks. "He's got a grim face, but then he doesn't look like the type who smiles very often."

"What…" Lindy craned her neck to get a glimpse of the bar, a jolt of surprise running through her at the sight of Roger sitting hunched over at one end.

"Isn't he the one you said was unsuitable?" Emily whispered, and a shot of something fierce and determined made Lindy snap, "He is *not* unsuitable. That was one impulsive comment made after I was pushed into it."

"Whoa." Ava held up a pacifying hand while Emily bit her lip, looking far too chastened. "I feel like we just hit a sore spot."

"Sorry." Lindy gave Emily an apologetic grimace. "I didn't mean to lash out. It's just…"

"You've got the hots for your unsuitable bloke?" Ava finished with a grin. "Go for it, girl."

"I don't," Lindy said, not entirely convincingly. She glanced again at Roger, alone at the bar. Ava had said he looked grim, but then Roger often looked grim. But why was he drinking alone at four o'clock on a Wednesday afternoon? He was the last person she'd expect here.

Then she suddenly thought of Ellen, and her heart lurched. "Oh no…" she whispered, and Emily touched her arm in concern.

"Lindy, what is it?"

"I just need to check…" she murmured, barely aware of her friends looking worried around her as she headed for the bar.

As she came closer, she saw that Roger had his hands flat

on the bar, and he was staring at the tumbler of whisky in front of him as if it were a chalice of poison.

"Roger…?" Lindy asked cautiously. She slid onto the bar and stood next to him. "Is…is everything okay?"

Roger sighed heavily, not breaking his gaze on the glass as he answered, "No. Not really. And it feels like nothing will ever be okay again."

Chapter Fourteen

T HE WORDS WERE melodramatic. He knew that. Roger was not the type of person to be prone to melodrama, and yet here he was, saying nothing would ever be okay again and staring at a glass of whisky as if it was his only hope. He didn't even like whisky, but it had felt like the right drink to order. You didn't drink a nice rosé while grieving your mother.

"What's happened?" Lindy asked softly. He could see her in his periphery, a cloud of dark hair and soft lips, not much more. It was enough. He felt his breathing steady, even as the grief remained, like a surging sea inside him, threatening to break loose. He couldn't let it.

"Nothing, really," he told her in a level voice. "Nothing that wasn't expected, anyway." He took a measured sip of whisky as if to make his point. It was hard not to grimace as the medicinal taste burned the back of his throat.

"You're not here because of nothing," Lindy said quietly. "Is it...is it your mum?"

It was, but he could tell from Lindy's expression—even

in his periphery—that she thought the worst.

"She's been recommended for palliative care," he stated flatly. "Which obviously should not be a surprise since, as I told you before, she has terminal, incurable cancer and she'd already been recommended to have no further treatment." He took another sip. It tasted just as bad. "Really, this is simply the next step in a process whose particulars I was aware of all along."

"Still, it doesn't feel that way," Lindy said quietly. "Does it?"

No, it most certainly did not. Somehow Roger couldn't get the words out of his mouth. What a surprise. He just shook his head, and forewent another sip of whisky.

"After my parents died," Lindy said after a moment, "about three months after, I was going through their things. I knew I had to do it, sort it all out, and I'd prepped myself for it, because I knew it would be hard." She paused, and Roger had the sense she was struggling with some greater emotion.

"But when I was actually there, pulling open the drawers, looking at the photos and books and the shopping lists in my mum's handwriting…it was so much harder than I thought. No amount of preparation could have ever helped me get through that moment."

Roger turned his head to glance at her, her expression distant and shadowed. "But you did get through it."

For a moment she looked as if she was going to disagree,

and then she nodded slowly. "Yes, in time, in my own way, I suppose I did. And you will, too." She rested her hand on top of his—slender, soft, warm. "But knowing that doesn't make it any less hard in the moment."

"It just feels too soon," he said quietly as he stared at their hands. "I thought she was fine. I mean, ill, yes, I know that. I'm not delusional. But still…okay." He drew a revealingly ragged breath. "But then today she reminded me of how tired she's been. How she falls asleep in the middle of a sentence. Going to dance class saps her energy for an entire week."

"I didn't realise…"

"She still wants to. She'll most likely keep going to your class until the bitter end. She loves it." He paused, risking another look at her even though he feared his eyes were becoming a bit damp. "Thank you for giving her that, Lindy."

"Oh, Roger…" Lindy pressed her lips together and shook her head, her eyes looking as suspiciously damp as he suspected his own were. "You don't need to thank me. For anything."

They remained silent for several moments, her hand still resting on top of his. Even with the wild sorrow locked inside, Roger felt a surprising, settled sort of happiness cloak him in comfort. They were just *being*, he realised, and it felt right.

"I was angry with my mother today," he said after a

moment. "Which is absurd, I realise. Absurd and reprehensible." The tone he'd taken with her in the hospital shamed him now. How could he have been such an idiot?

"Understandable, though," Lindy said. "In a situation like this, you feel like you've got to be angry with someone. I raged at a barista once, and it had nothing to do with the way she'd made my coffee." She gave him a shamefaced smile that he managed to return, sort of.

He let out a wavery, raggedy sigh. "I don't *want* this," he said. The words were infantile, futile—and yet he felt them. He had to say them.

Lindy squeezed his hand. "I know."

"I don't want to go through the next few months, or however long it takes," he continued relentlessly. "I can't stand even thinking about it. For the last year I've more or less been acting as if my mother doesn't have cancer. I don't let her talk about it. I'd rather pretend." He glanced at her bleakly, realisation thudding through him. "That isn't fair to her, is it?"

"No," Lindy said quietly. "It isn't."

He knew that, and yet he was glad she'd said it. He was glad, perversely, that she hadn't said something to make him feel better.

"What do I do now?" he wondered aloud.

"You don't drink any more whisky," Lindy said, the barest hint of a smile in her voice. "And you go back to your mum and you let her talk if she needs to talk. And you let her be quiet if she needs to be quiet. And you say the word 'cancer' when it's necessary."

He nodded slowly, like someone receiving instructions. "Yes. All right. I can do that."

"And you make the most of these months that you're dreading, because they're all you have left." There was a break in Lindy's voice that made Roger ache. "If I'd known…the number of times I didn't call or I cut it short or I didn't come home for the weekend…"

"Lindy…" He couldn't stand the sadness in her voice, but she shook her head fiercely.

"Never mind. This isn't about me right now. All I'm saying is, make the most of it, Roger. Celebrate every moment if you can."

Except he was not a celebrate-every-moment type of guy. Perhaps now was the time to change…and he knew, of course he knew, just how he could. He gazed down at his barely touched tumbler of whisky and then said, a bit aggressively, "I'll do it."

Lindy blinked. "Do…what?"

"The performance. The extravaganza. What have you. I'll do it."

He glanced at her as if she'd just delivered his death sentence, and was slightly heartened to see a smile of wondering incredulity blooming across her face. "Seriously? You will?"

"Yes."

"You don't have—"

"I know I don't have to," Roger cut across her. "I have been perfectly aware of that all along. But you're right about celebrating the next few months. I'll regret it if I don't. And I know...I know doing this dance performance, God help me, will make my mother happy, even if I fall on my face, which I most likely will do. So."

"Oh, Roger, that's wonderful." Lindy looked like he'd given her a million pounds, a feeling that would almost certainly desert her when she realised what this meant for the performance—ruination. "Thank you."

"Don't thank me, especially since you've already witnessed my dancing."

"It's not about being some sort of star," Lindy said a bit severely and Roger grimaced.

"Thank heaven for that."

"What are you doing for Bonfire Night?" she asked abruptly, and Roger blinked at the sudden swerve of subject.

"Er...I haven't thought..." He'd been planning to give the community fireworks on the village green a miss, because it would mean standing in the freezing dark while explosions went off all around him. Not his idea of a good time, although he realised he wasn't sure what his idea of a good time actually was.

"I'm going to be staying in," Lindy stated matter-of-factly, "because of Toby. The behaviour specialist from Blue Cross said the big bangs might scare him, so I thought we'd have a chilled night."

"Okay…"

"So why don't you and Ellen come over for supper?" Lindy continued. "It won't be anything fancy…chilli and jacket potatoes and maybe some sparklers in the garden, if Toby isn't freaking out too much. And then we could watch a film?" Her face suddenly fell. "Unless of course you want to spend the time together, just the two of you, which of course I'd understand." She shook her head, doing a mock face palm. "Sorry. I just rushed in with my idea without actually thinking…"

"No," Roger said quickly, before she could back out of the invitation entirely. "That sounds…" Lovely. It sounded lovely. "Nice."

Lindy grinned at him, and the sight of her obvious delight made him feel like grinning too, and yet he didn't. He gave a nod instead.

"Okay, then." She touched his arm again briefly. "Now go back to your mother, Roger."

"You make me sound as if I'm about ten."

"No, just a loving son of any age." Impulsively she leaned forward and kissed his cheek. It took all of Roger's effort to react normally, as if the brush of her soft mouth against his skin hadn't filled him with yearning. She eased back, smiling self-consciously. "You're a good man, Roger Wentworth."

The place where her lips had brushed his cheek was buzzing. Roger managed a small smile. "Thank you."

"I'll talk to you on Monday about details for Bonfire

Night," she promised.

"All right."

Roger watched Lindy head back to her friends in the back of the pub; they were all watching her avidly, and would no doubt press her for details as soon as she sat down, a prospect that gave Roger a visceral shudder of dread. Would she tell them about her Bonfire Night invitation? Would they think it was a date?

He knew his mother would, and he realised, with grim sobriety, that there was no point disabusing her of such a notion. Let her hope there was something going on between him and Lindy. By the time it was obvious there wasn't, his mother might not be here anymore—a thought that had Roger reaching for his whisky yet again.

"WHAT ON EARTH was that all about?" Ava demanded before Lindy had even taken her seat back at the table with her friends.

"Nothing," Lindy said as nonchalantly as she could. "I was just saying hello."

Ava gave her a blatant look of disbelief. "That was not a hello; that was an intense conversation. You touched his hand three times, and you kissed his cheek."

"You counted?" Lindy said with a little laugh.

"Of course." Ava leaned forward. "So, spill. What's going on with you and Mr. Unsuitable—"

"He's not—" Lindy began fiercely, and Ava held up a hand, laughing.

"Lindy, I know he's not. Of course I know. You were just talking intensely to him for the last forty-five minutes. That is the definition of suitability, not the opposite."

"Forty-five…" Lindy couldn't keep from gaping. Had it really been that long?

"Yes, and we were watching pretty much the whole time," Alice chipped in with a friendly smile. "It did look intense. Is everything okay?"

"Yes," Lindy answered after a pause. As much as she appreciated her friends' concern, right now their interest felt a bit too much like well-meaning nosiness. It wasn't her place to share Roger's grief or Ellen's diagnosis. "We were just…chatting."

"Riiiight." Ava looked amused and unconvinced. "Well, we won't pry, no worries. At least not right now. Drink up, everyone. I really do need to live vicariously."

Lindy was glad for the reprieve, and she did her best to contribute to the conversation as they chatted about village life—William, Ava's son, had started nursery in September; Emily and Owen were thinking about getting engaged.

"But nothing's settled yet," Emily insisted, blushing. "We're really still in such early stages."

"Don't worry, I won't ask Owen when he's going to put a ring on it," Ava teased. "Anyway, you'll just have this to look forward to—swollen ankles, stretch marks that make you look like a sunburned zebra…" She sighed, patting her bump, and Emily smiled.

"And a lovely little baby at the end of it all."

"Yes, there is that," Ava agreed.

Lindy glanced at Alice, surprised to see her looking stricken for a moment, before she chimed in with the murmurs of appreciation. Was that why Alice had seemed brittle the other week, over Sunday lunch? Were she and Henry trying for a baby and having no luck?

Lindy had assumed she was living the perfect fairy tale, but even fairy tales had their difficult moments. Poor Alice…it had to be hard, being happy for Ava and trying not to let her own fear and sorrow show.

Lindy sat back and sipped her wine, for the first time putting herself in similar shoes. Here was Ava, in her late thirties, having found Mr Right when she was thirty-five—the same age as Lindy herself. And now expecting her second baby… Lindy knew there had been some pretty significant bumps along the way—a first husband who'd died, two adult stepchildren who were nightmares, and the fact that William was Ava's first husband's rather than Jace's. But still, here she was, cradling her bump with a loving look, no matter how she pretended to moan and groan.

Could such things be possible for her?

In all her life, Lindy had never considered them to be. As a child and then a teenager, she'd been perfectly content travelling with her parents, living out all their adventures.

She'd never even thought about a husband and family of her own, not even in the distant, far-off future. And then after her parents had died…it had felt, in many ways, like an invisible concrete wall had come down between her and the rest of the world.

Other people went to their grandparents' for Christmas, or talked about their past boyfriends, or flew to Ibiza for a hen night with their five BFFs. They went to parties and barbecues and had cosy nights in with their loved ones. Not Lindy.

To be sure, she'd always had plenty of friends to head out to a wine bar on a Friday night, and she was first to sign up for the office Christmas party or summer picnic. She'd never been short of casual outings or social occasions, but it had never, not even once, gone deeper.

That person to ring in the middle of the night and simply say 'help'? Didn't exist. Never had. Not even Ellie, who was probably her closest friend besides Roger.

Could *Roger* be that person for her? Could she be that person for him? She couldn't let herself think beyond that; she wasn't going to spin dreams of happy families and white weddings and baby bumps. No way.

But even just a really good friend…the kind you could count on…that would be something. That would be a lot.

"Right, I should get back before I have to toddle home," Emily announced. "A cocktail in the middle of the day is making me a bit loopy."

"Me too," Alice agreed with a smiling grimace, and Ava rolled her eyes.

"Spoilsports."

Soon they were all heading back to Willoughby Close; while they'd been in The Three Pennies, dusk had fallen, and the high street was now cloaked in violet shadows, the air possessing that almost metallic bite of cold.

"Brr," Emily exclaimed as she zipped up her snowy-white parka. "It really is starting to feel like winter."

"And it's only November," Alice said on a sigh. "At least there's Christmas to look forward to—and the ball."

"How are the preparations going?" Lindy asked as she pulled on her gloves. It really was cold.

"Great," Alice enthused. "Henry has ordered the most enormous tree for the foyer—I think it's about twenty feet high! And I've gone a bit crazy with decorations… I'm going to do my best to wait until December first to put them up, but there'll be lots. You can help if you like. I think I'll need all the help I can get!"

"I'd love to," Lindy said. She'd spent the last fifteen Christmases alone, save one where she'd accepted the invitation of Christmas dinner with a co-worker, Melanie, but she'd realised belatedly it was Melanie's entire extended family and her. She'd been a pity invite, and despite her friend's cheerful efforts, she'd felt like one. Every other Christmas had been the same—volunteering at a homeless shelter to serve Christmas dinner, and then binging on

Christmas TV and ice cream. There were worse things, surely.

What would she do this year? If Alice got wind of her alone status on Christmas Day, Lindy had no doubt there would be an invitation forthcoming—and probably one from Ava, as well. She decided to keep quiet, at least for now—because she knew who she really wanted to spend Christmas with.

Chapter Fifteen

HIS MOTHER HAD been nearly incandescent with joy when Roger had told her they were both invited to Lindy's for Bonfire Night. She'd tried to hide it, of course, assuring him she knew they were just friends, and saying how kind it was for Lindy to include her. But Roger had seen the bright hope in her eyes, and he decided to do nothing to dampen it. Let his mum think he and Lindy were soon to be an item. It didn't do any harm, and Lindy wouldn't find out.

Although, scratch that, she probably would. Ellen would undoubtedly say something significant at some point. Still Roger decided to let it lie, for his mother's sake, and perhaps even a little bit for his own. Hoping felt kind of nice, even if he wasn't doing it actively. He was too sensible for that, and like Chris had explained, he was firmly friend-zoned.

They'd had their usual Monday banter in the office kitchen—Roger's reply had been he'd been washing his hair instead—and then Chris had asked about Lindy.

"Still in the friend zone?" he'd said with a commiserating smile, and Roger had shrugged.

"I'm not actually entirely sure of my location in regards to the woman in question," he'd said after a moment. He was thinking of Lindy's hand on his three times—yes, he'd counted—at the pub.

"Oh, yeah?" Chris's eyes had lit up with interest. The smell of his Lynx aftershave was overpowering and Roger's instinct was usually to make his escape as quickly as possible, but now he realised he wanted Chris's insight, as dubious a thing as that undoubtedly was. "What's been happening?"

"She's been quite…tactile," Roger said, and Chris stared at him, nonplussed.

"Tactile?"

"As in touchy. Touchy-feely." Words he hoped would never come out of his mouth again.

"Ah." Chris nodded knowingly. "Does she seem like she's doing it deliberately? Maintaining eye contact while she gives you a feel?"

Roger's mouth drew up in slightly prim distaste. "The touching in question was her hand upon mine," he felt compelled to clarify. "And no, I wouldn't say it was deliberate. More…unthinking. There was no eye contact involved." Although that was at least in part because he hadn't been making any.

"Ah-hah." Chris gave another knowing nod. "Sorry, my man, that doesn't look good."

"What?" Roger was startled by his certain-sounding assessment, although he tried not to show it. "Why have you reached that conclusion?"

"Because she's decided you're not a threat," Chris said simply. "Firmly friend-zoned, man. *Firmly.*"

Roger had stared at him in growing dismay as he realised the nascent hopes he'd only begun to cherish were already being turned into ash. "So what you are saying," he answered slowly, "is that if a woman unthinkingly touches or squeezes your hand—it's because she sees you as an impossibility in terms of romantic affection?"

"That's it exactly," Chris agreed sagely. "Sorry."

Roger had managed to draw himself up. "At least I know where I stand," he said as he took the teabag out of his mug and flung it rather disconsolately into the sink.

Now he was walking with his mother up to Willoughby Close, the reminder of his friend status weighing heavily on him. He'd been stupid to think even for a moment of anything else; he'd already got this message, loud and clear, and yet still he'd started to hope again. He was, quite clearly, an idiot.

Toby set to barking as soon as they came up to number two, and a few seconds later Lindy opened the door. She looked fantastic as usual—her hair in tumbled waves halfway down to her waist, her jumper one of soft blue cashmere, paired with a long, swishy black skirt.

"Come in, come in," she said, sounding almost exuberant, and Roger followed his mother into the cottage he remembered as being homely but surprisingly simple and even plain.

Toby capered around frantically as they divested themselves of hats and coats, and his mother effused about how kind Lindy was to invite them. Roger placed the bottle of wine he'd brought—quite a nice red—on the island in the kitchen area and Toby finally settled down, retreating to his bed by the windows.

"What a lovely little cottage," Ellen exclaimed. "So cheerful."

It *was* cheerful, with the wood burner going merrily and a colourful patchwork afghan across the back of the beige sofa, the aroma of chilli scenting the air. Yet Roger couldn't quite shake the feeling that Lindy had not imprinted her personality on any of it, and he couldn't help but wonder why. He thought about asking, but he had no idea how to frame the question. *Why does your home look so bland when you're so vibrant?*

No, better simply to sit on that one.

His mother was still chatting to Lindy, and so Roger took the opportunity to stroll around the room, noting a black-and-white photograph on the wall behind the wood burner. It was a candid shot, or what seemed like one, with Lindy and two older people whom Roger supposed had to be her parents.

They were caught mid-conversation, all laughing or smiling, Lindy's hair whipping across the front of the frame, while the background, what looked like some large, significant building—had been artfully blurred. It was all quite wonderfully done, capturing the sense of immediacy and joy, three people caught up in themselves in the best possible way, so even the Taj Mahal—Roger recognised it belatedly—faded into insignificance. He was still staring at the photo when Lindy came to stand beside him.

"My parents," she stated simply.

"They look as if they were lovely people." He meant it sincerely, and Lindy flashed him a quick, grateful look.

"They were. Truly, the best." She let out a little sigh. "I was so very lucky, you know? Sometimes it's easy to forget that."

"Yes." It occurred to him that he had not really considered feeling the same about his father—he'd had a wonderful man in his life for the first twelve years of his childhood—how many people could say that? He had been lucky, too. Blessed, even if, in later years, it hadn't always felt like it.

Blessed, too, Roger realised, to have had such an amazing mother. Ellen had selflessly put him first, accepted him absolutely, and loved him unconditionally for as long as he'd been alive. How many people could say that? Really, all the usual quibbles and complaints aside, he was a fortunate man indeed.

"Anyway…" Lindy shook off the moment of melancholy with characteristic cheerful vigour. "The chilli is ready—we can eat first, and then do sparklers?" She turned back to Ellen, who was inspecting the quilt over the back of the sofa with a bit too much concentration. How many private moments was his mother going to try to give them? Roger wondered. It could start to become noticeable, if not downright awkward. But then he was plenty used to awkward, and he could certainly handle a little bit from her.

Lindy started dishing up the chilli, and Ellen insisted on helping, taking the jacket potatoes, steaming in their crispy golden-brown skins, out of the oven. At Lindy's bidding, Roger opened the wine and poured three glasses. Soon they were all seated at the little table as night settled softly on the back garden, and really, it was all quite cosy.

"Tell me all about yourself, dear," Ellen said once they were seated, and Lindy shot Roger a questioning look that he was astute enough to pick up on. She was wondering what his mother knew about her already, and of course the answer was absolutely nothing because Roger had never said. Unfortunately he could not discern whether that was a good thing—he'd been discreet—or a bad one, because he'd seemed indifferent.

Gamely enough Lindy explained about her job in Manchester—Ellen was thrilled she'd been an accountant like he was—and then about her parents dying. She used the same matter-of-fact tone Roger always did, but it didn't fool his mother.

"Oh, you poor thing. You poor, poor thing." She shook her head sorrowfully, her face crumpling in sympathy. "Of course, no one wants to hear they're a poor thing, I know.

I'm sorry, dear. I'm sure Roger has told you about his own loss?"

"And yours, as well," Lindy replied quietly, and Ellen inclined her head in acknowledgement.

"It's been hard on both of us, there's no question, but at least we've had each other."

While Lindy hadn't had anyone. Roger glanced at her, amazed at how serene and confident she seemed, when she'd experienced such a devastating loss at such a young age. How did she do it? How did she stay so warm and approachable when life surely should have taught her to be wary? Perhaps that was a question he'd work up the courage to ask her one day.

LINDY HAD BEEN intending to do the sparklers after supper, but it was clear Ellen was starting to flag even before the meal was over. She'd barely touched her chilli or potato, giving Lindy a small smile of apologetic regret.

"I'm sorry, dear. It all looks delicious. It's just I don't have much of an appetite these days."

"No worries," Lindy said quickly, but her heart ached. Ellen looked as if she were fading right before their eyes, her skin papery and pale, everything about her diminished, although there was still a determined sparkle in her eyes that Lindy liked.

"I can't tell you how pleased I am that Roger has agreed

to participate in the performance," Ellen said after supper as Roger took her arm to help her over to the sofa and Lindy made coffees. "To think we'll waltz together! It makes me so happy." She shot Roger a rather adoring look that made Lindy smile, as much as seeing her son's strained response. This was hard for him, she knew, both because of the overt emotion and the nature of loss.

"Not just waltz, but foxtrot, rumba, and samba, too," she reminded Ellen. At last Monday's class she'd gone through the basic choreography of the routine she hoped her six mostly willing pupils would learn—it involved one minute of each dance, with a switching in and out of partners as they moved in a graceful hexagon around the ballroom. Ellen had been thrilled, Maureen grudgingly approving, Simon and Olivia mostly oblivious, and Helena worried but excited. Roger's one comment had been: "I can appreciate the geometrics of the endeavour," which had made Lindy laugh.

"I think it's going to be an amazing night," Lindy said as she handed Ellen and Roger their coffees before settling in the squashy armchair opposite them. Toby slunk round to lie docile and pleading at her feet and she gave him a quick, loving stroke.

"I'm already planning what I'll wear," Ellen told her as she took a tiny sip of coffee. "I have the most amazing dress—I wore it on a cruise years ago, before Eric died. Do you remember, Roger? When we cruised the fjords? You were only eight or so."

"Yes, they were quite interesting," Roger replied.

"It's purple, one-shouldered, with sequins. A bit much, I know—"

"I love it already," Lindy assured her. "And if you can't wear something fabulous for a ballroom dancing extravaganza, when can you?" She gave Roger a teasingly severe look. "I hope you're going to get in the spirit of things, as well?"

He looked as startled as a deer in headlights, or maybe more of a moose, blinking for a few moments before he found his voice. "I do not think I would look fabulous, as you say, in purple sequins."

Lindy let out a laugh, nearly spitting out her mouthful of coffee, and Roger gave her a small smile.

"How about a tuxedo?" she suggested. "With satin lapels? A ruffled shirt? A hot pink cummerbund?"

"Why not all three?" he parried back, and she nodded approvingly.

"Now you're talking."

"Roger does have a tuxedo," Ellen said. "From his university days. Do you remember, Roger, you took that lovely young girl to the May ball in your third year?"

Roger gave a terse nod, and Lindy tried not to feel a silly twinge of jealousy at the thought of this long-ago girl.

"I remember," he said.

"I think it'll still fit," Ellen continued musingly. "You haven't gained a pound since your uni days, I'm sure." She turned to Lindy. "He bikes to work every day. He keeps very fit."

"Mum," Roger protested, and then fell silent. Lindy did her best not to laugh. Was Ellen trying to elucidate all of Roger's finer points? She didn't mind. In fact, she was well aware of many of them already.

They continued chatting for a few more moments, but then Ellen put her coffee down, and she rested her head back against the sofa pillows, and in mid-sentence Lindy realised she'd fallen asleep.

"She does this quite a lot now," Roger said quietly as they both watched Ellen sleeping. "Falls asleep in the middle of something, even a meal. I was pretending not to notice, but…"

"At some point reality body-slams you," Lindy finished. "I'm sorry, Roger."

"We're making the most of our moments."

She nodded, taking a sip of coffee, not wanting to get too emotional for his sake. Watching Ellen sleep, seeing how translucent her skin was, how twig-like her wrists, it was hard not to realise she was a woman with only months left. Lindy just hoped Ellen would be able to stay strong for the Christmas performance in six weeks' time, but she had her doubts, none of which she wished to articulate to either Roger or Ellen.

"Should we wait until she wakes up, to do the sparklers?" she asked quietly, and Roger shook his head.

"She could be asleep for hours. I can wake her up now,

take her home…" He half-started to rise, but Lindy stayed him with one hand.

"No, no. Let her rest. And I'm sure she wouldn't want to disrupt the evening for anyone." She almost thought of saying something flirtatious about how she thought Ellen was trying to set them up, but she decided against it. She had no idea what Roger's reaction to such a statement would be. "We can do the sparklers, at least," she said. "It's probably better if Ellen doesn't—it's so cold outside."

"All right."

Lindy went to fetch the sparklers she'd bought in Witney, as well as a box of matches. Roger quietly opened the French windows and they slipped outside to her tiny garden, the night dark and thick all around them, the wood at the bottom of the garden no more than a humped shape of trees in the darkness.

The air was sharp with cold, the grass beneath Lindy's boots crunching with frost. In the distance, if she strained her ears, she could hear the sounds of the crowds gathering at the village green for the huge bonfire, soon to be followed by fireworks.

"Are you sorry that Toby's keeping you at home?" Roger asked, and she shook her head.

"Not a bit of it. This is much better than braving crowds and standing in the cold for the better part of an hour." She handed him a sparkler, her fingers brushing his. "And I prefer a simple sparkler to the whole dazzling show," she added. "Ready?"

"Ready."

Lindy struck a match and then lit both their sparklers in turn. The hiss and flare as it came alight and began first to sputter and then glitter always felt magical to her, a memory of childhood, of the wonder of small things, of simple joys, sparks against a night sky. She felt a rush of happiness as well as an ache of sorrow—to be able to stay in this moment, to keep it forever…

"Come on," she said, and stepped further into the shadows of the garden, holding her sparkler alight like a fizzing torch. Roger followed her, their sparklers snapping and glittering as they stood side by side, their breath making small puffs of frosty air in the perfect stillness, their sparklers held in front of them. The moment felt crystalline, precious and fragile, as translucent and fleeting as a bubble.

Lindy glanced at Roger—he looked so serious, so thoughtful, as he gazed at his sparkler popping and fizzing away, and yet she had no idea what he was thinking, or even what *she* was thinking. She knew she longed for something more, but she wasn't sure what it was or if she was brave enough to try for it. Thirty-five years old, fifteen of them spent alone, and trying for romance, or even just a deeper friendship, felt frankly terrifying. Letting someone in that much, letting them hear that cry for help in the middle of the night…

That was both appalling and wonderful. Frightening yet

needed.

And yet, despite the fears and uncertainties catapulting through her, she wouldn't trade this moment for the whole world.

Their sparklers died out and they were left in darkness, surprising in its totality after the bright lights that had been blazing right before their eyes. Lindy turned instinctively back towards the house, and Roger must have as well, for they bumped into each other as they moved, and then their extinguished sparklers fell to the ground and his hands were on her arms as they did an awkward, shuffling dance that bore little resemblance to anything Lindy taught in class, and yet felt far more exciting.

She let out a breathless little laugh and Roger's hands tightened on her arms as their bodies bumped—and she thought, she *knew*, he was going to kiss her. She could almost already feel it—how his lips would be soft and cold, and she felt as if there were trumpets blaring inside of her, as if fireworks were cartwheeling behind her eyes, all in anticipation of that wonderful, wonderful kiss.

The kiss that didn't happen.

Roger let her go and stepped back quickly, muttering "Sorry" under his breath, and Lindy refocused on the darkness and saw how severe he looked and realised she must have misread the moment entirely. Disappointment swamped her—enough disappointment for her to realise just how much she'd wanted him to kiss her. She'd wanted it with a yearning she felt soul-deep, one that was shot through her whole body like flecks of gold embedded in rock. She wanted it—and she didn't get it.

Roger started back towards the house, and after a few seconds of tortured deliberation, Lindy followed.

She might have been trying to convince herself she just wanted to be Roger's friend, but in that moment she knew otherwise. She was halfway—or more—to falling in love with him.

Chapter Sixteen

"ALL RIGHT, YEAR Sixes, I know you've got this." Lindy gave the twenty-eight pupils in various moods from ebullient to terrified to bored her biggest smile and a double thumbs up.

"One…two…three…go!" She switched on the music—Tchaikovsky's sedate 'Waltz of the Flowers'—and started clapping the time to the beat. Fourteen couples joined haltingly on the floor, some looking more tortured than others. "One step, two, heads up, look forward; smile like you're enjoying yourselves!" Lindy barked out commands in time to the tempo as she moved around the room, correcting kids' fumbling box steps with a smile here, a touch there. They weren't too bad, considering there were still four more weeks to go until the Christmas ball.

It was two weeks since Roger and his mum had come to her house for chilli and sparklers, two weeks since Lindy had been brave enough to acknowledge to herself, and no one else, that she might actually be falling in love with him. At least, she suspected that's what this strange, heady, bubbly up feeling was, mixed with a healthy dose of pure terror. She'd never been in love before, so she didn't really know how it was meant to feel, but if this wasn't it, she didn't know what was.

She *did* know that what she felt was deeper than mere interest or attraction—what she'd felt for Roger at the beginning, when she'd flirted with him so shamelessly, so seemingly harmlessly. It was more physical than the friendship she'd been aiming for, because she felt a driving need to touch him that she could only indulge in the merest of ways—the brush of a hand, the touch of his shoulder, and all the while her body felt as if it were on fire.

It was painful, living like this. It was also invigorating—had she ever felt so alive? Every morning she woke up and marvelled at things she'd always enjoyed, but never quite so intensely as this—the autumn sun gilding the frosted blades of grass in gold, the happy sigh Toby gave as he flopped at her feet, the crisp taste of her morning can of Coke. She revelled in each one, delighting in the smallest things, brimming with bonhomie for the world and everyone in it.

And she didn't even know if Roger felt the same way. In all truth, she thought he probably didn't; perhaps it hadn't even occurred to him, and yet somehow right now that didn't even matter. She was, Lindy realised, simply enjoying feeling this way—like she was *alive*, truly, gloriously alive, as if life mattered, and there was something bigger than herself in it. And yes, she did hope he might come to feel the same way in time—but if he didn't? She'd hug this precious secret to herself and enjoy every moment of it.

"Miss, Will is being sick!"

The terrified shriek of one of her Year Six girls had Lindy coming quickly out of her pleasant reverie. Fortunately, the boy in question was only pretending to be sick, hands clutched to stomach, because, like most eleven-year-old boys, he hated the waltz. Lindy collared him and then started partnering him, much to his dismay.

She persevered, careening around the room as she cracked jokes, and she was eventually rewarded with the smallest of smiles.

The bell rang a few minutes later, and Lindy dodged out of the way of the rush towards the school doors and freedom.

"Don't forget to practise!" she yelled after them. "Same time, next week!"

With a little laugh and a shake of her head, she started tidying up after the tornado that was a Year Six class—she found no less than seven discarded jumpers, two backpacks, a pencil case, and, rather worryingly, a single trainer. She dumped it all in the lost and found bin by the doors, and then turned off the music and packed up her own stuff. She needed to get back to Toby and give him his afternoon walk before he started to panic at being left alone for too long.

As she left the building, navigating through schoolyard three twenty scrum, her mind drifted back to the few times she'd seen Roger since Bonfire Night—two

Monday evening classes, and then a Saturday walk with Toby along the Lea River. She'd been toying with the idea of asking him out for a drink, and she'd composed various texts over the last few weeks, aiming for casual but friendly, except every time she went to press send, she knew what she felt wasn't either casual or friendly, yet what was the alternative? *I'm falling in love with you and trying to think of ways to spend time with you. Do you feel the same?*

Just the thought of typing those words, never mind actually sending them, set a shiver of terror through her. No, she couldn't do that. Not yet, maybe not ever. She just wanted to enjoy this feeling—this exciting-yet-safe sensation, for a little while longer, before she so much as attempted to catapult it to the next dizzying level.

"Lindy!"

Lindy turned to see Harriet Lang bearing down on her like a ship in full sail, a look of fearful purpose on her face. Lindy tried to smile.

"Hey!" she said, summoning enthusiasm. Harriet still scared her a little bit.

"How *are* you? I can't wait to hear all about this Christmas extravaganza of yours! Will won't tell me a word about it."

"Will…" Belatedly Lindy realised the pretending-vomiting pupil of earlier was Harriet's son. "Ah," she said, and Harriet gave a knowing nod.

"He's a handful, isn't he? If he's any trouble, I give you

my full permission to blast him." She shook her head. "He loves pushing both boundaries and buttons."

"His heart's in the right place, though," Lindy said, because she had a bit of a soft spot for Will Lang and his cheeky grin. "At least I think it is."

"Let's hope so," Harriet returned with a mock shudder. "Are you walking out?" She nodded towards the school gate, with the steady stream of parents and pupils going through it.

"Yes." Lindy couldn't keep the slight note of hesitation from her voice. She had a feeling, judging from Harriet's rather beady expression, that she was about to get a grilling.

"Good, we'll walk with you." She shouted for Chloe and Will who fell in line alongside them as they all headed towards the gate.

"So I feel as if I need to apologise," Harriet said frankly as Will and Chloe ran ahead. "Properly this time, for me and my big mouth."

"What—"

"That unsuitable comment I made, way back when, in Tea on the Lea." Harriet grimaced, looking slightly shame-faced. "I only meant to tease, but I think he heard and now that I know you're friends…" She paused. "*Good* friends…"

"Why does this apology feel like a way to get the gossip?" Lindy asked, smiling to take any sting from her words. Harriet let out a laugh.

"Because it is. I admit that unreservedly. But I am sorry.

I hate to think I hurt someone's feelings."

"I don't know if you did or not," Lindy said after a moment. "I haven't actually spoken to Roger about it, and he hasn't given any indication that he heard." Although she was almost certain he had.

"So…"

"We're friends," Lindy said firmly, in a tone she hoped invited no more questions. "Good friends."

"Ah." Harriet nodded with too much understanding. They'd reached the end of the school lane and were coming out to the top of the high street; Lindy knew Harriet's house, in Wychwood's slightly less well-to-do area, was up to the left, while she was going to head down the high street, back to Willoughby Close.

Chloe and William had already turned left, chasing each other up the street, as the last of the autumn leaves drifted down in yellow and reds. Lindy was about to say goodbye, but she saw that Harriet was hesitating, and with some trepidation she waited for whatever it was the other woman intended to say.

"Look, please don't take this the wrong way…" *Great beginning.* "Because I was once where you were. In Willoughby Close. Feeling…alone."

Lindy opened her mouth and then shut it. How did Harriet know she'd felt alone? Her presumption, along with her perception, silenced her.

"I only say that because I remember how you told us

about your parents dying when you were young," Harriet explained. "And, to be honest, I recognise the signs of self-sufficiency."

"I don't think there's anything wrong with self-sufficiency," Lindy said, her tone sharpening a little. "Especially when I've had to be self-sufficient since I was nineteen." Wow, she sounded both bitter and angry. How had that happened? She'd been feeling so happy, so benevolent. Harriet Lang had knocked both emotions right out of her, at least for the moment.

"Of course, I understand," Harriet said quietly. "I'm just saying…let Willoughby Close work its magic, as silly as that sounds. There are so many people who want to help you. Support you. It's hard to let them, to let people in, especially when you're used to doing everything yourself, or being the kind of person who does it for everybody else. That's how I was. But I ended up in Willoughby Close for a season—it's a long story—because I needed to be, and I needed friends. I found them there, and you can too."

"Thanks, Harriet," Lindy said, her voice a bit brittle, "but I'm not sure I need this pep talk. I've been hanging out with lots of the Willoughby Close gang." She'd had drinks at the pub and Sunday roasts at Willoughby Manor… What *was* Harriet talking about?

"I know you've gone out," Harriet answered, "and you're very good at accepting invitations. But I'm talking about something a bit deeper." She paused while Lindy simply stared. "You're very friendly, and yet you still somehow keep people at arm's length. I think you know you do it, as well. Maybe it's intentional?" Harriet gave her a sympathetic smile and Lindy found she could not reply.

How had Harriet seen that? No one had before, at least that she knew. No one had seemed to care enough. She was good for drinks and parties and the occasional evening out, but...real life? That call for help in the night, in the dark?

"I...I don't know what to say," Lindy said finally.

"You don't have to say anything." Harriet patted her arm. "Just think about what I'm saying." Dumbly Lindy nodded, and Harriet turned to Chloe and William, who were little more than specks far up the street. "Oy! You two! Wait up!" With a last, commiserating smile for Lindy, she started to jog up the street.

Lindy walked the rest of the way home in a bit of a daze. She was stunned by Harriet's comments, her courage in making them...and how spot on they actually were. Lindy had always attributed the invisible distance she felt from people to the simple, hard truth that for the last fifteen years she'd had to live on her own; everyone else had friends and family, close-knit communities that often proved impenetrable to her. Without that tribe surrounding you, it was hard to make inroads into community life the way everybody else did.

Now, in light of Harriet's comments, she had to ask herself if that distance existed because *she'd* put it there.

Intentionally. Wilfully. Because getting close to people often meant getting hurt. The devastation she'd felt after her parents' death…well, she'd put a lid on that box a long time ago, had soldiered on, declaring herself fine. Believing that if she acted fine, well, then she would be. And she was, she was sure she was, except…

She was starting to realise there had been an emptiness inside her all along that she hadn't wanted to acknowledge, even to herself. Being comfortable in her own skin, happy in her own company, all the tried and trite phrases that reassured her she was okay…suddenly they felt like so many catchphrases that were nothing more than salves. Placebos when what she needed was a whole-heart cure.

She'd told Roger she was like him in her sense of isolation, but she'd never realised it was out of choice. Out of fear. And even with this new, unwelcome knowledge, she had no idea how to change, or even if she wanted to. She might feel like she was falling in love, but was that all it was? All she wanted it to be? A feeling, and nothing more?

"STILL IN THE friend zone?"

The smell of Lynx aftershave assaulted Roger's nostrils before Chris's loud, cheerful voice registered on his eardrums.

"You haven't asked me about whether I've been to a rave this weekend," Roger replied, a bit disgruntled. He liked routine, and he'd also had his reply ready—*No raves, but I've found a new interest in grime.* Not that he actually understood what grime was precisely, although he had googled it—something about London and the Underground, it seemed, although that didn't really make sense.

"Sorry, I just couldn't wait to hear about your lady friend," Chris replied as he switched on the kettle, even though it had just boiled. "Is she still your lady…friend?"

"If by that, are you asking—again—if I remain in the 'friend zone,' as you termed it, then the answer would be yes." Roger tried not to sound dispirited. The last few weeks with Lindy had been lovely, although they hadn't actually seen each other all that much. Still, he'd found himself looking forward to the dance classes with more enthusiasm than he'd ever felt before, and their walk along the Lea River had been sweetly companionable.

Even so, the memory of that moment in the garden on Bonfire Night—the awkward dance they'd done as Roger had wondered whether to kiss her—remained singed into his memory. He still had no idea what that moment had meant—if it had been a disappointment or relief for Lindy that he hadn't, or perhaps she'd just been entirely oblivious to the tension he'd felt ratcheting through him. Maybe he was so firmly friend-zoned it wouldn't even cross her mind, and she'd just wanted to move past him, back into the house.

He had a sinking feeling that was the most likely case.

"Ah, sorry, man," Chris said as he poured the kettle over

his mug of instant coffee granules and then dumped two spoonfuls of sugar in. "That sucks."

"Mmm." It did, rather, although Roger would not have used such terms.

"You've got to make her see you differently—"

"So you've said," Roger cut across his young friend a bit acidly, "but I really don't see how." He couldn't change who he was, or how Lindy did—or didn't—see him. He definitely knew that much.

"You could just come out with it, you know," Chris said musingly. "It's not my style, but it works for some. Just spit it out. Tell her you've got *feelings.*" He imbued the word with such lascivious emphasis, adding a meaningful wiggle of his eyebrows, that Roger nearly blushed.

"I do not believe that is my style, either."

"What have you got to lose?"

"Her friendship, for a start." And he really didn't want to lose that, especially with his mother so ill. If Lindy suddenly cut off all ties, his mum would notice, and Roger couldn't bear for her to be disappointed at this stage. Her meaningful comments over the last few weeks—*don't forget the blue shirt, Roger! Is that cologne you're wearing?*—had been hard enough to take already; hearing her morose musings as to why Lindy's interested had cooled would be far worse.

Chris gave an understanding nod. "Do you think that would be it, if you told her? No second chances?"

"I…don't know." Lindy did not strike Roger as the type

of person to be so unforgiving, but the humiliation would be off the charts if he confessed his feelings and received a horrified, dumbstruck look in reply. He'd be as likely to sever any ties as Lindy, simply out of self-preservation.

"Well, maybe it's worth the risk," Chris said as he took a slurp of coffee. "You know, nothing ventured, nothing gained, and all that." He paused to adopt a serious and sentimental look. "And remember, it's better to have loved and lost than never to have loved at all," he intoned, as if offering a true pearl of wisdom.

"Many thanks for that sage advice," Roger replied tartly, and Chris grinned.

"I know it sounds like a load of tosh, but there *is* something to it."

Roger fished out his teabag and then picked up his mug. "Do you have a girlfriend, Chris?" he asked politely.

Chris's grin widened. "Nope."

"Ah," Roger said, and with a nod of farewell, walked out of the kitchen.

Despite his attempt to dismiss Chris's well-meaning words, Roger found he couldn't. What *was* the risk, exactly, of telling Lindy how he felt, or at least was starting to feel? If he could get over the embarrassment, he thought they might stay friends, although he suspected his confession would always be an unspoken awkwardness between them.

But what was the alternative? Never saying anything at all? Feeling this painfully sweet longing every single time he saw her? It would either make him wither away—or combust.

Roger continued to ruminate as he cycled back to the Park and Ride, and then drove back to Wychwood. After a quick check on his mum, who was flagging but still up for the class, he headed back to his house to change.

"Wear your blue shirt," Ellen had called after him, and Roger wondered if it would start to look weird, for him to wear the exact same clothes every week, simply because his mother thought he looked good in them. He decided to switch it up, and wear a pale green shirt today instead. Talk about living on the edge.

He'd just given himself a very small spritz of bay rum— aftershave, *not* cologne—when he heard a surprisingly frantic knocking on the front door.

Mum. Roger felt as if his heart had leapt right into his throat as he hurried downstairs and threw open the door, expecting to see his mum's neighbour Tina who occasionally looked in on her, a look of sorrow on her face. *She took a funny turn...*

Lindy stood there instead, Toby in her arms, her expression half-wild.

"Lindy..." Roger was at a loss for words; he'd never seen her looking so distraught. "What—"

"Can you take Toby?" she blurted, and he glanced at the dog, squirming in her arms.

"Is he hurt?" he asked in some alarm, and Lindy shook

her head.

"No, he's fine, but I—I have to go." Her voice wobbled and she took a deep breath. "Immediately. I'm sorry, I have to cancel tonight's class. I can't take Toby with me, and he knows you. It will just be for a night or two."

"Where are you going?"

"Derbyshire." Her voice splintered and a single tear slipped from her eye, like a drip from a leaky tap. "Home."

Chapter Seventeen

LINDY WAS TRYING to hold herself together, and obviously failing. She dashed the tear from her eye and nearly lost her grasp of Toby in the process. Roger lunged forward to take the dog, and Lindy let him. She was falling to pieces, and she couldn't seem to make herself stop.

"Lindy, what's happened?" Roger asked as he set Toby down on the ground and gave him a few soothing strokes. "You seem…traumatised."

That was probably a good word for it. She *felt* traumatised, far more than the situation surely merited, and yet even so she could not keep her emotions in check. They were running rampant, steamrollering over her sensibilities, making her gabble.

"Something's—something's happened," she said. "I need to take care of it."

"Let me help," Roger said simply, and for a second Lindy stared, remembering their conversation. Her cry for help. Well, here it was, and Roger was answering, as she'd known he would, even if she was still reluctant to take it, or anyone's.

"You are helping," she told him. "By taking Toby."

A pause, weighted with the unspoken yet felt. "More than that," Roger said quietly, and Lindy's splintered heart seemed to break. She wasn't sure she could take much more—of anxiety, of kindness. It all felt like too much. "What's going on, Lindy? What's happened?"

She shook her head helplessly, having no idea how to explain.

"You said you were going…home?" His brow furrowed in concerned confusion.

"Yes. The only home I've ever really had." She forced her voice to be matter-of-fact, her tone level. She could do this. It was ridiculous to be so affected. To feel so much grief—and yet it was there, a wild surging inside of her that she'd been suppressing for far too long. Fifteen years, in fact, all bubbling up to the surface now, and all because of a simple phone call.

Her old neighbour, Heloise, had rung her an hour ago. "Lindy, I'm so sorry, but something's happened to the house."

Lindy's heart had felt suspended in her chest; she'd had to tell herself to breathe. It had been a surprising reaction, because she didn't actually think about the house all that often. She hadn't been in over a year. But she'd always liked knowing it was there. She *needed* to know it was there. And she hadn't realised quite how much until Heloise had rung.

"What…" Her mouth was so dry she had to swallow and start again. "What happened?"

"I've been away," Heloise said apologetically. "Only for a couple of weeks, and you know nothing has happened in all these years…"

"I know." Lindy paid Heloise to look after the little cottage; to keep it dust- and problem-free, to mow the small square of garden and check no windows had been broken, no roof tiles blown off. For fifteen years Lindy had kept the house running and gone only a handful of times, but that had been okay. That had been fine.

"Someone broke in," Heloise said. "I'm guessing a couple of rough sleepers, or perhaps just some teens. There were beer cans, cigarette butts…"

"Okay." Lindy had taken a deep breath. She could handle a little clean-up.

"But I think they must have gone a bit crazy," Heloise said. "Perhaps they were on drugs? Because they…they went on a bit of a rampage."

A *rampage*? Lindy's stomach dipped. "What do you mean?"

"I'm so sorry, Lindy. The place looks like they took a cricket bat or a golf club or something to it. They broke everything they could break, including most of the windows. It must have happened soon after I left, because it was clear the rain had blown in, and some animals must have come in, as well…"

Lindy had closed her eyes, unable to speak.

"I'm so sorry," Heloise said. "What do you want me to do?"

"Secure it as best as you can," Lindy said, her voice wooden, sounding as if it were coming outside of herself, for all she wanted to do was howl. "I'll come up as soon as I can."

After the call she'd simply stood there in the centre of her cottage, her heart thudding hard, her palms going damp. She felt as if she were having a panic attack, but she hadn't had one of those in fifteen years, when she'd put the lid on that wretched box and never dared to pry it open again.

The house…oh, the house…

"Do you mean your parents' house?" Roger asked, and Lindy blinked him back into focus, wondering how long she'd been standing there, simply staring. "The house you grew up in?" he prompted.

"Yes. I've kept it all these years, just as it was." *Exactly* as it was, not a single curio out of place. She swallowed past the lump in her throat that was growing bigger by the second. "And now it's been…" Ruined. *Desecrated.* "Some rough sleepers or someone came in and made a mess," she said woodenly. "I need to go clean it up."

"Right now?" Roger looked startled. "It's almost seven o'clock in the evening—"

"I don't care." She sounded fierce, and he absorbed her emotion with a slow blink and a nod of his head.

"All right. You'll need to cancel the dancing class. Let me text my mum, and she can let everyone know."

"I don't want to trouble her—"

"It's no trouble."

"Can't you just go and tell everyone?" Lindy asked a bit desperately.

Roger gave her a steady look. "No, because I'm going with you."

"What—"

"You're in an emotional state, Lindy. You shouldn't drive all that distance alone—"

"But Toby—and your mum—"

"Blue Cross will have Toby back. That's what they'd prefer, anyway. And my mum will be fine for a night. I don't live with her, after all."

Lindy stared at him helplessly, and then she made the mistake of blinking. Tears slipped down her cheeks, one after the other. "I don't…" she began, and Roger frowned.

"Do you not want me to go? I won't, if you'd rather I didn't, but I'd feel better, knowing you weren't driving all that way alone."

"No," Lindy whispered. "I do want you to go." A lot. She'd been trying to be self-sufficient just as Harriet had said, but she didn't know if she was strong enough to handle this alone.

"Okay, then. Have you packed a bag?" She shook her head, realising how foolish and panicked she'd been. She didn't even have Toby's food or lead or bed. She'd just grabbed her dog and run out of her house like a madwoman.

"All right then, let me pack something quickly, and then we'll head back to yours. We can drop Toby off on the way to Derbyshire."

"But Blue Cross won't be open…"

"Marcia, one of the volunteers, lives in Burford and she takes them in when it's not opening hours."

Slowly Lindy nodded. Roger's steady manner, his utter unflappability, was calming her down. She felt her heart rate settle.

"Okay," she said, and tried to smile. She didn't quite make it.

Everything happened quite quickly after that. Roger went upstairs and came back down just a few minutes later with a small bag; Lindy had barely had time to look around the tidy downstairs of his cottage, all brown leather and masculine-looking tartans, exactly what she would have expected from someone like him. She'd only known to come to his house because he'd written his address on the registration form. She was glad she'd followed that reckless impulse.

Back in Lindy's car, they stopped by Ellen's to apprise her of the class cancellation, and then went on to Willoughby Close where Lindy threw a bunch of random clothes into a bag. By the time she came downstairs, Roger had heard back from Marcia, and she was ready and waiting for Toby.

Just twenty minutes later, they'd dropped her dog off

and were heading up the M40 towards Derbyshire. Roger had asked if she'd rather he drive, and Lindy realised she would. She felt too overwhelmed to focus on the motorway on a dark, windswept night, and yet without something to concentrate on, she found her thoughts roaming relentlessly back to the cottage and the damage that had been done. How bad was it? Could anything be salvaged? Surely something...

"You should ring the police at some point," Roger said after they'd driven in silence for some time. "Breaking and entering...destruction of property...these are crimes, serious ones. They should be notified, and perhaps they can discover who did it."

"Perhaps," Lindy replied rather listlessly. "I don't much care who did it, though, or even bringing them to justice. I just...I just want it back the way it was."

"How was it?" Roger asked gently, and once again Lindy's eyes filled with tears.

"The most magical place. Filled with treasures from all our travels...I kept it exactly as it always was, after my parents died. I didn't change even one tiny thing." A little sob escaped her and she drew her breath in sharply. "I'm sorry. I'm falling apart and I'm not even sure why. It's just a house. Possessions, not people. I know it shouldn't matter so much..."

"Perhaps the possessions matter, because the people aren't here any longer," Roger said quietly, and Lindy nodded.

"Yes…it's all I have left of them, and it may be gone. Wrecked." She scrunched her eyes closed as if she could will the thought away.

"Perhaps it's not as bad as you think."

"Perhaps it's worse."

He gave her that lovely little quirk of a smile. "I thought you were a glass half-full type of person."

"I *was*," Lindy replied, but now she wondered whether that had just been a façade she'd adopted to survive. Cheerful Lindy, always happy, always smiling. She certainly wasn't smiling now.

"Sometimes," Roger said after a moment, "the glass *is* half empty. You have to acknowledge that, whether you want to or not."

She glanced at him, noticing his serious look, and wondering if he was thinking about his mother. "That's a rather deep thought."

"Sometimes I can be quite thought-provoking," Roger returned with a smile. "Other times…not so much."

She laughed, at least a little, and then impulsively reached for his hand resting on the gear shift. "I'm glad you're here," she said. Roger glanced at her, a little startled.

"So am I," he said.

ROGER DIDN'T KNOW what had possessed him to volunteer

to accompany Lindy up to Derbyshire—and not even volunteer, but practically insist. Perhaps it had been the shock at seeing her look so distraught. Or maybe it had been a moment of recklessness born of his desire to help, as well as the affection he held for her, but as they drove northward he knew, with a soul-deep certainty, that coming with her had been the right thing to do.

Out of character, yes, and impulsive, certainly. But right. Definitely right. She'd cried for help and he'd come.

Not that it had been quite as easy as he'd assured her it was—he'd had to email his boss, asking for unpaid leave, which he suspected wouldn't go down well since he'd already taken all of his annual holiday, looking after his mother. Marcia had needed a bit of convincing to take Toby, as she'd been out at her knitting club, but she'd agreed in the end.

Still, he hadn't wanted to bother Lindy with those concerns. For her, he knew it needed to be simple. He just hoped whatever awaited them in Derbyshire wouldn't be as much of the disaster as Lindy seemed to think it was.

But if it was, and he suspected it might be, then at least he was here with her. Roger just hoped he was up to the job of caring and supporting her. It was definitely outside his comfort zone, even as part of him craved it. He wanted to be needed. He wanted to help. He just hoped he wasn't going to let Lindy down.

"Take the next exit," Lindy said after they'd been driving for two hours. "And then a left. It's just outside the village of

Hathersage."

For the next twenty minutes Roger followed her directions; it took all his focus to navigate the single track road on a moonless night that was as dark as pitch. Even with the main beam headlights on, he could only see a few metres of road in front of him.

Another few turnings and a few hundred metres down the narrowest lane Roger had ever driven on, with hedgerows brushing both wing mirrors, and finally they were there.

From the gleam of the headlights he made out a quaint-looking cottage, all topsy-turvy, clearly sixteenth century or earlier, with its wonky beams and windows that had settled in crooked lines with age. Windows, he saw, that were broken; the shattered glass making them look like jagged teeth.

Lindy started out of the car as soon as he cut the engine, and Roger called after her.

"Wait…I've got a torch."

He withdrew the heavy-duty torch from his bag and Lindy took it with a whispered thanks. Her face was pale, her eyes huge. Roger followed her to the front door; she unlocked it and then stepped into the tiny entry hall, letting out a soft gasp of dismay at all she saw.

Roger stayed silent as Lindy swung the torch around to reveal the devastation. Nearly every picture frame was broken, and the floor of the sitting room was scattered with broken pottery and glass. Roger could see that the place must have once been chock-a-block with curios and mementoes; every single one was now, as far as he could see, destroyed. Chairs and sofas had been tipped over, and in some cases the fabric had been slashed by a knife. Someone had clearly done something disgusting on top of the table in the dining room adjoining.

Lindy slowly moved through the rooms, leaving Roger no choice but to follow. The broken pottery and glass crunched under their feet. In the kitchen, the dishes had been hurled out of the cupboards and lay on the floor in broken heaps; Roger recognised a Willow Ware pattern similar to the one his mother had.

In the study off the sitting room, the beautiful mahogany desk, inlaid with hand-tooled leather, had been slashed at with a knife, and the heads had been lopped off all the pieces of a chessboard that was, Roger thought, meant to show the Battle of Waterloo.

The extent of the carnage was so severe, and so very vicious, that it took his breath away even as it made him burn with anger. What kind of person committed this wanton, craven destruction? It was more than merely reprehensible; it was truly evil.

Lindy hadn't said a word or even made a sound through this whole, terrible inspection. Now she merely turned from the study and headed up the narrow stairs to the bedrooms above. Roger had to duck his head to avoid a low beam as he followed Lindy to the first bedroom—the master, judging from the size of the bed; the sheets were rumpled and stank of something vile. Clearly someone had slept there, and more than once. The drawers had been pulled out and clothing tossed about, and the mirror above the bureau was shattered, but otherwise the room was whole, making Roger thankful for very small mercies.

The bathroom was unscathed, thankfully, and the second bedroom—Lindy's—was untouched. Perhaps the vile intruders had simply run out of steam. It looked as if they hadn't even gone into the small bedroom with its single bed, the sheets still drawn up, everything quietly pristine.

Roger glanced around the room, looking for some clues as to the girl Lindy had once been. Besides the single bed, there was a matching bureau and desk, and a bookshelf full of slightly old-fashioned childhood books—Enid Blyton, Arthur Ransome, LM Montgomery. They all looked as if they'd been well read. A few childhood trophies lined the windowsill, and some ribbons decorated the mirror. A ballroom dancing poster was stuck to one wall, peeling at the corners.

"At least this room is untouched," he said, and Lindy let out a trembling sound that was halfway between a laugh and a sob.

"I don't care about this room. This room is just *me*. It was the rest of the house that I cared about—*that* was Mum and Dad, not this." She swept one arm to gesture to the bedroom and all its time capsule contents. Her shoulders started to shake.

Roger had stepped forward and put his arms around her before he was fully aware of what he was doing. He knew it was the right thing to have done when Lindy clung to him, her head on his shoulder, her tears soaking his shirt. He didn't say anything, in part because he didn't know what to say but also because he didn't think there were any words. Sometimes, he knew, you just needed to cry.

He remembered his mother telling him the same thing soon after his father had died; he'd been keeping it all in, a pressure building in his chest, a rage taking over him that was fuelled by fear. Fear of what happened if he stopped being angry. Fear that if he let himself cry, he'd never stop.

She'd told him he needed to cry, that every tear he shed was one he wouldn't have to shed again, but 'they had to be got out.' And in her arms, twelve-year-old Roger had wept, hot, rage-filled tears that had emptied him out like a husk. Exhausted, he'd slumped on the sofa and fallen asleep for three dreamless hours.

He thought Lindy needed something similar now. Her tears kept coming, her body shaking with the force of them, and Roger just held her. After an indeterminate amount of time—an hour or a minute, he didn't actually know—she eased back and looked up at him with a crumpled, tear-washed face.

"Don't leave me."

"I won't," he said, because of course he wouldn't. It was

absolutely out of the question. "Perhaps we should get some sleep, though." It was after eleven, and he thought they were both exhausted.

"Yes…if I can. I don't know if I'll be able to."

"You can try, at least." He nodded towards her bed. "If you take the bed, I'll kip on the sofa downstairs." The bed in the master was currently unusable, thanks to the rough sleepers; although downstairs was freezing, due to the broken windows, and smelled rather nasty, it was preferable to the alternative.

"No." Lindy shook her head, her expression resolute. "I don't want you to sleep there."

Roger gazed at her, nonplussed, wondering if she thought he'd somehow desecrate her parents' space by sleeping on the sofa.

"Would you…" Lindy paused, looking hesitant. "Would you stay with me? Here? I don't want to be alone."

Stay with her? Roger stared at her blankly. Did she mean actually in the *bed*? It looked very narrow. And while staying with Lindy was unquestionably at the top of his priorities, Roger feared it would be an uncomfortable and potentially embarrassing night. But perhaps she didn't mean the bed, just in the room. That made more sense, and was certainly possible. In any case, he knew there was only one answer to give. Only one answer he wanted to give.

"Of course I will," he said.

Chapter Eighteen

LINDY STARED AT her gaunt face in the bathroom mirror, amazed at how weary, how *old* she'd looked, as if she'd aged in a matter of hours. Perhaps she had. Certainly it felt as if a lifetime had passed since Heloise had first called her. Even in her worst imaginings, Lindy had not pictured the extent of havoc that had been wreaked on her parents' home.

She swallowed down the need to sob—she'd cried enough, *surely*—and turned away from the mirror. She'd changed into her pyjamas, including thick socks and a fleece, because the house was freezing, and she was going to at least try to go to sleep. She had no idea how Roger felt about sharing the narrow bed with her; she only knew she needed him there. She couldn't bear to be alone, not tonight, with so many memories flocking around her like ghosts.

As she came into the bedroom, she saw he'd already changed—plaid pyjamas bottoms, a woolly jumper, and thick socks like her. It really was freezing. He also, she saw, had taken some blankets from the airing cupboard and laid them on the floor.

"You don't have to sleep on the floor," she blurted, and Roger looked flummoxed.

"Oh. Er." He lapsed into silence, and Lindy wished she knew what he was thinking. Did he not want to share a bed with her? Surely he knew she'd have no romantic designs on him tonight of all nights? She was hardly going to seduce him when her heart felt as if it had been shattered.

"What I mean is, I don't want you to sleep on the floor," she said stiltedly. "I...I want to be held." She flushed at how needy she sounded, but she couldn't keep herself from it. She simply felt too desperate for human comfort, for arms around her.

"Okay," Roger said, but he still looked uncomfortable, and the knowledge stabbed Lindy.

"Unless you don't want to? I mean, if you'd *rather*..."

"N—no," he said quickly, stammering slightly in his unease. "I wouldn't rather. I just didn't want to presume..."

"Presume away," she replied, and peeled back the covers. They were stale-smelling, with the faintest aroma of lavender to cover the more unpleasant smells of dust and damp, but she didn't care. She slipped beneath the sheets as Roger took the blankets from the floor and laid them on top of the bed.

"It's rather cold," he explained, and then he paused, looking down at the bed. Lindy looked at it too. It was *very* narrow. Were all single beds this narrow? She hadn't slept in one since her uni days. She took well over half of it now.

"Sorry," she half-mumbled, and scooted over to one side,

so she had a full butt cheek off the bed. Perhaps this wasn't the best idea, and yet she didn't want to do something different.

Gingerly Roger lowered himself onto the bed and stretched out. He wasn't a small man, and Lindy suspected his feet and even his ankles were hanging off the end, although he didn't complain. He lay rigidly next to her, and she thought he must have only one butt cheek on the mattress just as she did. Really, this wasn't sustainable.

"Held," she reminded him, and he gave her a look that was a mix of desperation and terror. Then, awkwardly and clumsily, he put his arms around her. He jabbed her in the eye with his elbow, and Lindy had to bite her tongue to keep from crying out. Still, with his arms around her she was able to snuggle in closer to him, her cheek on his chest, her arm around his waist. *This* was what she'd been talking about. Oh, yes. This felt very nice indeed. His heart was thudding under her cheekbone and he smelled like bay rum. His chest was wonderfully solid, his waist decidedly trim, everything about him steady and comforting and *right*.

And yet she realised she wanted to get even closer, if that were possible, in a non-sexual way…well, *mostly*. She slipped her knee between his so their legs were twined and then she hooked her other arm around his neck so their bodies were just about as close as they could be, her breasts pressing against his chest, her face nestled in the lovely, warm curve of his neck. He was solid warmth all around her, a cocoon of safety and comfort. She felt her body relax for the first time since that phone call. Here was another kind of home.

"Is this okay?" she whispered and Roger's voice was only slightly strained as he replied, "Yes. Of course."

"Good," Lindy murmured, and then snuggled even closer.

THIS WAS TORTURE. Pure, perfect torture. Roger didn't think he'd ever actually been as physically close to another person as he was with Lindy—not even the women he'd dated. He'd never lain with someone with every single body part touching, feeling practically *fused* together, her lips pressing against his neck...*so* many things pressing. He felt all of her, and he suspected she was very shortly going to feel all of him.

He was doing his best to keep that embarrassing prospect from happening, thinking of all manner of things that were not Lindy's body against his. Lindy's lips on his skin. Lindy's...

Stop. *Stop.*

He drew a quick breath as quietly as he could, and that's when he felt a droplet of damp on his neck, and he realised Lindy was crying.

"Hey." He eased back so he could see her face, although the room was so dark he couldn't see anything but the faint gleam of her eyes. "You're crying."

"I'm sorry."

"Don't be sorry."

"I didn't expect…" She drew a hitched breath. "I didn't expect this to affect me so much."

"I think this kind of destruction would affect anyone," Roger replied quietly. Somehow, seemingly of its own accord, his hand had begun stroking her hair. Lindy didn't seem to mind.

She was quiet for a moment, the only sound the gentle draw and tear of her breathing, as Roger kept sliding his hand over the silky, tumbling mass of her hair.

"It's more than that, though," Lindy said after a moment. Roger stilled his hand for a second, and then kept stroking. "After my parents died," she continued slowly, "after the funeral, I came back to this house and I tidied everything up—I hoovered, I spritzed and sprayed, I filed all the papers my father had left on his desk. It felt like grieving, to go through all their things that way. And when I was done, I walked out of the house, locked the door, and rented a flat in Manchester. I've only been back here a handful of times since, and always just to see that things are fine, never to stay." She drew a hitched breath. "And yet all along, it was so important that this house was *here*, that it remained just as it was. It felt…crucial."

Roger remained silent, in part because he didn't know what to say, and also because he didn't think there was anything he *could* say. He just needed to listen. "Now…"

Lindy said hesitantly, "I wonder if, when I locked that door, I locked my grief inside. I refused to let it out." Another shuddering breath. "And now that the house has been broken open, so has my grief. My heart." She twisted against him so she could peer up at his face in the darkness. "Does that sound crazy? Maudlin? Both?"

"It's an interesting way of looking at it," Roger said after a moment, and Lindy let out a muffled laugh against his chest.

"That's your polite way of saying it's mad."

"Not mad—"

"It's okay, Roger. It *is* mad. And yet I think it's true." She sighed. "I didn't even realise I was doing it. I just wanted to be happy. I thought that if I acted happy, I would *be* happy. And lots of times I was. But all the while…there was this grief. And I wasn't dealing with it." She nestled closer to him, burrowing her face into his chest, which was quite a lovely feeling. "And so it all came spilling out now."

"Better out than in," Roger said pragmatically, and Lindy laughed again. He hadn't meant to be funny, but he liked making her laugh.

"What about you?" she asked. "When your dad died? Did you keep it in?"

"Yes, for a while. But my mother told me I needed to cry, and that every tear I shed was one I wouldn't have to shed again. And I was a child. Crying didn't feel as unnatural, perhaps, as it does as an adult."

Lindy was silent for a moment. "Do you miss him?" she asked unexpectedly and Roger stiffened slightly before he tightened his arms around her.

"Yes. Every day."

"Sorry, that was a stupid question. Of course you do." She sighed. "As I do. Every day. Even if I tried to act or even feel as if I didn't, as if I was absolutely fine." She let out an unhappy little laugh. "Who knew I was so messed up?"

"I didn't," Roger said honestly, and she laughed again, this time with genuine mirth.

"Oh, Roger." She sighed and nestled again. He liked the nestling. After a few sweetly silent moments, Lindy let out an enormous yawn. Roger felt it vibrate against him. "I think I might actually fall asleep," she said slowly, with surprise, and then a few minutes later her breathing evened out. She let out a soft sigh and her body relaxed bonelessly into his and Roger knew she was asleep.

He, however, was not. Even though he was exhausted, eyes gritty, muscles aching, Roger didn't think he'd be able to sleep. His heart was too full, his body too aware. He felt too much…in all sorts of ways.

As carefully and quietly as he could, he let out a slow breath and adjusted his position; the movement just caused Lindy to cling all the more tightly to him, wrapping her body around his like a vine. A very lovely vine. Her hair was tickling his lips. She smelled like vanilla. Despite the devastation all around them, he didn't think he could remember a moment when he'd ever been happier.

LINDY WOKE SLOWLY to sunlight and warmth all around her. Wonderful, sleepy masculine warmth. She was still cocooned in Roger's arms, and she'd slept deeply and dreamlessly for several hours, at last. She didn't feel refreshed, not exactly, but she felt…good.

She stirred slightly, shifting in Roger's embrace, and he stirred too, and a sudden hot flare of pure physical yearning shot through her. Roger might not be awake, but he was…awake. In the most fundamental and masculine way possible.

In the next second he'd jerked away from her and rolled out of bed, raking a hand through his hair as he muttered something about needing the loo.

Oh-kay. Lindy rolled onto her back, staring at the ceiling, as the bathroom door slammed and then locked. She might be very inexperienced for the average thirty-five-year-old; in fact, she *knew* she was, but she'd also known what she'd felt and it didn't displease her. Of course, it was just a man's basic, bodily function, she knew that too, and yet…

Lindy smiled. The thought that Roger might react to her physically was…thrilling. There was no other word for it. Of course, the fact that he'd hightailed it to the bathroom might be a slight cause for concern.

A full five minutes later Roger returned to the bedroom,

giving her a tense smile. He'd brushed his hair and he looked like he should be going to work, except he was in his pyjamas. Somehow Lindy liked that.

"Sleep well?" he asked in a slightly croaky voice, and then he cleared his throat.

"Yes, like a baby." She smiled at him, feeling shy. "Thank you."

He waved a hand in dismissal. "It was my pleasure."

She hoped he meant that sincerely. She couldn't tell, in the predictably awkward silence that ensued.

"I suppose I need to start sorting all that out," Lindy said with a sigh, nodding towards the rest of the house and all the mess that still waited. Her stomach clenched at the thought.

"And you should call the police. This really is an atrocious crime."

"Yes." She leaned her head against the pillow, not wanting to deal with any of it.

"Look, why don't I get dressed and get us some supplies? Something to eat for breakfast, and some coffee."

Lindy's mouth curved. "I thought you didn't drink coffee."

"Tea, then. Something to get us going, and then we'll tackle everything else."

"Okay." A wave of exhaustion crashed over Lindy just at the thought of tackling 'everything else,' but she appreciated Roger's unstinting offer of help.

"I'll just get dressed," he mumbled, and grabbing his bag,

he beat a retreat back to the bathroom. Lindy half-wished they were still both in bed, cuddling.

What *was* the status of their relationship? she wondered as she listened to the sounds of the tap and flush from the bathroom. Surely you couldn't sleep entwined with someone all night and still just be friends. Yet the memory of the awkwardness and embarrassment that had descended on them that morning as soon as they'd both woken up made Lindy think that you could.

Except she didn't want to be, and yet she felt too frightened and fragile to risk telling Roger how she felt. Perhaps she'd just see how today went, focus on the house, and then go from there.

Roger emerged from the bathroom a few minutes later, freshly dressed and shaven, smelling as usual of bay rum. Goodness, but she loved that smell.

"Be back in a few ticks," he promised, and Lindy took the opportunity provided by his absence to have a long, hot shower—the bathroom was, thankfully, the only other room that had been untouched by the intruders—and then get dressed. With her damp hair pulled back in a ponytail, and wearing sensible jeans and a fleece, she felt ready to tackle another look at the destruction, and this time in broad daylight.

It was worse, Lindy discovered, in the harsh glare of the wintry sun, than she'd realised last night. They'd smashed *everything*. Her heart felt strangely hollow as she took in the extent of the damage—seashells they'd collected in Cornwall, her mother's set of Royal Doulton china shepherdesses, the delicate tea set of Chinese porcelain they'd bought at a street market in Jingdezhen. All of it was in pieces on the floor—pieces too small to glue back together, nothing more than crushed fragments, some of it ground into veritable dust.

"I'm sorry."

Lindy glanced up to see Roger standing in the doorway, holding a paper bag and looking regretful.

"Daylight doesn't improve matters," he remarked quietly as he closed the door behind him.

"No, it definitely does not."

"I took the liberty of stopping by the police station in Hathersage and notifying them about what happened. I hope that was all right."

"Yes, of course. I know they need to be involved."

"They mentioned there have been several houses in the area that have been similarly vandalised," Roger continued, "so at least it's not personal."

"Yes, there's that at least, I suppose." She sighed and stooped down to retrieve one of the larger shards of pottery—the arm of a shepherdess, the remnant of a pink sleeve. "It's just all so wanton, so pointless."

"I know."

"Do you think they had fun doing it?" she asked as she chucked the shard away. There was no point in keeping it.

"I shudder to think that they did."

"They'll never be found, you know."

"Perhaps not, although if they continue with other houses, there's a greater chance they will be." With a small smile, he withdrew a can of Coke, dewy with cold, from the bag. "Drink up."

"You remembered." Bizarrely and embarrassingly, she felt near tears. Again. And all because of a can of Coke.

"Of course I remembered. It was, after all, somewhat of an oddity." He moved past her towards the kitchen. "I think I'll give the kettle a good rinse before I use it."

"Wise idea."

With the tea made, Roger produced a chocolate muffin and banana each, and they ate in comfortable, companionable silence, standing by the counter because the table, one Lindy had sat at hundreds of times, had been hacked at with what she thought was either a machete or a sledgehammer. Maybe both.

"I also bought some bin bags," Roger said. "And some Marigold gloves."

"Roger, you are a marvel and a saint." Lindy shook her head slowly. "I honestly don't know what I would do without you right now."

A blush tinted Roger's cheeks and he buried his nose in his mug of tea. "I suppose it's a good thing you don't need to find out," he said, his voice slightly muffled by his mug.

Lindy had to agree. And, she realised, more and more she was hoping she might *never* have to find out. But was that too much to wish for?

Chapter Nineteen

"**Y**OU HAVE A lot of explaining to do."

Ava started wagging a finger at Lindy as soon as she opened the door. She'd been back from Derbyshire for less than twelve hours; after an endless day of cleaning and lugging bin bags to the tip, talking to the police and trying not to cry, she and Roger had finally driven home at nearly nine o'clock at night. Lindy had been exhausted and emotionally drained, and she suspected Roger was, as well. At least everything had been fine at home; Toby had been ecstatic to see her when they'd stopped by Burford to pick him up, and Ellen had answered the phone call Roger made from a service area on the M40 with surprising and encouraging chirpiness.

Neither of them had said anything about last night; not, Lindy knew, that there was even anything to say. They'd shared a bed. They'd slept. That was it. And yet, to her at least, it had felt like so much more. Still, she was content to wait and see how the next few days and weeks played out; at least that's what she was telling herself now.

When Roger had dropped her off, she'd barely had the energy to mumble a goodbye before she'd stumbled into her cottage with Toby, and then soon fallen into bed. Now it was Wednesday morning, and she had a full day of phone calls to make to deal with the repairs to her parents' house, and she wasn't sure she had the energy to deal with Ava's good-natured nosiness.

"Explaining?" she repeated a bit warily as she stepped aside so Ava could come in. "I'm not sure what you mean."

"Don't you? Alice stopped by yesterday to ask if you wanted to help put up Christmas decorations at the manor, and Olivia told her that you'd gone to Derbyshire with Roger Wentworth." Ava raised her eyebrows enticingly. "Do tell."

"There's nothing to tell," Lindy said a bit shortly. "My parents' house was broken into, and Roger came up to help me sort out the mess. He's a friend, Ava."

"Oh no, I'm sorry." Ava's teasing expression collapsed as she looked at Lindy in concern. "Are you okay?"

"Yes. Well, sort of." Lindy tried for a smile. "The house is a disaster, everything basically wrecked." She sighed heavily. "They even tore out the pages of the photo albums." Something she hadn't realised until a few hours into cleaning, when she'd found them blackened and half-burned on the fire.

"It's almost as if someone has a vendetta against my family," she'd told Roger, "even though I know that can't be the case, especially since the same was done to other houses."

"I think it's just a vendetta against humanity," Roger had replied. "Perhaps they're bitter about their own difficult circumstances."

"Perhaps," Lindy allowed. "That's some bitterness."

He'd given her that little quirk of a sympathetic smile. "Indeed."

Now Ava looked at her in wordless shock. "The photo albums—oh, Lindy!"

Before Lindy knew what she was about, Ava had enfolded her in a hug, which Lindy gladly returned.

"I'm so sorry. And here I was, swanning in, demanding the gossip! I'm a cow."

"No, you're just nosy," Lindy answered with a laugh as she stepped back and dabbed at her eyes. "But I don't mind."

"So I can ask about you and Roger?"

"No," Lindy answered, smiling. "But tell me about the Christmas decorations. I thought Alice didn't want to decorate until December."

"Well, she's a bit impatient now. She's got loads of stuff delivered and she feels like it's going to take an age to sort out and set up—she was hoping a bunch of us would come over on the weekend and help. Mulled wine and mince pies a must, of course, the first of the season."

"That sounds fun."

"You could invite Roger, if you liked," Ava said rather coyly.

"To a Willoughby Close gathering?" Lindy pretended to shudder, although actually, she didn't really need to pretend when she imagined the well-meaning questions, the kind curiosity, the incessant avid conjecture, at this stage in her and Roger's non-relationship. "No thanks."

"I don't blame you," Ava answered with a laugh. "Saturday afternoon sound all right? Alice said everyone can stay for a kitchen supper afterwards."

"Perfect."

After Ava had left, Lindy showered and dressed, and armed with her morning can of Coke, she set about making the calls to various builders and handymen to deal with the worst of the damage on the house in Derbyshire. Yesterday she and Roger managed to clear out all the wreckage, and Heloise had come over and helped for a bit, looking distraught.

"I'm so sorry this happened," she kept saying, even though Lindy assured her it wasn't her fault.

"What are you going to do?" Heloise asked, wringing her hands.

"Clean up as best as I can," Lindy replied, "and then get someone to repair the windows and secure the house. After that..." She shook her head slowly. "I don't know."

Now, a day later, as she made arrangements for all the repairs, Lindy still didn't know what she intended to do with the house. Part of her thought it would be best to sell it and invest the money, or even put a down payment on a house in

Wychwood. She didn't have to rent forever. Another, greater part resisted every aspect of that idea entirely.

With a sigh Lindy checked her phone, and of course there were no missed calls or messages. She'd had the phone beside her all morning, so she would have known if anyone had been in touch. If Roger had.

After all the intimacy they'd shared in Derbyshire—and yes, it *had* been intimate—she'd been hoping, and even expecting, for him to be in touch. To see how she was. To *care*. The fact that it was already afternoon and there had been radio silence shouldn't bother her too much—he was at work, after all—but it did.

This was why you didn't let people in, Lindy thought morosely as she made herself lunch. You gave them the ability to hurt you. Her parents had done that by dying; Roger was doing it in another, albeit much smaller, way. It still hurt, though. Too much for Lindy's liking.

THREE DAYS PASSED without Roger sending so much as a text. Stupidly, perhaps, Lindy didn't text, either, although she wasn't sure why. Because she didn't want to seem desperate? Because she wanted him to make the first move? This was *Roger*, she reminded herself. He was unlikely to make the first move. And yet still she didn't call or text, waiting for him.

She was kept busy, anyway, between overseeing the repairs on the house from afar, and also gearing her classes up for the performance in just three weeks. She'd booked in another weekly session with the Year Sixes, who were starting to drag their feet a little.

"It's just, waltzing's kind of boring," Rose, one of the reluctant Year Sixes, told her on Thursday afternoon, when Lindy was trying to rev them all up for a bouncy box step. "It's so, like, *old*."

"Do you know that it was considered scandalous when it was invented?" Lindy countered. "So scandalous that loads of places banned it." Rose looked unconvinced. "What type of dancing would you rather do?" Lindy asked, and the girl's face brightened.

"Street dancing. Hip-hop. Something that really makes you move."

"All right." Lindy thought for a moment. "What if we did a mash-up? We start with a very sedate waltz, we break out into some hip-hop, and then back to a waltz, but with a bouncier beat?"

Rose looked at her sceptically. "Really? You'd do that?"

"Why not?"

The girl looked even more sceptical, eyes narrowed. "Can you do hip-hop?"

"Of course I can," Lindy replied. She'd never tried, but with the help of a YouTube video or two she thought she'd be up for the challenge. "Why don't some of you show me your best hip-hop moves, and I'll incorporate them into our routine?"

A few pupils were eager to show her their skills, and Lindy watched as they spun and jumped and shook their booties. She decided a few of the less suggestive moves could easily be worked into their routine.

"This will be *wicked*," one boy enthused after she'd explained her idea to the whole class. "Everyone will be so surprised when the music changes!"

"Shake them up a bit," Lindy agreed, smiling. "I love it."

She was still smiling as she left the school to walk back to Willoughby Close. It was almost the end of November, and winter was definitely in the air. Several shops had already got their decorations out, including Waggy Tails, which had a lovely display of Christmas-themed dog biscuits in the window, among wreaths of holly and evergreen.

Lindy realised, for the first time in a long while, she was actually looking forward to Christmas. Maybe she wouldn't even spend it alone.

She checked her phone, but there were still no message. Lindy tried not to let it dent her optimistic mood. Roger hadn't said he'd call her, and in any case, he was probably busy. She'd see him on Monday, and hopefully she'd be able to gauge what was—or wasn't—going on between them then.

Saturday dawned brilliant and sunny, with a hard frost brushing the world in white. Definitely a Christmassy sort of day, Lindy thought as she headed up to Willoughby Manor that afternoon to help Alice with the decorations. The whole gang was out in full force—Alice and Henry, Ava and Jace, Harriet and Richard, Ellie and Oliver, Simon and Olivia, and Emily and Owen.

Lindy took in all the couples with a slight sinking sensation. Maybe she should have invited Roger. No, that would have been a cringing disaster, the most obvious set-up in the world. Still, she definitely felt like a third, or really, a thirteenth, wheel in this crowd.

Fortunately no one actually made her feel that way. With so many people, it was surprisingly easy to forget they were all couples and simply get into the spirit of the thing—arranging clusters of candles on the deep windowsills, hanging wreaths and ropes of evergreen and holly, and watching in awe as Jace, Henry, and Owen all brought in the enormous Christmas tree, its top brushing the vaulted ceiling high above.

As they trimmed the tree, Henry doled out mulled wine and Alice put on Christmas carols.

"I love Christmas," she confided in Lindy as they hung star-shaped baubles on the tree. She seemed happier now that she was busy with the decorating, with less of the brittleness Lindy had sensed from her before. "I never had much of one growing up, so I do go a bit overboard here. What were your Christmases like?"

"Oh, they were wonderful." Lindy scrolled back fifteen years to when she'd had amazing Christmases—either tucked up in Derbyshire or travelling the world. "We spent one Christmas when I was about thirteen watching the sun come up in Tonga. And then we had this amazing singing competition—it's a Christmas tradition there. And Christmas trees are decorated with balloons and candy. We celebrated with some Tongan people. My parents were brilliant at making friends wherever we travelled."

"That sounds amazing," Alice said, looking awed, and Lindy smiled.

"It was," she said simply. "I was so lucky." She'd always said that, had always insisted on it, chanted it like a mantra or waved it like a mascot, but she realised now there had always been some dark corner of her heart that had nurtured the bitter root of grief and insisted silently that she hadn't been lucky at all.

Now she realised she meant it, right down to her toes. She'd been lucky. She'd been blessed. And she still was. It was good to remind herself of it; it was even better to truly feel it, all the way through…and in no small part due to Roger Wentworth. If only he'd call…

"So what's this I hear about you and Roger Wentworth?" Henry asked when they'd all sat down to a supper of beef stew and dumplings in the cosy kitchen.

"Henry, don't," Alice shushed him. "You're being so nosy. Anyway, they're just friends."

Henry arched an eyebrow at Lindy, who laughed. "We really are friends," she told him and then added, with impish emphasis, "Good friends."

"Ooh, I knew there was a story there," Harriet said. "But I've pressed enough. You'll tell us when you're ready, won't you, Lindy?"

"Maybe."

"Next time, invite him with you," Alice insisted. "I've never even talked to the man—"

"He's lovely," Olivia said. "Truly."

Lindy sat back and sipped her wine, saying nothing. For once she didn't mind all their questions, because she knew every single one was motivated by kindness, and even love. How had she landed here in this comfortable kitchen, surrounded by people who knew and liked her? Admittedly, she'd never actually talked to Richard Lang before tonight, and she barely knew Owen, Emily's fiancé, but she liked them all and she'd count them as friends.

But not *good* friends. Not yet. Not like Roger.

She was still brimming with a sentimental sort of bonhomie when she tottered home to an undoubtedly anxious Toby a few hours later, under a silver sickle of moon. Simon had offered to walk her home, but Olivia had been deep in a chat with Alice, and Lindy hadn't wanted to break up the party. Besides, after so much conversation and commotion, she'd had a hankering to be alone, in the quiet of a still winter's evening.

As she came into the courtyard, she took out her phone. She'd resisted looking at it all afternoon and evening, and now her heart did a little dive as she saw the blank screen. No missed calls. No messages.

"Screw it," she muttered under her breath and she swiped to make a call. A few seconds later Roger's phone was ringing.

"Lindy?" He sounded concerned as he answered after the second ring. "Is everything all right?"

"Yes, why wouldn't it be?" she asked as she fumbled for her house key.

"Because it's nearly eleven o'clock at night, which I believe is considered an inconvenient time to telephone."

Oh, but he sounded so much like himself, and Lindy actually liked it. A lot. "True," she said solemnly as she unlocked her door and stepped inside. Toby skittered up to her and thrust his nose between her knees, as he always did. "Sorry, did I wake you?" she asked.

"No," he said after a pause. "Was there a reason why you were ringing?"

"Does there have to be one?" Lindy asked, realising as she said the words that she might be a bit tipsier than she'd thought. She had a reckless desire to say something she might regret later—but what if she didn't regret it?

"Usually there is a reason for someone ringing," Roger replied. "At least, that has been my experience of exchanges over the telephone."

"All right, then, the reason I called was because I wanted to hear your voice." Lindy flung herself onto an armchair and closed her eyes as Toby sprawled happily at her feet, relieved now his mistress was home. Had she really just said that?

"Hear my voice?" Roger repeated after a moment, sounding flummoxed. "Why?"

"Because you haven't rung or messaged me since we got back from Derbyshire. I was expecting you to."

"Were you? I don't believe I had given any indication of intending to do so."

"Oh, Roger." Lindy let out a groan. "I know you didn't *say*, but I thought you *would*. Don't you understand that?"

A long silence while he contemplated her question, or perhaps just stared into space. Who knew? "I suppose," he said after a moment. "You were hoping I would call to see how you were, after the incident in Derbyshire?"

"What incident are you referring to?"

"The damage done to your house, of course."

"Oh." She thought he'd meant their night together. Of course he hadn't meant that. Suddenly she felt horribly flat. This conversation wasn't going at all the way she'd been hoping it would.

"What incident did you think I meant?" Roger asked and Lindy opened her eyes to stare out at the dark night, her tiny garden gilded in silver by the slender crescent of moon.

"I just thought," she began stiltedly, "after everything

that happened in Derbyshire, we were—friends. The call-in-the-middle-of-the-night kind."

A pause that felt horrid. "I see," Roger said.

"Are we not?" Lindy asked, sounding far too woebegone.

"No—that is—we are. I'd like to think we are." He released a frustrated breath. "It's just, I'm not very good at this."

"At what?"

"Having a conversation on the phone, for a start. I never know what to say. And I can't see your face, so I don't know if you mean what you say or something else."

"I pretty much just told you what I meant," Lindy pointed out, but she felt a little cheered by his honesty.

"I know you did. I'm sorry, Lindy. I'm just…I'm really no good at this." He sounded both aggrieved and aggravated by his own failure in this matter, and more het up than she'd ever heard him before.

"Well, why don't you try to get better?" she suggested.

"How?"

"Well…" Lindy took a deep breath and forced herself onward. "You could ask me out."

The silence that followed was like a thunderclap. Lindy bit her lip to keep from taking the words back. *Still* more silence. What on earth was he thinking? Had she appalled him? Wrecked their friendship forever?

"Ask you out," he repeated neutrally. No help there in terms of what he might be thinking.

"If you wanted to," Lindy said, feeling the need for a caveat.

"Do you mean…" Roger paused. "On a…a date?" He sounded so hesitant, so incredulous, that Lindy didn't know whether to laugh or groan.

"Yes, of course I meant on a date, Roger," she exclaimed rather recklessly. "Do you want to go on a date with me?" Another pause, this one far too long. "*Say* something, Roger," she cried. "Don't you realise how I'm putting myself out here?"

"Very well, of course I want to," he practically snapped, and Lindy let out an incredulous laugh. She hadn't been expecting *that*.

"Oh…"

"I just didn't think that you…that you were… Oh, it doesn't matter."

"What *did* you think?"

"That we were friends. You kept saying how we were friends all the time."

"Good friends—"

"Yes, but *friends*. Very much friends. My colleague at work told me I'd been friend-zoned. Firmly friend-zoned, were his actual words."

"You talked to someone at work about me?"

"I didn't mention your name," Roger informed her stiffly. "I was merely asking for advice."

Lindy realised she was grinning. He'd been asking for

advice…! About *her*. "So are you going to ask me out?" she demanded. "On a date? A proper date?"

Yet another pause, but Lindy didn't mind this one so much. "Yes," Roger said at last, sounding surprised. "I believe I am."

Chapter Twenty

S O THIS WAS it. Make-or-break territory. An actual date. He'd been on plenty—well, several—before, so why was he so terrified?

Roger straightened the collar of his blue shirt—yes, he was wearing it again—as he gazed at his reflection in the mirror. Boring brown hair. Boring brown eyes. Crow's feet too, that were becoming more pronounced, and streaks of grey above his ears. He was getting old. The thought depressed him, not because of what he saw in the mirror, but because of where he was in life. Single. Childless. He wanted those things—a wife and a family—the same as most any other man, even if he'd never dared to think he could obtain them.

But now he had a date—and not just any date, but with someone he genuinely cared about. Someone he both feared and hoped he was falling in love with. Hence, the terror.

Taking a deep breath, Roger turned away from the mirror. He'd had to tell his mother about the date, because they normally watched telly together on a Saturday night—what a

life he led!—and she'd been, predictably and a bit worryingly, ecstatic.

"Oh, Roger." She'd clasped her hands together, eyes
shining. "I'm so happy for you. You and Lindy are perfect
for each other. I knew it from that first evening—"

"We're just going out to dinner," Roger warned her.
"Not getting engaged." Just saying the words felt forbidden,
dangerous. He feared he was going to start having heart
palpitations.

"I know," Ellen replied with a roll of her eyes. "But it's a
start, and remember, you're not getting any younger."

Thinking of his crow's feet and grey hair again, Roger
knew she spoke the truth—yet he still didn't want to rush
things, for his own safety as well as Lindy's. Well, mainly for
his own. The chance of humiliation, of hurt, was simply too
great.

He'd agreed to pick Lindy up at Willoughby Close, and
then they were driving to a restaurant on the outskirts of
Burford, a Michelin-starred place that he hoped wouldn't be
too la-di-da. He'd wanted to go somewhere nice, somewhere
neither of them had been before, but as he drove towards
Willoughby Close he wondered what on earth he'd been
thinking in choosing such an unknown. He didn't like
surprises. He didn't do well with them, and enough about
the very fact of tonight felt unexpected. At least he'd been
able to view the menu online, and decide what he was going
to order. That was one potential minefield avoided.

Willoughby Close was cloaked in darkness as Roger parked and walked up to the door of number two. He rapped smartly twice, and Lindy opened almost immediately.

"Hello, Roger." She smiled shyly, and Roger stared back, finding himself utterly silenced. She looked magnificent in a knit dress in forest green that clung in all the right places and then flared out around her calves. Her hair was half-up, half-down, so a few tendrils framed her face and the rest tumbled down her back. In her matching green heels, she was only an inch or two shorter than he was. When he tried to speak, he smelled vanilla, and he found suddenly he could neither speak nor think.

"Aren't you going to say hello?" she asked teasingly, and Roger managed to bark out, "Hello."

Lindy's eyes widened and he amended quickly, "I mean, hi. You look…" *Amazing. Gorgeous. Like the most beautiful woman I've ever seen.* "Green."

Lindy's eyes widened further as her mouth curved. "Green?"

"Great," he amended. "You look great." He exhaled in relief that he'd managed to navigate that moment tolerably well. At least Lindy was smiling.

"Thanks," she said, and she stepped out of her cottage, locking the door behind her.

They didn't speak in the car as they drove through the darkness towards Burford. Roger tried desperately to think of something to say, but his mind was insistently, utterly blank.

He focused on the road.

"How is your mum?" Lindy asked after a few minutes of tense silence.

"Good." He was barking again, each word bitten off and offered tersely, even though he didn't mean it to be. It just kept happening.

"Has she been very tired?"

"Yes."

"Oh."

Lindy turned to look out the window. Roger cursed himself.

"How are the rehearsals going for the performance?" he asked, grateful that he'd finally thought of a question. "The Year Sixes and the junior class?"

"The Year Sixes are going brilliantly," Lindy replied. "The junior class is a bit of a disaster, but I don't think anyone will mind. Seeing Ollie in his tuxedo will be enough of a show, I think." She let out a little laugh. "They have fun, at any rate, and they burn off a lot of energy."

"That's good."

And that was their conversation over. If Roger hadn't been driving, he would have closed his eyes. He could usually, with effort, make acceptable conversation, but tonight it felt impossible. The stakes were simply too high. The pressure in his chest felt too great.

"Where are we going, as a matter of interest?" Lindy asked after a few moments.

"The White Hare, outside Burford. It has a very good reputation and atmosphere."

"Sounds nice."

More silence. Thankfully they were almost there. Roger made an extra effort to seem as if he had to concentrate on driving, simply as an excuse not to talk. When it came to the companionable silences they'd once spoken about, he reflected miserably, this definitely wasn't one of them.

At last he pulled into the car park of the restaurant, which was lit by fairy lights, the sixteenth-century stone building decorated with Christmas holly and evergreen and looking both quaint and welcoming. The next few minutes were spent walking into the restaurant and then being shown to their table, precluding the need for conversation.

Their waiter handed them menus, and it only took Roger a few seconds to realise the menu had completely changed since he'd looked it up online three days ago.

"This isn't your menu," he blurted, while Lindy looked at him in surprise.

"It is, sir," the waiter replied smoothly. "We change our menu every few days, to make best use of fresh ingredients that are locally sourced."

"But I was going to have the sautéed chicken breast with tarragon cream, charred leeks and Reblochon pomme puree." He'd said the name of the entire dish, and belatedly he realised that was a bit weird. It was also weird that he was making a fuss about it, but it was just he was *thrown*.

"I would be happy to help you find an alternative dish on the menu, sir," the waiter said after an excruciating pause.

"No, no, that won't be necessary." Roger buried his nose in the menu as he tried to cover his gaffes. "I was simply taken by surprise."

The waiter gave a little bow and left and Roger inspected the short menu with an entirely affected studiousness, simply so he didn't have to look at Lindy and no doubt see the appalled expression on her face.

"You don't like surprises, do you?" she murmured after a few moments.

"I prefer to be prepared for all eventualities, which is why I looked at the menu online before we came," he said stiffly, knowing he probably sounded like a complete arse.

"Well, is there anything you like on this menu?" Lindy asked, her tone both reasonable and gentle and making him feel like even more ridiculous.

"I'm sure there is," he muttered, still staring at the menu. "I just wasn't expecting the change."

"I know."

More silence. Not companionable. This date, Roger was quickly realising, was a mistake. He'd much rather be Lindy's friend than wreck any potential romance. He'd far prefer holding her in his arms—and what exquisite agony that had been—than push her away completely. And his behaviour so far was definitely pushing her away. How could it not be?

"Have you reached a decision?" the waiter asked in a professionally urbane and deliberately blank voice. The man had already decided he was going to be a difficult customer, Roger was sure of it.

"I think I have," Lindy said. "Roger?"

In all his intent scrutiny of the menu, he hadn't actually managed to read it. "Ladies first," he said, as he scanned the list a bit frantically.

Lindy ordered the prosciutto starter and a steak, and in a moment of panicked recklessness Roger decided to order the fish, even though he didn't actually *like* fish. This was another unfortunate default of his—to panic and pick the worst option rather than the best or even the middling, mediocre one.

"I'll have the Cornish crab to start, and the sea bass with prawn tortellini, fennel puree, and the white wine sauce for my entrée."

"Very good, sir. And would you like any wine with your meal?"

Roger glanced at Lindy, who shrugged and smile. "I wouldn't mind a glass of your house red."

"I'll have the same. Thank you." He handed his menu back to the waiter, and so did Lindy, and then there they were, staring at each other with nothing to say, just as Roger had feared.

"Roger, you seem nervous," she said quietly, and for some reason he puffed up indignantly.

"I am not nervous."

"Well, I am," Lindy said candidly. "We're friends, and now we're on a date. It's a bit weird, isn't it?" She smiled, and Roger managed a small smile back.

"I suppose it is, a bit."

"Perhaps it doesn't have to be," Lindy suggested. "If we just remember that we're friends and we can talk to each other?"

Which had the effect of making him completely tongue-tied.

"I've decided to sell the house up in Derbyshire," Lindy said after a moment, clearly doing her valiant best to keep the conversation going. "I think it's time."

"You should do the repairs first, or you won't get a good price for it." Lindy stared at him, and Roger realised how unfeeling he'd sounded. "What I mean is…" He cleared his throat. "How do you feel about that decision?"

She smiled, and he breathed a hopefully silent sigh of relief that he'd navigated that potential pitfall without falling straight into it. "Sad but also at peace."

"Did you spend much time at the house, considering all the travel you did?"

"Enough. It was always the place that felt like home, and even more so after my parents died. Does that make sense?"

"I suppose, in a way," he said, and Lindy laughed.

"Oh, Roger, you don't think it does. It's okay. You can tell me so."

"I would expect that it felt far more of a home when your

parents were in it, but I suppose, upon reflection, I can understand that you might have been projecting more emotion onto the place than your actual experience warranted."

"Hmm. You might be right, there."

The waiter came back with their wine, which was a relief. They hadn't even had their starters yet and Roger already couldn't wait for the evening to be over. This was all so much more difficult than he'd hoped.

"Well, to first dates," Lindy said with a somewhat shaky laugh, and they clinked glasses. She took a sip of hers and then she replaced her glass on the table. "If you don't mind, I'll just nip to the loo."

"Of course." He lurched upright to a standing position, banging into the table and almost causing both of their wine glasses to topple over, as she smiled and excused herself. Roger slumped back into his seat. He felt exhausted, not to mention depressed by his own poor performance. What on earth was Lindy thinking?

LINDY WAS GLAD the ladies' was empty as she closed the door behind her with a sigh of relief. Goodness, but this was hard work. She'd been so looking forward to tonight ever since she'd rather recklessly asked Roger to ask her out, but in the forty-five minutes since he'd picked her up, she was starting to wonder if trying to turn their friendship into a romance was a good idea.

Roger certainly didn't seem to think so, judging by how awkward and difficult he was being. The man who had held her in the night, who had stroked her hair and been her rock, felt like a stranger. A fantasy.

But he wasn't, Lindy reminded herself as she touched up her make-up, frowning at her reflection in the mirror. The real Roger was the man who had held her in his arms, not this fussy stranger. This was just nervous Roger, the face he presented to the world because he found social situations difficult. She *knew* that, so she didn't have to let it bother her. She just had to find a way to get back the man she'd been falling in love with.

But how?

Well, she certainly couldn't do it while she was hiding in the loo. Briskly Lindy washed her hands, gave her reflection one last determined look, and then headed back into the fray.

By the time she got back to their table, their starters had arrived, and Roger was looking at his crab with something like dismay.

"Is everything all right?" Lindy asked as she took her seat.

"Yes, fine." He gave her a tense smile as he picked up his fork. "I was just waiting for you."

"This looks delicious," she said, and Roger didn't reply. She took a few bites of the melt-in-her-mouth slivers of prosciutto, only to glance up and see that Roger was toying with the first bite of crab that he had not yet eaten.

"Roger…?"

"Yes?"

"Is everything all right with your starter?"

He swelled up in that silly way of his that had once annoyed her but now made her want to smile. "Of course. Why wouldn't it be?"

"Well, because you're not eating it."

Roger sighed and put down his fork. "That's because I don't like fish. Well, not just fish. All seafood, but fish in particular."

"What?" A bubble of surprised laughter escaped Lindy as she looked at him in incredulity. "But didn't you order the crab *and* the sea bass?"

"Yes." He grimaced. "I have an unfortunate habit of panicking in a moment of crisis, and then choosing the worst option."

"What?" Lindy exclaimed. "I don't believe that. When I was flipping out all over town about my parents' house, you were as solid as a rock. Completely unflappable."

"Well, that's different."

"How?"

He shrugged. "It's not picking something off a menu, I suppose."

"So you panic with small decisions like what to eat but not when life is throwing its worst at you?"

"I've never thought about it in that particular way, but

perhaps."

"Well, I'd rather panic about what I order in a restaurant than fall to pieces when life gets hard."

He gave her a small, unhappy smile, and something reckless yet certain solidified in her centre, and then spread out. She *loved* this man. She really did. He could be quirky and difficult and sometimes just plain odd, but he was also steady and generous and tender and warm-hearted. She loved him. Lindy let out a laugh of pure, incredulous joy, and Roger gave a knowing, dispirited sigh, as if he thought she was mocking him rather than revelling in what she felt.

"You must be deeply regretting this whole endeavour," he said.

"I'm regretting this restaurant, yes," Lindy replied. "Because, to be honest, I think it's bringing out the worst in both of us."

"Not in you," Roger protested, and Lindy shook her head.

"I've been a mass of nerves. I might be the tiniest bit better than you at hiding it, though." She leaned forward, a new excitement sparking in her belly. "Do you want to get out of here?"

Roger's eyes widened. "What…?"

"Let's get out of here. I don't really want to eat this meal, and I don't think you do, either. It's a waste of money, I know, and I'll pay half—"

"You will not—"

"But let's just go. Let's run out of here and do something else. Something we want to do, rather than what we think a date should be."

She gazed at him, willing him to agree, wanting him to be brave enough to be uncharacteristically spontaneous.

"Just...leave?" Roger said as if he couldn't credit such a notion.

"Yes. Right now."

"I need to pay—"

"Okay, then. Pay, and we'll go."

He stared at her for another moment, and then he raised his hand for the waiter, who hurried over to their table. "The bill, please." Lindy grinned.

"I'm sorry, sir...?"

"We wish to leave early. Could I have the bill, please?"

"But the chef has already begun to make your main course—"

"I'll pay for the lot. There's nothing whatsoever wrong with the meal, we just wish to leave." Roger kept his gaze on Lindy and the excitement she'd been feeling flamed into something more elemental. Was she imagining that almost dark, dangerous look in his eye? This was Roger, after all.

"Very good, sir," the waiter said after an unhappy pause. Neither Lindy nor Roger spoke as they waited for the bill; she was afraid of breaking the sudden spell that had come over them, drawn them together. Her stomach was fizzing.

The waiter returned with the bill, and Roger paid it with

alacrity. Then they were taking their coats and heading out into the wintry night, the air sharp enough to steal her breath, the sky scattered with a million stars.

Lindy let out a shout of laughter as they came into the car park. "That was amazing."

"I've never done such a thing before in my entire life."

"I haven't, either," she confessed as she turned to him. "It was brilliant."

"It actually was," Roger said, sounding wondering. "Strangely."

"What shall we do now?" Lindy asked. The evening stretched ahead of them, empty yet filled with possibility.

"What would you like to do?"

They'd reached the car, and Lindy turned to him, about to suggest a takeaway and Netflix, but he was closer than she realised and, startled, she stumbled a little. Roger steadied her by putting his hands on her shoulders, and his eyes darkened as a thrill ran through her like lightning.

He kept his hands on her shoulders and she kept her gaze on his, parting her lips slightly, everything in her willing him to do what she desperately wanted him to do.

And then he did.

His mouth came down on hers as he kissed her, and it was everything she'd hoped for and more. His lips were soft and warm, and yet somehow they were hard and cool at the same time. They were perfect. His kiss was perfect, too—gentle yet firm, asking permission yet taking command.

Making her whole body spark and then flame. As far as kisses went, she'd never had better—and she never wanted to stop.

But Roger did stop, lifting his head to scan her face with his gaze as if asking a question, and with a trembling laugh Lindy answered it.

"You may panic in a crisis, Roger, but you certainly know how to kiss."

Chapter Twenty-One

"ONE, TWO, THREE; one, two, three!" Lindy clapped out the beat as four six-year-olds skidded around the floor, doing a vague approximation of a box step. Very vague.

Not that Lindy cared. Her junior class would win everyone's hearts no matter what, and the Year Sixes, since the addition of the hip hop mash up, were all working hard to produce a stellar routine. Her Monday class was also working hard; Simon and Olivia had finally decided to buckle down, and Helena was gamely partnering Maureen while Ellen valiantly continued on with Roger, even though she'd had to take several rests during the rehearsal.

Over a tea break she'd suggested to Helena that she invite her father to the performance; the young woman had let it slip that he lived in Cheltenham, not too far away, and impulsively Lindy had put the idea forward.

"Oh, I don't know…" Helena had looked both yearning and appalled. "What if he said no?"

"What if he didn't?" Lindy countered with a smile.

"You only live once, my girl," Maureen pitched in. "So you might as well give it all you've got, until you can't anymore." She grimaced as she rubbed her hip. "Trust me, I know."

"I'll think about it," Helena promised, and Ellen gave her an encouraging smile.

"You never know what could happen," she said warmly. "Life is full of surprises."

For a woman facing terminal cancer, it was a heart-rendingly optimistic viewpoint.

The performance was only two weeks away, and Lindy desperately hoped Ellen would have the energy for it. She knew Roger was worried, and he'd practised his dancing with an endearing diligence. He would never be light on his feet, but the man was certainly trying. And Lindy loved him for it.

She loved him, and she had a strange and nearly over-whelming urge to tell everyone so, although fortunately she had managed to curb the impulse. Still, the words kept bubbling up, and she found herself laughing suddenly, for no seeming reason. People probably thought she was going crazy, and maybe she was. She felt like dancing down the street, singing out loud, floating. Everything made her happy. The world felt as if it were sparkling.

It helped that, with the onset of December, Wychwood-on-Lea had gone into full Christmas mode. The high street was decked out in lights and evergreen, and every little shop had a magnificent window display of candles, wreaths, lights, or all three. There was an enormous Christmas tree in the centre of the village green, and Lindy and Roger had watched the lights being switched on one frosty night, holding hands, hearts full. At least Lindy's was.

They hadn't actually gone on many dates since that first sweetly sizzling kiss in the car park. After Roger had kissed her, he'd grinned self-consciously and they'd got in the car and done just what Lindy had hoped—had a takeaway while watching a movie back at her cottage. And they'd kissed again—and again—although it hadn't gone further and Lindy was actually just fine with that. She suspected she and Roger were more tortoise than hare when it came to romance.

They were also pretty uncommunicative when it came to the status of their relationship. There had been no 'we're now dating' conversation, which Lindy had thought Roger would have wanted to have, since he liked to be prepared for all eventualities. However, he seemed as content as she was simply to let things unspool in a glittering, golden thread. Where it led was not something either of them felt the need to discuss as of yet.

"So, I hear there's a new man in your life," Ishbel remarked when she was picking up Emma from the junior class, after the four tykes had tired themselves out racing around and pretending to waltz.

"I do," Lindy replied, feeling a slightly scary sense of liberation in admitting it. The last time she'd had a boyfriend had been over five years ago, and it hadn't lasted long. Already things with Roger felt far more serious, at least in her own head. Her own heart.

"Exciting stuff. Tell me more?"

Lindy glanced at Will and Liz, who were both listening in on the conversation with undisguised interest.

"There's not much more to tell," Lindy said. "It's all rather new, to be honest. How did you even know?"

"Nothing's secret in this village," Ishbel said with a laugh. "A friend of mine saw you and a tall bloke holding hands during the Christmas-tree lighting. She recognised you as the Year Six dance teacher."

"Ah." Lindy nodded knowingly. "Word does seem to get around."

"Is he a dancer?" Ishbel asked, and Lindy thought of Roger's stiff, deliberate movements around the dance floor.

"Yes," she said. "He is."

"Well, good luck," Ishbel said with a smile. "It sounds exciting."

"It is," Lindy assured her. "And thank you."

She was humming as she left the dance studio; she'd agreed to meet Roger at his cottage, so they could drive into Oxford for the afternoon and go Christmas shopping. Another date. Was it silly that she felt so excited? Lindy didn't care.

Her heart turned over simply at the sight of him opening

the door, looking so very Roger-like in his off-duty uniform of a button-down shirt and khakis.

"Do you own a pair of jeans?" Lindy asked after she'd stepped inside and Roger had kissed her cheek. He stepped back, frowning slightly.

"Is there a reason why you're enquiring about the nature of my wardrobe?"

"Just curious," she answered with a smile.

"Well then, the answer is I do possess one pair. I usually wear them for painting or other DIY projects."

"That makes sense," Lindy answered, and Roger shook his head.

"Why are we talking about this?"

"I was just wondering." She laughed at the perplexed look on his face. "Don't worry. I don't care what you wear."

"Good, because I thought you were about to give me a makeover," Roger replied dryly. "Shall we go?"

IT WAS EXCEEDINGLY pleasant, to wander down a festooned Cornmarket Street in Oxford, holding hands with Lindy and admiring all the Christmas-themed window displays. Almost too pleasant, because as much as he tried, Roger couldn't shake the feeling that this was all going to go up in smoke at any second, as soon as he put a foot wrong or Lindy came to her senses. It was only a matter of time; that had been his experience before, after all, although he didn't feel he could even compare his past relationships to what he felt for Lindy.

With Lindy, he could be himself. It amazed him that she didn't actually want him to change, and yet even so he couldn't keep from wondering if there was an agenda, or perhaps just a disappointment, underneath her smiling cheer—what had been that remark about jeans, anyway? He knew his clothes were boring; *he* was boring. Was Lindy only just coming to realise that? Would it put her off, as she began to realise the extent of his non-jean-wearing self?

As they stopped in front of an enormous Christmas tree and listened to a pair of talented buskers belt out 'Hark the Herald Angels Sing' to the rather surprising accompaniment of an acoustic guitar and a tambourine, Roger did his best not to worry about it. He just wanted to enjoy this moment, as he had every other with Lindy since he'd kissed her outside of The White Hare, and their friendship had turned into something wonderfully more.

Two weeks on, it still felt new and strange, and rather miraculous.

"Alice and Henry up at Willoughby Manor have invited us for dinner," Lindy told him when they were having a coffee in the Waterstones café overlooking the busy street. She spoke casually, but there was a deliberate lightness to her voice that Roger suspected was affected rather than real.

"Alice and Henry?" he repeated guardedly. "I don't believe I know them."

"You don't, but they know about us—" this was said

with a slight blush "—and with the dress rehearsal for the performance less than a week away, they'd like to get to know you."

The dress rehearsal. That was something else Roger had been trying not to worry, or even think, about. Despite several weeks of rehearsals, he was still as heavy-footed as ever. He was going to look ridiculous, trying to foxtrot and samba, but at least Maureen, Helena, Simon and Olivia weren't all that much better. His mother was the best of the class, and she was determined to shine. Too bad he wouldn't be shining with her, but he'd given his word and he would go through with it, even if the prospect brought only dread.

"Roger?" Lindy prompted. "I thought we could go to dinner on Wednesday. The dress rehearsal is Friday, the ball Saturday. A busy week."

"I am aware of the dates of those events," he replied, his tone a bit sharp to hide his unease. Lindy didn't look fooled.

"I know you are," she said with a smile. "So dinner is okay?" She looked so anxious, her eyes clouded as she nibbled her lip, and somehow that hurt. *He* was making her anxious, because she feared a simple dinner with friends might be beyond him. And the truth was, she could be right.

"Dinner is okay," Roger repeated. At least he hoped it would be.

Lindy's smile was like sunlight breaking through clouds. "Thank you, Roger," she said, touching his hand, and he gave her a rather tense smile.

"Don't thank me until it's over."

She reached over to kiss his cheek, and Roger breathed in her vanilla scent, a burst of happiness in his chest at the sight and feel of her. "I'm thanking you before, because I know having dinner with people you don't know in a place you've never been is not your favourite thing to do. And I'll thank you after, for doing it."

"Hopefully you will," Roger muttered, but he was smiling simply because of her.

"MY MAN, ROGER." Chris clapped him rather forcefully on the shoulder. "How is the great romance going?"

Roger had informed his colleague last week that he had 'moved decisively out of the friend zone,' to which Chris had crowed with delight and given him a fist bump that Roger had rather clumsily returned. Now, on Monday morning in the office kitchen, Chris forewent any banter about raves for the lowdown on Lindy, not that Roger had any intention of imparting many salient details.

"It's going very well, thank you," he said, and poured boiling water into his mug.

"Yeah?" Chris looked pleased. "Any hot dates planned for the weekend?"

"While I would not use such a term, we are going out to dinner with some acquaintances on Wednesday." Roger paused, wondering why he was actually contemplating asking for romantic advice from a spotty-chinned, gel-haired twenty-three-year-old. "I confess I'm slightly apprehensive about the evening, and what it might entail for our relationship."

Chris's forehead wrinkled as he considered Roger's statement. "You're nervous?" he finally said. "Why?"

Roger shrugged as he poured milk into his tea. "You might be able to surmise, considering your experience of our working life together, that I am not the most adept at social situations."

"Ah, Roger." Chris clapped a hand on his shoulder again, making Roger spill the milk. "I'll admit, when I first met you, I thought you were a bit of a spod, but once I got to know you, I realised you were all right. More than all right."

Roger didn't know what a spod was, but he thought he could guess. "Hence, my apprehension," he told Chris tartly. "Upon our first acquaintance, you remained unimpressed."

"Well…yeah." Chris nodded in agreement as he took a slurp of sugary coffee. "But, you know, be friendly and all that and you should be fine."

"Thank you for that excellent advice, as always." Roger turned to go with his tea, still feeling apprehensive about Wednesday evening.

"And, you know, Rog," Chris continued with a surprising earnestness, "you want people to like you for who you are, not who you are trying to be. So…just be yourself. If they think you're an anorak, then so what?"

An *anorak*? "Why would they think I was a raincoat?" Roger asked in bafflement, and Chris let out a bray of laughter.

"An anorak! You know, a nerd, someone who would never leave the house without an umbrella."

"Or an anorak."

"Exactly." Chris grinned at him.

Or a handkerchief, Roger thought, remembering Lindy's teasing comment about his own neatly pressed one. He was indeed an anorak, it seemed.

LINDY WAS FEELING nervous, more nervous than she'd expected to, and mainly on Roger's behalf. As the days had passed she could tell he was semi-dreading this evening's dinner with Alice and Henry, and that in turn was making her anxious. What if it all went pear-shaped? Was this just the beginning of a lifetime of smoothing things over when they got awkward or uncomfortable?

"Don't get ahead of yourself, my girl," Lindy told her reflection as she touched up her eye make-up and then glanced critically at her outfit—a silk blouse in forest green with a pair of dark skinny jeans and her requisite high heels. Smart but casual, or so she hoped. She pressed her hand to her middle as butterflies swarmed.

She couldn't figure out if she was nervous for Roger's sake, or for her own. Was she worried he'd decide the effort of relationships—including the one with her—wasn't worth the aggro? Or was she worried *she* was going to decide that?

Lindy took a deep breath and let it out slowly. Sensing her agitation, Toby pressed his bony head against her leg and she bent down to give him a quick, loving stroke. She'd been on her own a long time, and Roger even longer. The last few weeks had been wonderful, but they'd also been fairly low-key. A walk along the river, the afternoon in Oxford, an evening watching Netflix. It was as if they were both afraid to ramp it up, to get intense.

And yet at the same time, Lindy thought, part of her *craved* that. Part of her wanted to grab Roger by the lapels and ask him to marry her, while another part wanted to hide under her duvet. She felt schizophrenic in her emotions, careening wildly from one extreme to the other, backing away even as she longed to lunge forward, and vice versa. Did Roger feel the same?

She knew this was new territory for him, as well, and new territory was uncomfortable, uncertain, sometimes difficult. What if he decided to back off? What if she did?

The doorbell rang, and Toby sent up a chorus of frenzied barking, a habit she'd yet to train him out of. With one last, fleeting look in the mirror, Lindy hurried downstairs.

"Roger!" She smiled to see him standing there, looking so severe. "You look nice."

"I'm wearing my blue shirt."

"So you are."

"I do own other shirts, of course, but my mother keeps insisting I wear this one to any social function."

"I like your blue shirt," Lindy assured him, and then because he looked so serious and really rather adorable, she put her arms around him and kissed him.

Roger pulled her closer, kissing her quite thoroughly, reminding Lindy that while certain aspects of their relationship might have their concerns, this one did not. She didn't think she'd ever get tired of kissing him.

Roger pulled away slightly, his hands resting lightly yet firmly on her waist. "I might make an idiot of myself tonight," he told her. "Be warned."

"I am warned," Lindy said with a laugh. She laid one hand against his cheek. "And I don't care if you make an idiot of yourself tonight, Roger."

"You don't?" He looked at her seriously, and she nodded.

"I just want to be with you, idiot or not."

"I suppose that is something of a compliment."

Lindy laughed again, and kissed him once more for good measure. "It is," she said. "Trust me."

THEY WALKED HAND in hand towards Willoughby Manor, the trees and bushes that lined the sweeping drive bedecked with sparkling Christmas lights. It was only a little over a fortnight until Christmas, and Lindy was starting to feel rather festive; Wychwood-on-Lea was decorated to the hilt, and besides the ball, there was a full run of holiday events—a community carol sing, several services at the church, an evening of the requisite mulled wine and mince pies at Ava and Jace's. She was looking forward to it all.

She'd bought Roger a Christmas present, although she still didn't know whether they would spend the day together as they hadn't had that discussion, and she felt a bit nervous bringing it up. Perhaps he wanted to be alone with Ellen, since it would most likely be her last Christmas. In any case, no matter how they spent the day, she could still give him a present. It had been nice to have someone to buy a present for. She'd enjoyed selecting it and wrapping it, and she wanted to watch Roger open it, whether that was on Christmas Day or not.

"So this is the manor," Roger remarked as they came to the front door of the stately building, candles glinting and flickering in its downstairs windows and a large wreath decorating its front door. "Where I shall meet my dancing doom."

"I thought you did very well in Monday's rehearsal," Lindy reassured him. Admittedly, all three of her classes had stumbled a bit as they'd practised their routines for the last time before the dress rehearsal this week, but their hearts were all in the right place and she firmly believed—well, hoped, anyway—that once they were in the manor's ballroom, with its mirrored walls and chandeliers, the music swelling up and everyone watching, they would rise magnificently to the occasion, Roger included.

"Lindy!" Henry threw open the door as soon as Lindy had knocked, and gave her a wide smile and then Roger an appraising look.

"And you must be Roger."

"You are correct," Roger replied as they shook hands. As she looked at the pair of them, Lindy realised they were wearing almost identical outfits of khakis and blue button-down shirts; the only difference was Henry's shirt was a darker blue and had cufflinks. For some reason the realisation made her start to laugh.

Both men turned to look at her in politely baffled enquiry, and their expressions were so similar that Lindy found herself laughing harder, one hand clutching her stomach.

"What on earth's going on here?" Alice asked, smiling, as she came round the corner, only to stop as she took in the sight—Lindy now helpless with laughter, and Henry and Roger standing side by side, both looking bemused. "Oh," she said.

"Roger and I are scratching our heads here, trying to figure out what's so funny," Henry said, doing his best to be a genial host. Lindy feared she might be annoying him with her amusement, but honestly, there was just something hilarious about them standing together like that.

"It's just," Alice said, "you look a bit like twins."

"Twins…you mean, what we're wearing?" Henry asked as he inspected himself.

"We are wearing quite similar clothes," Roger allowed.

"It's more than the clothes," Alice said thoughtfully, her hands on her hips. "I think...actually...you're quite similar in looks and perhaps even in personality. Henry, you have darker hair, and Roger, you're taller, but...there is definitely a vibe going on."

"A vibe?" Henry repeated blankly.

"I think," Roger offered, "that your wife is implying we are of a similar nature." He paused. "That is, I think we might both be...anoraks."

"You mean raincoats?" Henry exclaimed, truly baffled now, and Lindy laughed harder, all her anxieties swept away in a moment. As Henry and Roger gave each other commiserating smiles, she thought the evening was going to be just fine.

Chapter Twenty-Two

"I T'S A GOOD thing everything's going wrong, right?"
Lindy's voice took on a ragged, manic edge as she gave
Alice a half-crazed look. It was the Friday afternoon before
the ball, and the day of the dress rehearsal for the performance.

Lindy had thought she'd been organised—having her
four six-year-olds come first, and then the Year Sixes, and
finally her evening class, which was how the order of perfor-
mances would go on the night. Everyone had practised,
outfits had been approved, the speakers set up, and Lindy
had even made flyers to hand out to guests in case they were
interested in classes.

Despite all that, at half past four on Friday afternoon she
felt as if things were falling apart. First there had been Ollie,
her little superstar who was so excited to perform at the
ball...until he'd tried on his beloved tuxedo and found it no
longer fit.

"He's had a growth spurt," Will explained helplessly.
"He's devastated."

So devastated he no longer wanted to dance in the performance, which had left Emma without a partner, and therefore in tears. Lindy had only just managed to cheer Ollie up enough to at least try dancing in the ballroom with the cool mirrors when she'd received a text from Dan Rhodes, the primary school's head teacher, telling her that five of the twenty-eight Year Sixes were backing out.

"Five?" Lindy had told Alice. *"Five?"*

"Cold feet?" Alice had surmised with a sympathetic smile, but Lindy had felt like tearing her hair out. She was going to have to re-choreograph the whole thing, and it meant one pupil was without a partner.

"Nothing had better go wrong with the evening class," she told Alice rather savagely as she downed a cup of tea in the manor kitchen. The house was decorated to the hilt and looked absolutely gorgeous—scented with evergreen and cinnamon, the tree in the foyer its crowning glory. It was eleven days before Christmas and yesterday morning it had actually snowed. Only a little—barely a dusting—but Lindy had been happy to see it.

In general, until this disaster of a dress rehearsal, she'd been very happy indeed. The dinner with Alice and Henry had been, somewhat to both her and Roger's surprise, a roaring success—Henry and Roger had talked business and then detective novels of all things while Alice and Lindy had gossiped about village life and then they'd both glanced at Henry and Roger nattering away—well, Roger was mainly listening, but still—and Alice had rolled her eyes.

"BFFs, those two are," she said.

Later, in the kitchen, Lindy had helped with the washing up while Henry and Roger had gone to bring in more firewood.

"Hunting and gathering at its modern best," Alice had teased. "I'm sure they feel very manly."

Lindy had enjoyed chatting with Alice, and she'd even been bold enough to ask her if everything was all right; there had been that brittleness from before, and occasionally Lindy wondered if it was back again.

"Everything's wonderful," Alice assured her and then said with a little, uncertain laugh, "Actually brilliant. It's too early to start shouting it from the rooftops, but…I'm pregnant."

"Oh, Alice, that's wonderful!"

"I only found out a few weeks ago," Alice confessed. "And we've been trying for a while. I even had some tests done, when I was worried something might be wrong. But nothing was, and now I'm pregnant and it's wonderful, but I feel as if I'm walking on eggshells. I'm afraid something's going to go wrong." She gave an abashed smile as Lindy hugged her.

"I don't blame you, especially when you've been working yourself down to the bone over the ball! You must let me help more."

"I'll take you up on that, actually," Alice said. "I'm exhausted."

"That went better than I expected," Roger told Lindy later, as they walked back to Willoughby Close. "Far better."

"Perhaps we can do it again sometime," Lindy had said teasingly, and Roger had given her a serious look.

"Sometime," he agreed, "but not too soon."

That had only been two days ago, but it felt like a lifetime as Lindy had dashed about the village, sorting out last-minute costume changes—the Year Sixes were all wearing black with either red or green sashes, but it had been late in the day when Lindy had realised they needed more fabric—as well as completing the safeguarding assessments and checking she had permission slips from every parent.

She'd also been doing her best to take some of the burden of preparation off Alice, and had been running around fetching last-minute decorations for the ball—another dozen champagne flutes, ten more yards of crimson ribbon. Her head felt as if it were in a thousand places, and she'd nearly cried with relief when Roger had shown up at the manor at three o'clock with a six-pack of Coke and a smile.

"Why aren't you at work?" she'd exclaimed as she'd reached for one of the cans.

"I took the afternoon off. I need to get ready for my big performance." But what he'd actually done was help her with all the last-minute details, including giving Ollie a cheering speech and the offer of a fedora, which Ollie decided he'd prefer to a tuxedo.

"I did not think you were the type of man to have a fedora," Lindy told him, and Roger had raised his eyebrows as he gave her what she thought was meant to be a mysterious look.

"There are many things you don't know about me," he said, and then, smiling wryly, added, "It was a joke gift at an office Christmas party. Do you think he'll mind that it's made of plastic?"

Fortunately Ollie didn't.

"Back into the fray," Lindy told Alice a bit grimly as she finished her tea and headed out of the kitchen. She needed to do a final run through with what remained of the Year Sixes before the last practice for her evening class. Roger had already left to fetch his mother.

"It's going to be fine," Alice assured her. "And remember what you said yourself—it's not about having a performance of superstars, it's about getting a community together and supporting one another, as well as having fun."

"Right." Except now that the moment had almost arrived, Lindy realised she'd like to be able to show off a little, or at least not have her performance be a complete disaster.

"Right, you lot," she told the Year Sixes who were milling around the ballroom, having been plied with Penguin biscuits and hot chocolate, "it's time to get down to business. I know we've made some changes, but I'm sure you can do this."

To compensate for the poor girl who no longer had a partner, Lindy had choreographed a switching in and out of partners for the waltz sections, with one person whirling in and out of the couples. She just hoped it worked. At least the hip-hop section still did; the deserters hadn't been keen on that part either, and she hoped the whole performance was stronger without the lurkers, although she still wished they'd decided to take part.

"Ready, one, two, three…!" She turned on the music, and the dancing began. It did work, she realised, even with a bit of stumbling and fumbling, and the kids who were here were glad to be here. Her heart filled up with hope and gratitude, and she laughed out loud when the music changed to a street beat and the pupils moved from a waltz to break dancing.

"That is brilliant," Alice enthused as she came to the doorway of the ballroom. "I absolutely love it."

Forty-five minutes later, the weary Year Sixes were trooping out, and Lindy headed back to the kitchen to grab a quick bite with Alice and Henry before her last rehearsal of the evening. Roger and his mother had been hoping to join them, but as the rehearsal ended, Lindy got a text saying they'd have to eat at home to conserve Ellen's energy.

"How is she doing?" Alice asked with a frown as she dished out beef stew and dumplings and Lindy collapsed into the armchair with the cat Andromeda on her lap.

"She's hanging in there," Lindy said as a pang of sorrow tore at her heart. She'd seen Ellen several times in the last few weeks, and on every occasion she'd seemed just a little more tired, a little bit *less*. It was heartbreaking to watch, and yet she couldn't help but admire Ellen's steely spirit. She was determined to dance.

"How are all the preparations for the ball going?" Lindy asked as the three of them dug into their dinners. "The house looks amazing."

"I think it's all in hand," Alice as she glanced at Henry. "You did pick up the champagne, didn't you?"

"Of course I did," Henry assured her. "As well as some sparkling elderflower cordial." He gave her a smiling look and Alice blushed prettily.

"We're having the food catered—just hors d'oeuvres and cakes—but Henry was in charge of the alcohol."

"A fearsome responsibility," Lindy said with a smile. She was looking forward to the party part of the evening, at least once the dancing was over. Butterflies swarmed again as she thought of all her pupils, ready to dance their hearts out. She so hoped it went well, for their sakes more than her own.

She knew what a huge confidence booster it could be to dance well in public; when she'd taken part in several local competitions during her Sixth Form years she'd felt as if she were flying on top of the world. She wanted that for her pupils—for them to feel good about themselves and what they'd accomplished, not least of all Roger, who she knew was still approaching the performance the way someone might a tooth extraction. Necessary but painful and deeply unpleasant.

Lindy helped Alice clear up after dinner, and then went to set up for her last rehearsal of the day. Outside night had fallen, and the ballroom, with its mirrors and chandeliers, felt both cosy and elegant.

Helena arrived first, her cheeks red with cold as she unwound a massive scarf from around her neck. "You'll never believe it, Lindy! My dad is coming tomorrow night!"

"Helena, that's wonderful." Lindy gave her a quick hug. "I'm so, so pleased."

"Now I just need not to fall on my face," Helena said wryly.

"You haven't yet," Lindy reminded her. "And you are very light on your feet."

Simon and Olivia came in next, followed by Maureen, and as Lindy greeted them all she sneaked a peek at her phone, hoping for a message from Roger, but there was nothing. It was after seven and she needed to start the dress rehearsal, but she hated the thought of beginning without Ellen.

"Why don't I start walking you through the steps," she suggested, and Olivia gave her a worried look.

"Is Ellen okay?"

"Yes, she's just conserving her energy." Lindy tried to look cheerful. "She'll be here soon, I'm sure. I know she wouldn't miss it for the world."

"Of course not," Olivia returned quickly, and an unhappy silence followed as they all contemplated why Ellen might miss it. But no, of course she couldn't. Wouldn't. She'd had so much strength and good humour so far, Lindy thought. Surely she could keep going another twenty-four hours?

"They're here," Maureen announced in a tone of great satisfaction. "I knew Ellen would come."

"Roger…" Lindy almost ran to hug him before she remembered that she'd kept their dating status on the down low for her dance class, at least until after the ball, mainly to avoid Maureen's unfiltered comments.

"Hello, everyone." Ellen's smile was wan but determined and she clutched Roger's arm. She looked as if a single breath could blow her away, and for a moment Lindy wondered if she should even be here. What if this was simply too much for her?

"Is this going to be okay?" she asked Roger in a low voice as she set up the music. "I don't want your mum to do something that could endanger her…"

"She's absolutely insistent." Roger smiled tiredly. "I told her not to come. She's been sleeping all day, and she hasn't eaten anything since yesterday." His mouth tightened as he shook his head. "But she refused. This is what she wants."

Lindy laid a hand on his arm. "I'm so sorry…"

"She's happy," he said simply. "That's what matters."

Still, Lindy strove to keep things easy as she put on the music and had everyone walk, rather than dance, through their steps. Roger had brought a chair for Ellen to sit in between practices, and she ended up sitting out the samba, assuring everyone she was fine but she wanted to conserve her energy, and she was "brilliant at the samba, anyway."

"You certainly are," Lindy agreed, even though her heart was breaking. There was something so tragic about Ellen's determination, as well as incredibly inspiring.

"I'm trying not to cry," Olivia whispered during their tea break, "but if you're wondering why I keep nipping to the loo, that's why."

Lindy gave her a sympathetic smile. She'd felt near tears herself on more than one occasion, but she was doing her best to keep a stiff upper lip for Ellen's sake. She knew how important this was to her.

"I know you're trying to keep things low-key for my sake," Ellen told her when she'd taken the cups back to the kitchen, following her into the cosy room with an effort that alarmed Lindy, "but please don't. I'm well aware this is my last hurrah, Lindy. I'm conserving energy for *this*, not for something later."

"But there's still Christmas…" Lindy protested rather feebly. She didn't know how to handle the steely glint in Ellen's eye.

"By Christmas I'll be in hospice. Roger doesn't want to admit it, but it was always going this way. I made the reservation myself. I can go in the day after the ball."

"Does Roger know?" Lindy asked, because he certainly hadn't mentioned it to her.

"I've told him," Ellen said with a sigh. "But he always

says we can talk about it later. Unfortunately, that only works for so long."

"But I'm sure he'd want to be with you for Christmas," Lindy said gently. "Don't you think so? A…a last Christmas together?"

"I'd rather hoped he'd spend it with you," Ellen told her with a smile. "You love him. At least, I think you do." Lindy blushed, and Ellen smiled in understanding. "I'm afraid I've become a bit plainer in my speech. That happens when you know your days are running out."

"I do love him," Lindy said in a low voice. "Although I haven't told him yet."

"There's time enough for that. But I can't tell you how much it helps, knowing he won't be alone. I realise how difficult and prickly Roger can be sometimes, but I'm sure you know as well as I do now what a good heart he has."

"I do," Lindy assured her.

"Please be patient with him," Ellen entreated quietly. "He doesn't do well with emotions, especially hard ones. He might…he might shut down when I go into hospice. When I die." Her throat worked but she managed to continue steadily, "He did a bit, when his father died. Didn't want to talk or even see anyone. It took a lot of effort, a lot of love, to bring him out of himself. Please don't take it to heart."

"I won't," Lindy promised, even though she quailed inwardly at the emotional challenges that were sure to lie ahead. "But in the meantime, let's think about you and what you need—"

"What I need," Ellen assured her, "is a night of dancing. So let's get on with it!"

Back in the ballroom everyone was milling around, waiting for the final practice of the performance. Taking a deep breath, Lindy turned to them all with a purposeful smile.

"This is it, everyone! Last chance before the big day. So give me your brightest smiles, your best moves—heads up, shoulders out, feet moving! Let's go!"

She started the music as the three couples took their positions. Her heart expanded with love at the sight of Roger holding his mother so tenderly, moving her around the floor with both gentleness and surprising finesse. Simon and Olivia were actually doing okay too, and Maureen and Helena were gamely whirling around, Maureen taking the lead. Lindy's heart filled with both hope and joy. It was going to *work*. It was going to be beautiful.

In the next moment everything seemed to shift and tilt—Ellen stumbled, and Roger caught her in his arms. Olivia noticed, and took a step away from Simon, and even as the music continued and swelled, Lindy felt as if it had stopped, as if the whole world had gone silent.

"Ellen…" she began, only to stop in horrified surprise as Ellen sagged in Roger's arms, her head lolling back as she went unconscious.

Chapter Twenty-Three

"SHE'S BEEN PUSHING it a bit too hard, I'm afraid."

The A&E consultant gave Roger a sympathetic look and he nodded mechanically back. There was a buzzing in his ears, a blankness in his brain. He didn't think he'd said anything coherent since he'd come to the hospital in Oxford two hours ago. He hadn't even *thought* anything coherent. From the moment his mum had collapsed to now—the call to 999, the ambulance that had come, the terrifying ride while she'd lain so still and unresponsive and they'd given her oxygen—all of it had created a white, buzzing blankness inside him that he couldn't seem to shift. Even now he simply stared at the consultant who seemed to be waiting for him to speak. There was a plastic holly wreath on the door of the little room where he'd been asked to wait.

"But..." Roger licked his lips as he finally spoke. "She's going to be okay, isn't she? I mean..." He trailed off, because of *course* she wasn't going to be okay. His mother terminal cancer; she was determined to go into hospice in just two days' time. She was dying. She wasn't *okay*.

"Her cancer has certainly progressed," the consultant answered carefully. "According to her notes, she was going into hospice shortly…?"

"Yes, but…" Again he trailed off. He'd refused to engage with his mother about the hospice thing *still*. It had been foolish but had felt necessary, but now he saw it was only selfish. He hadn't wanted to think about it. He'd just wanted life to be simple for a little while, to enjoy his time with Lindy without worrying about anything else, including his own mother.

He was a *cad*.

"So what happens now?" he asked into the void of ignorance he'd allowed himself to linger in.

"Your mother is insistent that she go directly into hospice," the consultant answered. "She can stay in hospital here overnight, and be transferred to the hospice in Burford tomorrow."

"Tomorrow?" Somehow, even now, he hadn't expected this. "But the ball," he said stupidly. Of course his mother wasn't going to the ball. She wasn't going to dance the way she'd intended to. The way she'd dreamed.

"Why don't you talk to her?" the consultant urged. "She's awake now, although she's tired. I'm sure she'd be very happy to see you."

Wordlessly Roger nodded. He left the depressing little room he'd been sitting in where people received bad news. Lindy had wanted to accompany him to the hospital, but

Roger had refused. He hadn't wanted to detract from the preparation for the ball, her big day, but he also hadn't wanted her to see him in such a moment of weakness.

In any case, he knew this turn of events would detract from, if not completely derail, the ball. Everything had changed, and yet nothing had. It was just he hadn't wanted to realise it had already changed.

Slowly he walked to the ward where his mother was. The curtains had been pulled around her bed and he slipped between them quietly. Ellen opened her eyes as he came in, smiling wanly.

"Roger." She raised one hand towards him and then let it fall back onto the bed. "I'm sorry to have caused so much fuss."

"Don't," Roger said, his voice thick with emotion, "be sorry. For anything."

Her eyes fluttered closed briefly before she opened them again. "I hope you're not here to argue with me."

"No, I'm not," Roger replied. He felt as if his heart were breaking—literally rending in two. He had an urge to clutch at his chest.

"I'm going into hospice tomorrow," Ellen stated firmly.

"Yes." He drew a breath. "If you're absolutely sure…"

"I'm sure."

"But Christmas…"

"You can visit me on the day, Roger." She paused, closing her eyes again in a way that made Roger panic. *Don't close your eyes*, he wanted to say. *Don't leave me like that.* "I'm not trying to hurt you," she said, her voice so soft he had to strain to hear it. "But the truth is, I'm amazed I got this far. I'm tired, Roger. So very tired. I can't cope for another two weeks, putting a brave face on it. I just…can't." The words seemed to exhaust her, and she sagged against the pillows, her eyes closing once more. For a few moments, as Roger watched in helpless misery, he wondered if she'd fallen asleep.

Finally, after several endless minutes, she opened her eyes again. "Spend Christmas with Lindy," she urged.

Roger had nothing to say to that. He and Lindy hadn't spoken about Christmas; really, they hadn't spoken about anything. They'd been existing in a happy bubble of romance and kisses, but the problem with bubbles was, they broke. They didn't last.

"Roger," Ellen prompted. "Tell me you'll spend Christmas with Lindy."

"I…" Roger shrugged helplessly. "I'll talk to her about it."

"Good." Ellen closed her eyes again, resting once more before she opened them and gazed at him with steely determination. "And promise me one other thing."

"What other thing?" Roger asked, even though he knew it didn't matter. He'd promise his mother anything.

"Promise me you'll dance at the ball. With Lindy."

"The ball…" He stared at her in shock. "Mum, I can't go

to the ball now—"

"You can and you will. I've been looking forward to it for too long to miss it now." She smiled faintly. "The nurse has told me I can watch it on my laptop, on Zoom, of all things."

"Zoom…"

"Yes, she'll set it up, and all you have to do is bring your laptop to the ballroom and make sure the camera is aimed at the dance floor. It's apparently very simple. Please, Roger. For me." Exhausted by her little speech, Ellen let her eyes flutter closed again before she opened them and gave him a rather beady look. "Say you will."

Wordlessly, helplessly, Roger nodded.

THE NIGHT BEFORE the ball, Lindy barely slept. She'd returned from Willoughby Manor in a daze, worried and heartsick about Ellen…and Roger. She wished he'd agreed to let her come to the hospital with him; perhaps she should have insisted. Yet the last thing she'd wanted to do was insert herself into an important moment between mother and son.

Still, she longed to hear something from Roger. She'd texted him twice, and then spent an hour pacing the downstairs of her cottage while Toby watched her and whined. Alice, Olivia, and Helena had all texted her, and Maureen had rung, everyone asking for news, but there wasn't any. Lindy's nerves were completely shot from the uncertainty and fear. *What if…*

But, no. She couldn't let herself even think it.

Then, finally, at a little after eleven, Roger rang.

"She's going into hospice tomorrow," he said abruptly, without any greeting, while Lindy breathed a silent sigh of relief that the news wasn't worse.

"I'm so sorry, Roger."

"She won't dance at the ball. Obviously."

"No…"

"She wants us to do it instead."

"You and me?"

"Yes, apparently a nurse said she could watch it on Zoom."

"Oh, well that's—"

"I should go," Roger cut her off. "I'm tired." And then, before she could reply, he disconnected the call. Lindy stood in the centre of her living room, holding her phone and trying not to feel hurt. Trying not to feel like Roger was pushing her away.

He was overwhelmed. He was hurting. And Ellen had told her to be patient. Lindy let out a shuddering breath. Part of her wanted to drive over to Roger's cottage right now, give him a big hug and tell him she loved him. Tell him she would be there for him the way he'd been for her.

But what if he didn't let her? What if he didn't want her?

Fifteen years of being on her own meant she had a whole load of insecurities. Lindy knew that, and yet it was hard not to feel them as she put her phone down and got ready for bed, her heart heavy inside her. Tomorrow it was the ball; next week was Christmas. From her upstairs window Lindy could just see the fairy lights glinting on the hedges and bushes outside of Willoughby Manor. As she looked, they blinked off, no doubt turned off by Henry. The world was cloaked in blackness. With a sigh, Lindy turned from the window and slipped into bed.

THE DAY OF the ball was bright and wintry, the whole world glittering with a hard frost, as if a Christmas fairy had sprinkled everything with glittery dust. It was perfect weather, and yet Lindy woke up with her stomach in a tight knot of nerves; when she checked her phone, there were no messages. She texted Roger to tell him she was thinking of him and to let her know if there was anything she could do, but there was no reply and she felt as if she'd both done too much and not enough.

She'd promised to help Alice with all the final preparations for the ball, so at least she wouldn't be sitting around worrying and waiting for Roger to message. She knew she would drop everything in a split second if he asked her to come. If he said 'help.'

But as the hours passed and she rushed around tweaking decorations and putting out champagne glasses, he didn't ask. And while her phone was lighting up with texts and WhatsApp messages from parents and pupils alike, none were from Roger.

At lunchtime she broke and called him, but it went to voicemail. Her stomach clenched, even as she told herself this was stupid. Roger would be settling Ellen into hospice, no doubt feeling overwhelmed by it all. Still, she couldn't shake the feeling that he was intentionally withdrawing from her, that he'd decided she wasn't worth the risk.

She knew how quickly things could change and unravel. She knew how a life and all its hopes could vanish in an instant. She just hoped that wasn't what was happening now.

At four o'clock Lindy left Willoughby Manor and a fluttery, nervous Alice to return home and get ready for the ball. What she had thought would be a time filled with excitement and hope was tinged with both anxiety and sorrow.

She'd bought a new dress for the ball—a fairy-tale dress of crimson satin, strapless with a diamante belt cinching her waist, and a matching spangled wrap.

She kept her make-up understated but elegant—smoky eyeliner and a bit of lippy, but not much more. She curled her hair and piled it on top of her head, letting a few curls cascade down her shoulders like Marie Antoinette, and completed the outfit with a pair of faux diamond chandelier earrings.

Gazing at her reflection, Lindy thought she'd looked very nice indeed—if only she didn't appear so miserable. Outside the bright, beautiful day had darkened into a perfect Christmassy night, the sky sparkling with stars, the air cold and sharp with festive promise.

Willoughby Manor was ablaze with lights as Lindy walked up to it a little after six; the ball started in an hour, but she'd asked the Year Sixes and juniors pupils to arrive half an hour early, and she wanted to be on hand to help Alice with any last-minute needs.

"Lindy!" Alice, looking lovely in a sleek, off-the-shoulder navy gown, and she even seemed to be starting to bloom a little, at least now that Lindy knew she was pregnant. Alice gave her a quick hug as Lindy stepped into the hall. "Have you heard from Roger today?" she asked, a crinkle of worry appearing in her forehead, and speaking past the lump in her throat, Lindy shook her head as she answered.

"No, not yet."

"I hope everything's okay. Poor Roger. Poor Ellen."

"I know." Lindy tried to smile but it was hard. She'd been so looking forward to this evening—to the ball, to the performance, to celebrating with Roger, to Christmas—yet now everything felt both tarnished and fragile. "Ellen is insistent that Roger still dance tonight," she told Alice. "With me as his partner. She's going to watch it on her tablet."

"Oh, that's wonderful! I'm glad she'll be able to take part, at least in some small way. How do we set it up?"

"Roger will, I think. When he comes." *If* he came. Lindy was starting to wonder.

SOON THE OTHER residents of Willoughby Close were coming in, everyone wanting to pitch in to help make the Christmas ball a success. Lindy exchanged hugs with Emily and Olivia, Ellie and Ava and Harriet. Everyone asked for news, and each time Lindy had regretfully had to shake her head. She still had no news, no word from Roger since last night.

Soon enough she didn't have time to wonder or even think about it, because her pupils were arriving and she was racing to and fro, attending to final costumes fixes and soothing the inevitable jitters. At the very last minute, a Year Six who had bowed out appeared, wanting to dance after all, and in a flurry of panic Lindy had had to rejig the whole routine yet again. Fortunately her pupils seemed up to the challenge, fizzing with both nerves and excitement.

Seven o'clock, and the first guests were arriving in a flurry of greetings; a string quartet was playing Christmas carols in the hall while waiters circulated with trays of champagne and mulled wine. Still no sign of Roger.

Lindy had gone ahead and set up a Zoom link for Ellen on her own tablet, but as she didn't have Ellen's information to connect the call, she felt helpless. She needed Roger. In so many ways.

Don't panic, Lindy reminded herself. *If he doesn't come, the performance can still go on.* It would have to. But where was he? And what about Ellen?

"You look gorgeous," Ellie told her as she gave her another hug. "Absolutely amazing. I can't wait to see the performance, Lindy. I only wish things were a bit happier."

"Me too."

At quarter past seven as she paced the entrance hall, Lindy's phone rang, a number she didn't recognise, and she snatched it up breathlessly.

"Hello?"

"Hello, Lindy."

To her shock, it was Ellen on the line. "*Ellen…how…how are you?*"

"I'm very well, dear. I've got my tablet set up for Zoom, and I'm looking forward to tonight very much." Ellen's voice sounded wispy and tired, but there was humour and cheer in it too. Lindy's eyes stung.

"We've got the camera all ready," she assured her. "I'm just waiting for Roger to come and invite you to the online meeting so you'll be able to see everything."

"I can't wait. I've given him strict instructions, so you must hold him to account."

"I'll try."

"And do visit me when you can."

"I'd love to, Ellen."

"All right, then. I'll see you online!"

Lindy had just put her phone away when she felt someone behind her and she whirled around. *"Roger…"*

He looked amazing in his tuxedo, if a little tired, and Lindy longed to rush into his arms. Something in his expression, or perhaps in her own heart, held her back. She waited instead, hovering uncertainly as he gave her as inscrutable a look as she'd ever seen.

"You're here," she said after a moment, when she realised he wasn't going to say anything.

"I am," Roger agreed.

"Your mum just called—she wanted you to set up the link so she can watch online."

He nodded mechanically. "I'll do it," he said, and brushed past her without another word or glance.

WILLOUGHBY MANOR WAS ablaze with candles and lights, bedecked with garlands of evergreen and holly tastefully tied with ribbons of crimson velvet. The cheerfully frantic melody of 'God Rest Ye Merry Gentlemen' was reverberating through the air and everyone seemed to be in full festive spirits, chatting, laughing, and drinking with both alacrity and ease.

Roger glanced at the huge Christmas tree festooned with glittering baubles and had a mad urge to pull the tree down, watch the ornaments scatter and break, to see something wrecked and ruined amidst all this merry beauty. He didn't want to be here. He certainly didn't want to *dance*.

The only reason he'd come was for his mother—his mother, whom the consultant, the perfectly amenable and yet wretched Ms Weston, had informed him had only a few weeks left to live, if that. *Weeks.* Roger had been as breathless as if she'd punched him in the gut.

How it all happened so fast? How could he possibly be here, in this place?

He fumbled with his phone, wanting to focus on doing something constructive, even though he didn't want to set up a stupid Zoom call. He didn't want to dance with Lindy, even as he longed to take her in his arms, bury his head in her shoulder and just breathe her in. Let her steady and anchor him.

When he'd seen her in the foyer, looking so anxious and sad, something had held him back. Going to her had felt like both the most natural and unnatural thing in the world— what he craved, and yet he couldn't.

Wasn't that how he'd always been? Imprisoned by his own ineptitude, his own fear? Could he even *do* a healthy relationship? The last twenty-four hours, the isolation and despair he'd felt and his utter inability to do anything about either, made him think he couldn't. He never would.

The guests were arriving, everyone mingling and chatting and laughing, and Roger felt a million miles away from it all. He almost felt invisible, skirting the room, trying to avoid everyone, even Lindy. He was in no mood to make idle chitchat, not that he ever could, and the performance loomed in front of him like a bottomless chasm that was just waiting for him to fall into.

He couldn't do this. Any of this. He'd been stupid and

naïve to think that he could.

"You must be Roger!"

He turned to see a woman he didn't recognise giving him a conspiratorial smile. "Lindy's new man. I've heard about you." She giggled a bit tipsily while Roger regarded her stonily, saying nothing. "I don't actually know Lindy," the woman confided, "but she teaches one of my children, a Year Six."

"I see," Roger said, although he saw nothing.

The woman leaned forward so her champagne almost spilled from her glass. "I don't know why she thought you were so *unsuitable*. I think you're very sweet."

Roger stared at her, unable to form a reply. *Unsuitable.* He'd actually almost forgotten about that comment Lindy had made months ago now, when he'd seen her in the teashop. Almost forgotten how humiliated he had felt, how ludicrous the idea of a romantic relationship between them had seemed—not just to him or even to Lindy, but to everyone. Apparently the comment had been circulating Wychwood, because he didn't think this woman had been in Tea on the Lea on the day.

He didn't think Lindy would stand by that comment now—at least he hoped she wouldn't—but even so he wondered if it mattered. He *was* unsuitable. He'd always known it. Unsuited to romance, to relationships, to the kind of intimacy he found so baffling. Without a word, he turned and walked away from the woman, away from the ball, slipping through a set of French windows that led out onto a night-cloaked terrace. Alone in the freezing darkness, he closed his eyes and wished that everything were different. That he was different.

THE PERFORMANCE WAS about to start. Lindy stood on the side of the ballroom, Emma clutching her legs and Ollie cavorting around, as she waited for the signal to start from Alice, and wildly scanned the room for Roger. Where was he?

"Are you ready?" Alice asked as she hurried over. "I'll get Henry to tell everyone to gather round, if you are."

"Er…" Lindy looked around again. No sign of Roger. The Year Sixes were getting antsy, and Ollie had about fifteen minutes more of good behaviour in him, if that. She couldn't delay any longer, and yet she didn't want to start without Roger. "Give me one sec," she said, and gently removing Emma's arms from around her waist, she hurried from the ballroom, peeking in all the other reception rooms, hunting for the one man she cared about more than any other. The man who had been there for her, and now she wanted and needed to be there for him…if he'd let her.

Why had she hesitated, when she'd first seen him to-night? Why hadn't she put her arms around him and told him she loved him? Held him close and never let him go? Instead she'd simply followed his lamentable cues and now she was wandering around, wondering where he was. What he was thinking and feeling.

She couldn't find him anywhere downstairs, and as the seconds passed, the window for having a successful performance was surely closing. Feeling she had no choice but to go forward without Roger, Lindy started towards the ballroom—and then her heart leaped into her throat as she saw a shadow beyond the French windows. Could it be...

Ignoring Alice's enquiring look from across the room, she practically ran across the ballroom and slipped between the open windows. The cold air hit her like an electric shock, gooseflesh prickling over her skin. But Roger was there, standing by the balustrade, his back to her, moonlight limning him in silver.

"Roger..."

He didn't turn as he spoke. "I can't do it."

"The performance?"

"Any of it."

Her heart felt as if it were sinking like a stone inside her. Lindy drew her wrap more tightly around her shoulders, little protection against the cold though it was. "What do you mean?" she asked, although she was afraid she knew.

"This. You. Me." Finally he turned around, but then Lindy wished he hadn't. His expression, only just visible in the moonlight, was so very bleak.

"Roger, please..."

"I'm sorry, Lindy. I wish...I wish I was different."

"I don't." She took a step towards him, purpose firing both her words and movements. "I don't wish you were different at all. I love you, Roger. I love you exactly the way you are."

Something flickered across his face and then was gone.

"You don't believe me?" Lindy challenged. "You don't think I could love you, all of you?"

"I think," Roger said after a moment, his voice both heavy and taut, "I'm too *unsuitable*."

Lindy flinched. She knew, of course, what he was referring to, although she hated to think that it might matter now. "Yes, I said that—I thought that—at the beginning. But then I came to know you, and appreciate you…and fall in love with you." His expression didn't change and a frustrated panic seized her. "Tell me you're not going to hold one remark I made eons ago against me."

"No, I'm not." Roger sighed heavily. "That would be completely childish. It's just…it made me realise, Lindy, how hard all this is for me." He gestured to the space between them. "And as for going out there…I'm not sure I can do it, even for my own mother's sake."

"You can, Roger," Lindy urged. "With people supporting you, loving you. It doesn't have to be you against the world. It doesn't even have to be *us* against the world. There is a whole community out there longing for you to succeed, and more than ready and willing to pick you up when you don't. I know, because I've made friends with them. I've been alone my whole adult life and I made myself not mind, but that's not the same as being able to rely on other people for help and support and love, and that's what I've finally been learning to do now. What I've needed to do all along." She took a deep breath as she continued steadily, "Let me love you. Don't turn away from me now just because it's hard or scary or uncertain, because I *get* that. I know it's all three, and I'm still here. Still in love with you."

The words had poured out of her so fast that Lindy had barely been aware of what she was saying, and yet she knew she meant all of it. Utterly. She loved this man. She should have told him sooner. She should have let her love, rather than her fear, direct her actions, but at least she was here now.

"When I was alone in the night and I needed help you came," she said softly. "You were there. Let me be there for you. Please. That's all I want. That's all I'll ever want."

Slowly, holding her breath, Lindy extended her hand to Roger. "They're waiting for us to dance together—you and me. Your mother is, too. It won't matter if you do the samba or if you fall on your face. Everyone there is on your side, and I'll still love you no matter what happens. All of you."

The seconds passed, each one an agony. Then, slowly, achingly, Roger took her hand.

"I might actually fall on my face," he warned, and Lindy let out a shaky laugh of both relief and joy.

"I'll fall with you. Happily."

With their fingers twined, they headed back to the ball-room.

ROGER'S LEGS WERE shaky and his heart full as he and Lindy walked hand in hand into the ballroom; almost as one, the crowd turned to appraise them, and it took him a moment to realise everyone was smiling. Ollie, fedora rakishly tilted over one eyebrow, was jumping up and down in excitement.

Alice was beaming as she hurried towards them. "Ready?" she asked, and Lindy glanced at him.

"Yes," Roger said as he squeezed her hand. "Ready."

The music started up, and Roger watched hand in hand with Lindy as the juniors started. They were crazy, careening around the floor with both pizzazz and polish. Then came twenty-four Year Sixes, all in black with red or green sashes, stumbling slightly through the complex choreography, but with smiles on their face. When the hip-hop section came, everyone clapped and cheered. Neither act was perfect, but they were both obviously roaring successes. And Roger realised Lindy was right. Everyone here wanted them to succeed. Everyone here was on his side.

Finally, it was their turn. All the eyes—including his mother's—were on them. He glanced at the tablet posi-tioned in the corner of the ballroom; he could see his mother sitting up in bed, looking tired yet alert. Roger turned to Lindy; she'd never looked lovelier, like a queen, regal and yet gentle, her head held high, her eyes warm with love as they took their places in the ballroom, the mirrors reflecting the glittering light from the chandeliers.

He was a lucky, lucky man, Roger knew, to have a woman not just love him, but fight for him as well. He was also a foolish man, for nearly throwing it all away—and for what reason? Because he was afraid? Because he hadn't wanted to be rejected? Because loving someone was the riskiest thing you could ever do, and he'd learned not to take risks. But he wanted to take this one.

If a guess was an informed estimation, then love was a calculated risk. A wonderful, terrifying, all-or-nothing gamble that he knew he wanted to take on and on, to forever—with this gorgeous woman now floating in his arms.

"I should have said this before," he said in a low voice, as Lindy's eyes widened at his serious, rather severe tone, "but I love you, Lindy. I love you completely and utterly, without reservation or qualification. Comprehensively, in fact, in all conditions or circumstances." He let out a breath. "So."

Lindy's lips curved in a knowing smile and Roger realised there had probably been a smoother way to say that, but then he'd never been smooth. Fortunately, it didn't seem to matter.

"And I love you just as completely, utterly, and comprehensively," she told him, grinning. "In all conditions and circumstances. Does that cover everything?"

"I believe it does," Roger answered seriously. "After all,

we want to be prepared for all eventualities."

He took her hand and Lindy laughed out loud, as the music swelled and they began to dance.

Epilogue

"WHO'S THAT, DO you think?"

Lindy's nose was nearly pressed to the glass as she watched the rather battered blue estate pull up to Willoughby Close.

"I have no idea who that is," Roger replied, "especially as I cannot actually see out the window, and therefore have no view of the person in question."

"I think someone's moving into number three!" Lindy said excitedly. A woman was climbing out of the car, one hand to her back like she had a crick in it. "Who could it be?"

"Again, I have no idea."

"I know you don't," Lindy replied, laughing. "But I'm curious."

She turned to give him a smile, which he returned warmly. Two weeks on from the ball, nearly New Year's, and everything still felt new, precious, and just the tiniest bit fragile.

Their dance had been a triumph—they'd stumbled, yes,

and once they'd almost fallen, but still. Lindy wouldn't have changed a single thing about it—especially not when they'd finished by turning to the camera where they could see Ellen sitting up in bed, tears trickling down her cheeks and a wide smile stretching across her face. Around them everyone had clapped and cheered, and Roger had looked surprised and a bit shaken by the enthusiastic applause. Several Year Sixes had high-fived him, and Ollie had rugby-tackled his legs. Roger had looked pleased, and Lindy's heart had expanded with love.

The rest of the ball had passed in a happy blur, and a week later they'd spent Christmas together—a bittersweet and beautiful day.

Lindy had woken up to snow falling like icing sugar, and she'd thrown on clothes before running over to Roger's cottage.

"Merry Christmas!" she'd yelled, and he'd looked bemused, still in his pyjamas. Lindy had gathered up some of the first snow to make a snowball, but it had been too powdery and had fallen apart in her hands. She'd laughed and thrown it anyway, dusting Roger's pyjamas in white, and he'd caught her up in a kiss that felt magical, the beginning of everything.

But that Christmas had been an ending of sorts, as well. They'd gone to the hospice that morning to visit Ellen and there had been something both sad and sweet about the scene—the Christmas tree in the entrance of the hospice, the fairy lights spangled on the end of Ellen's bed.

"It's still Christmas," she reminded them with a papery smile. "And I'm still here."

They'd sat by her bed as they'd opened presents—Lindy had bought Ellen a pair of fluffy slippers, which she'd oohed and aahed over, and Roger had given her a watercolour of her cottage, to hang in her room. They'd stayed for Christmas dinner, even though Ellen had insisted they have a proper one later.

"I hope you're cooking a turkey," she told her son severely, and Roger assured her he was. They'd decided, after the ball, to spend Christmas at Lindy's cottage, so Toby wouldn't be left alone for too long. As they said goodbye to Ellen, Lindy promised to visit her again soon. Ellen squeezed her hand and gave her a look full of love.

"You don't know happy you've made me," she said.

"And you don't know how happy your son has made me," Lindy returned with a smile.

Ellen had given her a knowing look. "Oh, I think I do," she said.

Back at the cottage, Toby had scampered around while Roger had got the turkey ready and Lindy had put on Christmas carols and made mulled wine. It had felt surprisingly easy, to move around each other in the little kitchen, to exchange quick smiles or even a kiss as Nat King Cole had belted out 'The Christmas Song.'

This was what normal, regular people had, Lindy thought. What they took for granted, and yet she didn't think she or Roger ever would. They knew how precious it was, how every moment felt like a miracle, and for that she was grateful.

While the turkey cooked, they'd opened their presents under Lindy's little tree while Toby tried to eat the wrapping paper.

Lindy had got Roger a blue shirt—surely a man couldn't have too many—and a huge, polka dot umbrella.

"Because if you're going to be prepared," she told him, "you can at least do it with style."

Roger had reduced her to sentimental tears by giving her a watercolour of Wychwood's high street and a small wooden box with a picture of Cornmarket Street painted on its lid.

"To start a new collection of treasures," he'd explained, and Lindy had thrown her arms around him in loving gratitude. She didn't think Christmas got any better than this.

Since then, they'd spent the last week with Ellen, who was fading a little more every day yet was peaceful about it, or by themselves, walking Toby or watching movies, simply being with each other. On New Year's Eve they'd gone to Ava and Jace's for a party, but they'd both been glad to get home to simply be with each other.

"It's a woman," she told Roger now as she twitched the curtain to make it a little less obvious that she was blatantly snooping. "With two kids, I think," she added as a lanky, sulky-looking boy unfolded himself from the back of the car, and an older girl with long, dark hair and fingers flying over her phone walked into number three without even looking up. "Teenagers. And a dog!" The smiley-faced golden retriever loped behind them, ears perked and tongue lolling. Lindy reached down to pet Toby, who was seeming anxious by all the unexpected activity. "No dad, though, at least not with them. Perhaps he's coming separately."

"Perhaps you'll find out in time, from the woman herself," Roger said as he came to the window.

"We could invite her over for dinner," Lindy suggested and Roger slid his arms around her waist.

"I suppose we could," he agreed. He was warming up to social occasions, slowly but surely, and they had Simon and Olivia's wedding to look forward to next week.

"I don't know what I was thinking," Harriet had whispered to Lindy at Ava and Jace's party. "He's not unsuitable at *all*. In fact, he's completely gorgeous."

"I know," she replied, brimming with both pride and love. "I've snagged myself quite a catch."

Now Lindy rested her head against his chest as she let the curtain fall and her musings about her new neighbour were momentarily forgotten.

Really, she had everything she wanted right here, she thought, as Roger's arms tightened around her and he rested his chin on top of her head, for now and always. For ever.

The End

Find out about Willoughby Close's newest resident in the next book in the series, Remember Me at Willoughby Close*!*

Join Tule Publishing's newsletter for more great reads and weekly deals!

If you enjoyed *Christmas at Willoughby Close,*
you'll love the next book in the….

Return to Willoughby Close series

Book 1: *Cupcakes for Christmas*

Book 2: *Welcome Me to Willoughby Close*

Book 3: *Christmas at Willoughby Close*

Book 4: *Remember Me at Willoughby Close*
Coming January 2021!

Available now at your favorite online retailer!

More books by Kate Hewitt

The Willoughby Close series

Book 1: *A Cotswold Christmas*

Book 2: *Meet Me at Willoughby Close*

Book 3: *Find Me at Willoughby Close*

Book 4: *Kiss Me at Willoughby Close*

Book 5: *Marry Me at Willoughby Close*

The Holley Sisters of Thornthwaite series

Book 1: *A Vicarage Christmas*

Book 2: *A Vicarage Reunion*

Book 3: *A Vicarage Wedding*

Book 4: *A Vicarage Homecoming*

Available now at your favorite online retailer!

About the Author

After spending three years as a diehard New Yorker, **Kate Hewitt** now lives in the Lake District in England with her husband, their five children, and a Golden Retriever. She enjoys such novel things as long country walks and chatting with people in the street, and her children love the freedom of village life—although she often has to ring four or five people to figure out where they've gone off to.

She writes women's fiction as well as contemporary romance under the name Kate Hewitt, and whatever the genre she enjoys delivering a compelling and intensely emotional story.

Thank you for reading

Christmas at Willoughby Close

If you enjoyed this book, you can find more from all our great authors at TulePublishing.com, or from your favorite online retailer.

TULE
PUBLISHING

Made in United States
North Haven, CT
08 February 2023

32226109R00205